MY SECOND CHANCE Cowboy

DESIREE HAMMOND

My Second Chance Cowboy

For information about special discounts for bulk purchases, please contact Ollie Boy Publishing at sales@ollieboypublishing.com.

ISBN 979-8-9928197-0-0

To my beautiful girls,

May you always possess the courage to embrace new adventures and step outside your comfort zone. This story is for you—I hope it reminds you that love and determination can light the way to your own happily ever after.

Author's Note

I write Happily Ever After romantic stories that celebrate love, resilience, and the beauty of new beginnings. My novels aim to whisk readers away on emotional journeys filled with hope and heartwarming connections, reminding us all that love can blossom even in the most unexpected places.

This particular book delves into deeper themes such as death, divorce, family loss, and abandonment issues. While these topics can be challenging, they are integral to understanding the complexities of love and relationships. Through the characters' struggles and triumphs, I hope to shine a light on the healing power of love and the importance of finding one's way back to happiness after facing life's hardships.

All of my stories are closed-door, sweet romantic comedies, focusing on the joy and humor found in romantic entanglements without explicit content. I believe that love can be both delightful and entertaining, providing readers with uplifting experiences that leave them smiling.

My goal is to create stories that resonate with readers on multiple levels, offering both entertainment and reflection. Each character's journey is crafted with care, drawing on the real emotions and experiences that shape our lives. I believe that within every story of heartache lies the potential for growth and renewal, leading us toward our own "happily ever after."

I want to clarify: no dogs or hogs were harmed in the making of this book!

Thank you for joining me on this adventure, and I hope you find inspiration and joy within these pages. Your support fuels my passion for storytelling and encourages me to continue exploring the many facets of love in my future works.

Chapter One

Finley

"Texas?" My eyebrows fly up my forehead as I stare at my giddy assistant. Donna nods enthusiastically, completely ignoring my surprised and likely frightened look. '

"It'll be perfect for you, Finley," she insists. "Have you even heard of a dude ranch? It's like a vacation but with horses, fresh air, and maybe some hunky cowboys."

"Uh, Donna," I interject, "I'm a city girl through and through. Not to mention, I have absolutely no experience with horses or any outdoor activities. I'd be completely out of my element."

"Exactly!" she exclaims, clapping her hands together. "That's what makes it so perfect! It's a total change of scenery, and it'll force you to step outside your comfort zone. Trust me, Finey, it'll be good for you."

"I don't know, Donna," I say hesitantly, twisting my hair around my finger. The thought of leaving my familiar surroundings and venturing into the unknown is daunting, to say the least.

"Finley, please believe me on this one," she insists, her eyes pleading with me. "You deserve a break – a chance to heal."

"Alright, alright," I relent, holding up my hands in surrender. "I'll think about it, okay?"

"Promise?" Donna asks, her voice hopeful.

"Promise," I confirm, nodding.

"I think this is just the thing you need to get you back to your old self," she gushes with a little too much exuberance.

Satisfied, Donna leaves my office.

I adore my legal assistant, Donna Mullins. Although she is only 12 years older than me, she has been like a second mother to me. She makes sure that I go home at a decent hour, pick up my dry cleaning, and remember to eat. She always keeps my office stocked with healthy snacks in case my hypoglycemia rears its ugly head. She has worked for me for five years and has helped to lift me up during one of the most difficult times in my life.

Andrew passed away about a year ago, and despite being back at my job as the lead corporate attorney for BryantMed Medical Supply Corp. in Boston, I have only been going through the motions. I'll admit, I am keeping things together professionally, thanks greatly in part to Donna, but I am an empty shell of the woman I was before Andrews's death.

I step back to the reality that just unfolded in my office. My days have become an endless loop of reviewing contracts, attending meetings, and drowning in paperwork – all while trying to ignore the constant ache in my chest. Donna, who has been my rock and quite literally saved my job and this department while I was a functioning Zombie, is pushing me to find a place or a treatment that will help me unthink. She insists that Texas is the medicine my brain needs to help me heal. I'll admit,

three weeks in the Texas countryside with nothing
to do but be a cowgirl sounds very intriguing.   So
far, the spa retreat and the week-long girls' trip to
Cabo haven't done much to lighten my spirit.

"Finley Prescott, you need something," I
whisper, twisting a strand of hair around my
finger as I ponder if this is that "something." My
analytical mind is at war with my broken heart,
and I know I need a change. I guess maybe this
Cavenaugh Ranch thing couldn't hurt.

When I arrive home that night from the office, I
get a message from Kaity asking me to meet her for
dinner. Dr. Kaitlyn Cooper, to be exact.

I check my reflection in the bathroom mirror. My
once lively green eyes now seem dull and lifeless,
and my fair skin is even more pale than usual. I
touch up my makeup with a bit of concealer and
run a brush through my hair. "As good as it gets,"
I say to myself as I go downstairs to make the short
walk to dinner.

I walk to our favorite Italian place in the North End and order a glass of wine while I wait for her. When she gets there, she does the same, and we order our dinner. While we wait for our salads, I notice Kaitlyn is a bit antsy.

Then she blurts it out. "So, are you going to go to Texas?" It's then that I realize I have been tag-teamed by my assistant and best friend. She proceeds to tell me that she and Donna have been working together to find me a suitable retreat. One that will be far enough away from Boston that I don't have any familiar triggers and long enough to relearn how to live in the moment. "They probably don't even have real cell service down there," she adds with a smirk.

"Really?" I asked skeptically. "I am trying to wrap my head around the idea of trading my high heels for cowboy boots. Do you honestly think a city girl like me can survive on a ranch? I couldn't even handle camping in my backyard with my brothers when I was a kid, let alone wrangling cattle or whatever they do on ranches."

"Finley Prescott, there isn't anything you can't do when you set your mind to it," Kaitlyn replies, her words full of conviction. "This might turn out to be exactly what you need."

"That's absurd, Kaity! Me? At a dude ranch?"

"Think this through logically, Fin. Pros: Fresh air, new experiences, getting out of this rut you've been in since... well, you know," Kaitlyn adds, trying to appeal to my analytical side.

"Cons: Dirt, bugs, horses –" I pause, tapping my fingernail on the table. "– potential embarrassment from lack of coordination and poor sense of direction."

I stare at Kaitlyn briefly before adding a single pro to the list: "Possibility of healing." I would love to heal from the pain of losing Andrew and find some semblance of happiness again.

"Finley," she whispers. "Give this a shot."

"Okay, okay," I sigh, a small smile tugging at my lips as I feel a tiny spark of excitement ignite within me. "I'll give it a try. But if I end up falling off a horse or getting lost in the wilderness, I'm blaming both of you."

She lets out a sigh of relief. "I was hoping you would say that because I already booked it for you, Fin." "Love you!" she adds, looking slightly guilty.

I should be annoyed that they ganged up on me, but in my heart, I know that they both want the best for me, and I love them for it.

We have a nice dinner, talking about everything and nothing. Kaitlyn informs me that my flight leaves next week and she has generously agreed to keep my plants alive for the next three weeks while I am gone.

"Let's get our dessert to go and see if your closet has anything worth packing." Kaitlyn whispers something to the waiter as she hands him her credit card.

We enter my apartment, and I turn to Kaity with a concerned look.

"Kaity, I have no idea what to pack for 3 weeks in Texas."

She pulls out her phone and starts scrolling. "Hmm, what to pack? Here it is. The website says you should be prepared for all kinds of weather." "That's not very helpful," I scoff. "Boston has seasons. Where the heck are you sending me?"

"I'll be right back," I tell her. I head to the guest room, pull out my two largest bags from the top of the closet, and wheel them into my room, where Kaitlyn is standing in front of my closet, staring at the rows of clothes and shoes.

"You should have plenty of room in those. That one looks like it could fit me," she jokes, pointing to the largest suitcase.

"You should come with me!"

"I can't. My surgery schedule is pretty booked for the next few weeks. Besides, I got you the last available spot for their next session.

"Andrew and I had talked about heading to Texas; Austin, actually. He wanted to check out the South by Southwest film festival. Austin always intrigued him with its music, film, and quirky atmosphere. He has a cousin there and we had always planned to visit someday."

"I didn't know that. I've been to Austin a couple of times. I don't think you would like it. It's eclectic and weird."

"What is that supposed to mean?" I say defensively. I know exactly what she means, but bantering with Kaity is always fun. My analytical self has a hard time relating to free-spirited, uninhibited people. Andrew was always that bridge. He was more easy-going than me—the ying to my yang.

"Andrew, look what Kaity's got me doing," I say to his picture on my dresser. "She's got me heading to a part of Texas nowhere near Austin, to a dude ranch that claims to have all four seasons during a three-week stay."

"I love that picture of him. It's the one you used for his funeral, isn't it?

"It is. It's from the day he passed the Bar."

"I wish I had gotten to meet him before the accident. As his neurosurgeon after the plane crash, I never got to see him awake. His smile is radiant."

"It's contagious. That was such a happy day. It makes me smile when I see it."

"And Fin, four seasons is not what I said."

"Yeah, I know. But it means packing a lot of stuff. I'm not sure I have everything I need. Maybe I should postpone and go when I have more time to get ready."

"I know you're a little nervous. But you have to be brave. Andrew would want you to go on this adventure, experience new things, and meet new people. Maybe even a new man type of people."

"I'm not ready for that yet, Kaity."

"I'm not pushing you, Fin; I'm just being optimistic."

"Kaity, I miss him so much. Andrew would have loved this trip - he always did have a soft spot for cowboy boots."

"Speaking of footwear, how are things with Dr. Ben, the podiatrist?" My attempt to change gears in our conversation is met with a stink face from Kaity.

"Boring and predictable."

"How so?"

"He always wants to go to the same two restaurants and orders the same thing every time. I'm probably being overly critical. He's so nice and a total gentleman. I'm not quite sure what I'm looking for, but I'm sure Ben isn't the ONE. I need to break it off with him. He's a really great guy, just not the one for me."

"That's too bad. You two look good together."

"I know. He's good-looking and in great shape, but there is absolutely no spark. I need some excitement, Fin."

"He'll make someone a very good minivan-driving, suburban husband someday."

We laugh for a few minutes as I pull some packing cubes from the armoire.

"Packing cubes, Fin? Do you want me to hook you up with Dr. Ben when you get back?"

"I like to organize all my clothes so it's easier to find things when I arrive. Also, one of my biggest travel fears is to see my luggage going around on the airport conveyor split open with my undies hanging out for the world to see."

"I know, I just like messing with you," Kaity says, taking one of the cubes off the bed.

"I saw that happen to a guy in Chicago, O'Hare airport once, and I can never unsee his Virgina is for Lover's boxers trailing behind his open suitcase on the belt in baggage claim."

"My luck, it would be my thong undies everywhere. Alright, girly, let's get you packed," Kaitlyn says as she starts to attack my closet.

I take a deep breath, and we start with the basics. I grab a few tank tops, several pairs of comfortable jeans, a couple of T-shirts, and a light jacket. I add a few long-sleeved t-shirts, plenty of socks and undergarments, and a light sweater for nights by the campfire to the pile. Kaity quotes something from the website's warning about the weather and grabs my light raincoat and a sunhat as I pull my hiking boots from the back of the closet. "I don't have any cowboy boots, but these will work if I'm going to be trekking through the wilderness," I say, holding them up for Kaity's approval.

"What about some cute stuff for going out?"

"Where will I be going out?" I ask her.

"Oh, who knows? Maybe some handsome cowboy will take you two-stepping. Or there will be some kind of hoe down or whatever they call those dances."

I can't even imagine going out dancing just yet at this stage in my life.

The look of shock on my face has Kaitlyn doubled over in laughter. "You should see your face. Priceless!"

"But seriously, Fin, pack a few cute things. Even if you don't go out, it will make you feel pretty, which will be good for your mood."

I hate to admit it; I haven't gone out of my way to look pretty in a while. I put on makeup and still dress professionally, but I wouldn't say I'm aiming for pretty.

"Okay, fine!" I grab a few sundresses and a pair of sandals, just in case.

Kaity adds a bikini to the pile, which I promptly exchange for a more reserved one-piece. "That one was for Andrew, not the public," I add putting it back in the drawer.

"Okay, fine. But you absolutely must take this cute pair of denim shorts."

We sit on the edge of my bed, surrounded by the huge pile of clothes.

"This is going to be an adventure," I say more to myself than Kaitlyn.

"I like your positivity, Fin."

I take the denim shorts from her and add them to the pile.

Look out, Texas...here I come.

Chapter Two

Brady

Adeline walks into my office as I finalize my feed order for the week and start to shut down my computer.

"I have the roster for the next session for you."

"You could have just emailed it, Addie."

"Brady, I know you. You wouldn't have even looked at it until they were already here," she says with a satisfied look.

"We're going to be full. I had a last-minute addition a few minutes ago."

"Great! Twelve campers, or Yuppies, or Instagrammers, or whatever they call themselves. I can hardly wait."

Adeline rolls her eyes at me and hands me the paper. "I know how much you like to kill trees, Brady," she adds as she glances at my desk area.

I have a paper calendar on the wall and there are sticky notes on many of the flat surfaces. I'm an old-school paper guy, and I don't see what's wrong with that.

Speaking of wrong, having campers on the family ranch that Cavanaugh's have owned for over 150 years is wrong. Cavanaugh Ranch is a working ranch, one that I run now. My dad, William Cavanaugh Junior, Bill to those who know him, has taken a step down to enjoy a bit of retirement and be smothered by my mama since his heart attack. I am doing the best I can to keep this well-oiled machine going. Unfortunately, my sisters have convinced the family that we need to be thinking of the future, and to them, the future is having any number of strangers come to the ranch for 3 weeks and pretend to be cowboys. Every time one of these "camps" is supposed to start, my stress level goes up, and I get even grumpier than usual.

"I also came to tell you dinner will be a little late. We're waiting on Cody. He should be getting dropped off in a few and then we'll eat."

"K. Thanks. I'll be up at the house in a few minutes."

"Brady, I know you hate this, but you don't have to be so negative. Not everyone who visits is going to be like Amber. News flash, most people aren't like her and actually do want to come here to have a fun experience working on the ranch."

"I don't think everyone is going to be like Amber." My voice wavers a bit, and I can taste the lie on my tongue. "I just don't like city-slickers running around our ranch."

" I wish you'd get on board; the Dude Ranch is good for business," Adeline adds as she walks to the door.

I was outvoted by the family, my sisters have my parents and at least two of my four brothers wrapped around their little fingers. I never stood a chance when that topic came up about a year ago. And the greenhorns have been coming to the ranch three weeks out of every month for about six months now. Some sessions are better than others, but it never fails to amaze me that despite the very detailed description on the website that my sister, Addie, created, some New York doctor or lawyer will come here expecting room service and nightlife.

We converted ten of the twenty cowboy cabins into guest bungalows, which, according to some fancy pants guy from a travel website that came out during the initial week, are considered four-star accommodations. Everybody who comes here should be expecting to roll up their sleeves and jump into the experience. Some do, but some don't seem to understand what a working ranch consists of. It's a lot of hard work that I've done my whole life, but I wouldn't want to do anything else.

On the corner of my desk is the new brochure Adeline left for me a few days ago. The colorful paper gleams proudly: "Welcome to Cavanaugh Ranch Retreats! Experience the Cowboy Life." In smaller print beneath, it lists activities like "horseback riding" and "yoga under the stars" along with more absurd things like "cowboy poetry" and "line dancing lessons." I sigh heavily, my annoyance growing with each word I read.

"Hey, Brady!" I look up from my desk to see my brother Cody in the doorway, holding two guitar cases. "I saw the light on when we pulled up and figured it was you hiding out in here."

"I'm not hiding, just finishing up for the day," I say as he sets his guitars down and I get up and grab him into a hug. We slap backs a few times, and I sit back down. "Did you just get in from Nashville?"

"Yeah. The guys just dropped me off on their way to Molly's B&B. I figured I'd stop by and see the fam; maybe get my boots dirty for a few days. We open for Treaty Oak Revival at the Iron Horse in Wichita Falls next week and John Pardy in Fort Worth the following. Adeleine asked us to play a set here in town, so here I am."

"That's fantastic. So proud of you, Man."

"Thanks," he adds sheepishly.

"Well, it's good to see you. We can always use the help. I've got a couple of guys doing the circuit right now, so we're a little short on cowboys with the patience for Addie's dude ranchers."

"Oh, It can't be that bad, brother." Cody laughs.

"How did the recording go?" I ask, trying to change the subject to something less stressful.

"It was amazing! We were able to lay down all the tracks for the album. There will only need to be some minor mixing in post-production. The record company even has an artist working on some cover art options, so it should be ready for release in a month or so. I'm psyched but a little nervous,"

"That's a first for you isn't it?" I ask, surprised by his admission.

"That's because it feels like sharing a small piece of my soul with the world. You know I'm not that outgoing. The whole public side of making music is a little daunting. I've been performing my whole life, but it's always been for people I know. This is different."

We both sit there for a moment, lost in thought.

Cody stands abruptly. "I'm starving. You coming to supper?" he asks as he grabs his cases and heads to the door.

"Yeah. I'll be right there."

I head out of my office located in one of the horse barns and take in the rolling hills that seem to go on forever. I am overwhelmed by the site of this land, dotted here and there with cows lazily grazing.

I can't believe it. My family's ranch, a once proud cattle empire, is being reduced to a tourist attraction. And all because my sisters think it's a good idea to expand our business. What happened to the days when we were content with raising cattle and tending to the land?

I shake my head and make my way to the main house for supper.

Most of the family is already there by the time I wash up and change. Meals at the ranch are usually a family thing since most of us live on the ranch. Mom and Dad built this house right before my brother

Carter was born 29 years ago. He was the fourth boy, and the old homestead was getting a little cramped for what turned out to be seven kids. Five boys and two girls would have made that old farmhouse a bit cramped. Most of us live in various wings of this huge, 20,000 square-foot, Spanish-style main house that will eventually accommodate most of our families as well. Or, at least the families of my siblings anyway. I've soured on the idea of settling down with somebody again after my divorce from Amber. So, I'm a 36-year-old man living in one room of what is supposed to be my family's part of Cavanaugh House. But thinking of her and her gold-digging family makes my head hurt, and I know my forehead is furrowed as I enter the kitchen.

"What's wrong with Brady?" my youngest sister, Maddy, asks as she pokes her finger between my eyebrows. Did somebody hide your favorite saddle again?

"He's just grouchy because the next camping session will start next week," her twin Sawyer adds without looking up from the task of setting the table.

Adeline is chatting with Dad and raises her volume across the din of the kitchen to add "We are seeing a significant uptick in interest and are almost booked through the end of the year."

"Woo Hoo!" I add as I kiss Mama on the cheek and take the vegetables from her hand and set them on the table.

Addie and Madison give me a look as I take my seat but they both look like they are biting their tongues for a later time. They know my feelings about this new aspect of our ranch but sometimes I just can't contain my mood.

As mom brings the platter of steaks to the table and sets it down near my dad, he wraps his arms around her hips and proceeds to tell me, "All you need is a good woman, son. You should have seen me before your mama finally agreed to go out with me. I was a mean ole rascal till she tamed me."

"Now Bill, don't go spillin' our secrets," Mama says with a wink, patting his arm as she goes to sit at the opposite end of the long farmhouse table that could comfortably seat 16 people.

I look around the table as most of my family sits down and wonder what I am doing wrong. I seem to attract the same kind of women, the ones who look past me to the dollar signs instead of the man. I naively thought my college girlfriend was the one. She had me fooled into thinking she loved me, and that money wasn't that big of a deal to her. Everything changed when we returned from our honeymoon in Paris, though. Amber hated living on the ranch, preferred to stay in Dallas or Houston, and spent more money on clothes and shoes than most people spend in a lifetime. After only three years, we called it quits, and thanks to her snake of an attorney, I continue to pay her a monthly allowance. I'm grateful that we didn't have any kids together. Don't get me wrong; I LOVE kids, and I always thought I'd have some by now. Amber never wanted to ruin her figure and told me that if we ever had them, we would go the Kardashian route and use a surrogate. I'm glad we never pursued that option because Amber isn't what anyone would consider the motherly type.

Sawyer breaks the silence and my internal tirade. "Cody, It's good to have you home. How long are you staying?"

"I'll be here for a few weeks. Gonna play a few local gigs before we start promoting the album."

"Do you think I could get you to do an Insta live with me while you're home? I know my followers would love a behind-the-scenes of Cody Cavanaugh – before his career skyrockets." Maddy looks at Cody with a grin, clearly excited about the idea. Cody chuckles, shaking his head. "Well, Miss Madison, I reckon I could spare a few minutes for your fans. But don't expect any wild stories or scandalous confessions," he teases, shooting her a wink.

Madison's eyes sparkle with mischief as she claps her hands together. "Oh, don't you worry, Cody. Our siblings can provide enough juicy details to appease my followers," she replies playfully.

"Speaking of siblings, does anyone know when Wyatt will be gracing us with his presence?" Cody inquires. "I haven't seen him in ages."

"As a matter of fact," Addie replies. "He will be here on Sunday morning."

Wyatt, the self-proclaimed eternal bachelor, is usually in Houston handling the oil side of our business. I think he likes avoiding family time. Wyatt has always been the odd one out in our family, never wanting to settle down with anyone. As the conversation flows around the table, I feel a pang of jealousy toward Wyatt. He claims he's happy with his life unencumbered, and his carefree attitude keeps him from falling prey to gold-diggers.

"Is he still dating that actress, or was she a dancer? I can never seem to keep track of his revolving door of girlfriends." Cody scans the table, hoping for clarification.

"She was a model, y'all, and I don't think they are still together. I saw a recent post of hers, and she's been in Europe for the past month," Madison adds as she stabs her salad a little to aggressively, causing lettuce to land on the table.

"Is Europe a sore subject, Mads?" Her twin Sawyer inquires.

"If you are insinuating that I am upset about Josh being in France right now, the answer is NO! We broke up again. I'm done with him. Besides, we were talking about Wyatt's love life, not mine."

"You know," I say, cutting into my steak, "Wyatt might be onto something here. Maybe we should all take a page out of his book." My siblings look at me with raised eyebrows, clearly surprised by my statement.

"What do you mean?" asks Carter.

"I mean, maybe we should all just focus on ourselves and our work instead of trying to find love and getting married. Look at all the stress and heartache it's caused most of us." I motion around the table to emphasize my point.

"Brady, you can't give up on love," says Mom, her voice gentle but firm. "You'll find someone someday who loves you for you, not your money."

"I'm not sure you're right, but thanks," I say, frustration creeping into my voice.

"Maybe you need to stop looking for love in all the wrong places," suggests Adeline. "Maybe you need to try something new, like online dating or a matchmaking service." I snort at the idea.

"All of you will find the right person and settle down when you're good and ready. Now quit with this kind of talk, and let's eat this delicious meal your mama made for us." Dad's rebuke silences all of us.

I take a deep breath and try to push away the thoughts of my failed marriage as I cut into my steak. The meat is cooked to perfection, as always, but my appetite is not quite there. As we eat, the conversation shifts to the upcoming camping session and the various activities that will be offered to the guests. I listen half-heartedly, my mind wandering to the current state of my love life.

When the meal wraps up, my siblings start to clear the table, and I volunteer to wash the dishes, hoping to distract myself from my thoughts. As I stand at the sink, scrubbing a pot, I hear the sound of footsteps behind me. I turn to see my sister, Madison, looking at me with a concerned expression.

"Brady, are you okay?" she asks, placing a hand on my arm.

"I don't want to be a topic on your next Instagram, Maddy."

"Can't a concerned sister just check up on her big brother once in a while?"

"That's not usually how you roll, and you know it!" I say – a little too harshly.

"I don't even have my phone on me right now," she insists. "It's charging in my room, if you must know. Besides, you've already been highlighted on my page plenty of times!"

I sigh, knowing that I can't keep my feelings bottled up forever. "Sorry, Mads. I'm a little down. I just feel like I'm never going to find someone who loves me for who I am, not for what I have; what we have."

Madison nods sympathetically. "I know it's tough, but you can't give up hope. None of us can. I personally, am not looking for my forever yet, but I know there's someone out there for each of us. You'll find your forever person eventually, Brady. I just know it." She laughs before adding," Maybe she'll love you even more when she sees you in your Superman pajamas!"

"Yeah, but she's probably really ugly and has only one good eye, brother," Cody teases as he heads to the fridge for a post-dinner snack.

"We can't all be rockstars with an entourage of adoring fans and groupies ready to throw their panties at us while we sing for our supper," Maddy says jokingly as she whips a kitchen towel at his bicep. "Yeah, and it's kinda gross if that is your idea of a turn-on," she adds before hanging up the cloth to dry.

"That's only cuz you're not a dude, Mads!" He responds with a chuckle and then makes a break for it with a third of a cherry pie – still in the tin.

Maddy shakes her head with mock exasperation. "Anyways, ignore him. He's an idiot. The future Mrs. Brady Cavanaugh will definitely find you one day!"

"Thanks for the pep talk, Mads, but let's keep it real for once: I'm destined for spinsterhood and old-cat-lady status, or whatever they call old men like that."

"See. I can be serious when I want to!" she snorts in laughter, and after giving me a playful wink, she turns on her heels and flounces out of the room, no doubt ready to spread her newest musings to her zillion loyal followers on social media.

I let the water out of the sink, and while the pessimism still lingers in my thoughts, I head to my suite at the far end of our house. I know that I need to focus on other things besides my love life – or lack thereof.

Chapter Three

Finley

I take one more look around the room and one last glance at Andrew's picture on the dresser and smile. "Wish me luck, babe," I whisper. "I'm going to need it." I close my suitcases, ready to start this new adventure!

As I am about to zip up my carry-on, I notice a small book tucked away in the corner of my dresser. It's a leather-bound journal that Andrew gave me on our first anniversary. He knew how much I loved to journal and wanted me to have a special place to keep my thoughts. I flip through the pages, reading some of my old entries. It's been a while since I've written anything down, but I feel a sudden urge to start again. I tuck the journal into my bag, feeling a sense of comfort knowing that I have him with me on this journey.

June 4

Andrew,

It has been quite some time since I opened this beautiful journal to write down my thoughts. Life has felt so difficult without you by my side, and I have simply been going through the motions. I miss you every day.

You will never believe what Donna and Kaitlyn have talked me into doing. You know Donna, but unfortunately, you never got the chance to know Kaitlyn. She is the amazing doctor who cared for you until the very end and has become such a rock in my life - she's probably my closest friend right now. Anyway, they convinced me to take a trip to Texas! Can you imagine? I'm feeling nervous and a bit scared, but also excited at the opportunity to try something new and take my mind off things for a while. Oh, and yes, I am currently twirling a lock of hair around my finger as I write this. That old nervous habit of mine that always made you laugh. It seems to be happening more often these days.

I know you would be proud of me though. I finally filled the open position in my department with a new guy named Jason. He's only 26 years old but full of drive and energy, just like you were. I feel like I can trust him to handle things while I'm away for a few weeks. And get this - he even went to BU, too! You would have gotten along well with him. He looks much younger than his age, and Donna loves to tease us by calling him my little brother, but you know how she is.

Oh, sweetheart, how I wish you could join me on this trip. You always had such an adventurous spirit and loved trying new things. I am trying to channel your enthusiasm and optimism during this trip. Please watch over me while I'm there and make sure I don't fall off any horses or get lost in the wilderness. I love you and miss you more than words can express.

They started boarding my flight, but I'll write more soon.

Forever yours,

Finley

The flight to Texas is long but uneventful. I spend the rest of my time reading, napping, and watching movies. When we land in Dallas, I can feel the heat in the air. It's a stark contrast from the cool, damp Boston weather I just left. I grab my luggage and continue to the pickup area.

A tall, rugged-looking man is holding a sign with my name on it. He introduces himself as Cole, the driver who will be taking me to the ranch. He insists on taking my bags, so I follow him to a luxurious SUV with just my purse and small carry-on bag. When I climb inside, I am introduced to Dr. Michael Baker and his teenage daughter, Claire. They will be my travel companions for the two-and-a-half-hour ride from DFW Airport to the Cavanaugh Ranch. There is a nice basket of snacks and a cooler of drinks, so I grab a water and sit back to take in the sights. It strikes me how flat it is as we make our way north on the highway. Unlike Boston, I can see for miles in every direction.

The shuttle hums along as we leave the city behind, and soon, we are surrounded by an endless expanse and open sky. I feel so small against the vast Texas landscape. My fingers subconsciously twist a strand of hair as I stare out my window,

First time in Texas? Dr. Baker asks, breaking my train of thought.

"Is it that obvious, Doc?" I ask with a nervous laugh.

"You've got that 'I'm not in Kansas anymore' look about you," he smiles warmly. "Please, call me Michael," he adds.

"Kansas? More like Massachusetts."

"My daughter and I are from Fresno, California. I've done extensive research on the ranch and other places like it." He speaks almost as if he's reciting a brochure when he adds, "We're sure to have many new and exciting experiences."

"Since my D I V O R C E four years ago, I try to take Claire on a father-daughter adventure every summer."

"Dad, UGH! Did you seriously just spell out the word divorce like it was a curse word? This lady doesn't care," says the teenager who, up until a second ago, had appeared to be asleep with her Airpods in.

He looks slightly embarrassed as he responds, "Ah, teenagers! Am I right?"

I give Michael a sympathetic smile.

The remainder of the ride is spent listening to the faint sounds of a country western station on the radio.

I must have dozed off, but I am awakened by loud complaining. Claire is sitting against the door with her arm at the top of the window, phone in hand.

"I can't get a signal," she says, her voice tinged with frustration and disbelief. "I can't post our arrival."

Michael glances up from his tablet, his brow furrowed but seemingly nonchalant. "You don't need to post it right now," he says in a surprisingly gentle voice. "We can record it, and you can post it from the ranch when you have a stronger signal."

Claire's shoulders slump slightly, and the corners of her mouth turn down. "Fine," is all she says, in a tone that is anything but. I wonder what she is trying to post and to whom. But I decide not to ask. I will probably find out soon enough.

The ranch is nothing like I expected - it's quiet and peaceful, with nothing but fields and horses as far as the eye can see.

We are met by several more cowboys who unload all our bags from the SUV. I notice how fit and attractive they all are. It looks like some type of cowboy modeling agency. Cole lets me know that my bags will be in my bungalow and directs me to the rustic building in front of me to check in for my keys.

"Good evening, Ma'am. I'm Addie Cavanaugh. Welcome to Cavanaugh Ranch." The young woman who greets me is a strikingly beautiful tall blonde with perfect hair, teeth, and makeup like she just stepped off the cover of a magazine. I feel matronly by that greeting, and I imagine I look a bit worse for wear after such a long day of travel.

I smile politely, "Hi, I'm Finley Prescott, and I am checking in."

"Of course, Mrs. Prescott, I have you in the Bluebonnet Bungalow. It's the third one down the path to the left. Cole should already have your bags in your room by the time you get there. Dinner will be back here in the dining room at 7. So, if you'd like to freshen up or take a swim, you have some time. Please let us know if there is anything you need."

She hands me some papers with my emergency contact info to verify and sign.

"Mrs. Prescott, you will probably want to put that beautiful engagement ring in your room safe so you don't damage it while you're here. It's on a shelf in your closet and can be set to whatever four-digit code you choose. I'm sure Mr. Prescott would be pretty disappointed if something happens to it while you are here," she adds innocently.

My throat tightens, and I can hardly focus. I order myself not to cry as I hand the documents back. I manage to squeak out, "Mr. Prescott is deceased."

"Oh heavens! I am so sorry. I had no idea. Please forgive me." The poor girl looks like she might cry as she hands me my keys.

"Of course," is all I manage as I take the keys from her and walk out the door to find my bungalow.

I quickly type out a text to Kaity.

> Got here okay. A little freaked out.

Just as I hit send, the phone rings in my hand, causing me to jump as I open the door.

"What's wrong, Fin?" she says when I answer.

"Nothing really," I force out, trying to keep my breathing steady. "Just a little reminder that I'm no longer Mrs. Prescott," I recount the conversation with Addie and how it hit me so suddenly.

"You will always be Finley Prescott in your heart, but maybe it's time just to be Finley for a bit. I'm sure she didn't mean any harm by her comment."

"Oh, I know," I say numbly. "It just hit me hard when she suggested I take my rings off to keep them safe." My eyes well up with tears that threaten to spill over again. "I haven't taken them off in years. This will be weird."

"Are you going to be okay?" Kaity asks with concern in her voice.

"I think so," I lie, swallowing hard against the lump in my throat. "I held it together all the way to my bungalow. No tears for the first time in a long while. I'm going to be okay."

The line goes quiet for a moment before Kaity speaks again. "Ok. Well, if you need anything, you know where to find me."

"I know. Thanks for listening. Everything will be fine."

"Soooo. How are the accommodations? They are supposed to be four-star?" Kaitlyn asks, attempting to change the mood.

I look around for the first time since entering the room and give Kaity the complete tour via Facetime. I am pleasantly surprised by my surroundings. In sharp contrast to the rustic exterior, the room is contemporary and pleasantly inviting. A king-sized bed dressed in soft, fluffy bedding sits in the center of the room, calling my name. I plop myself down, and it feels so comfortable and amazing. Two comfy chairs and a small table are arranged into a cozy sitting area, and a little kitchenette complete with a small fridge, sink, and coffee pot line one wall.

"Kaity, I think I will be fine. Thank you so much for this trip and for calling me so quickly." I smile warmly for the first time in a long time. "I am going to freshen up, put on my big girl panties, and make the most of my time here."

"Love you, Fin. Have some fun, and call me anytime."

"Thanks. I will and love you, too. Bye for now."

I hang up and feel a sense of peace and determination. My room opens to a luxurious bathroom with a soaking tub and a steam shower. I wash up, change clothes, and start to unpack. I put many of my clothes into the built-ins in the closet and find the safe on the shelf. As difficult as it is to remove my rings, I set them in a little tray built into the safe. I add my small purse and set the code. My wedding anniversary date seems appropriate as a four-digit code I will not forget. I grab a light sweater and my key and head out the door to explore the ranch a bit before dinner.

The sun is starting to set as I return from my walk around the Ranch. The pinks and oranges of the sunset directly in front of me are breathtaking.

I am almost at the main building when I hear shouting.

"NO Bandit! Stop! Drop it! Stop!"

I am almost run over by a medium-sized, black and white dog running at full speed in my direction. It takes me a minute to figure out what it has, but I laugh out loud as I do. The dog is running away with a very large, very pink brazier in his mouth. One cup is on his head, and the other is flapping behind him in the wind like a large parachute. More tears are running down my face as I arrive at the scene of the crime. These are good, satisfying tears.

Standing with her hands on her hips, yelling at several large cowboys, is an older woman, most likely in her sixties or early seventies. A giant suitcase is on the gravel behind an SUV limousine with its back hatch open. The bag must have toppled out when the door opened, and clothing is spilled on the ground. She turns around, and I am confident that the garment I saw a minute ago must belong to this woman.

"He went that way," I interject as I approach the scene. "Towards the bungalows."

"Thank you, honey, Barbara Hirsh, The Bubbe from Boca. I'm sure you've heard of me." She introduces herself as she snaps her fingers and points at Cole, my driver from earlier. "John Wayne, after that dog!" she commands, pointing in the direction I had indicated. The big cowboy ambles off after the dog while two others gather the enormous suitcase and remaining clothing from the driveway and carry it off in the same direction.

"Geoffrey, follow them and make sure that no more of my unmentionables get stolen by mangey dogs on the way to my suite." She is snapping orders to a forty-something man who is obviously on his phone and holding up a hand to indicate that he is busy. This doesn't seem to faze her as she continues to bark orders at him like he works for her. "Geoffrey, now, go with them!"

"Mrs. Hirsch, please accept my apologies. Bandit is still a puppy and just wants to play. Cavanaugh Ranch will happily reimburse you for your property loss." The same girl from earlier, looking a bit frazzled, is approaching.

"It's Ms. Hirsch. Pronounce it like a z, my dear. Mizzz!"

"Yes, Ma'am. Sorry, Ms. Hirsch. As I said, if the boys can't get your garment away from Bandit without damage, we will surely get it replaced."

"I should hope so; those babies are quite pricey." She puts her hands on her hips and pushes her chest forward to accentuate her very ample bosom.

"These girls didn't come cheap, and neither do their containment."

I snicker as I leave the chaos that appears to be Barbara Hirsch. I almost collide with a very handsome but grumpy-looking cowboy approaching the situation.

"Pardon me, Ma'am," he says gruffly as we make the briefest eye contact. There is something interesting behind his baby blues. I can't tell if it's anger or sadness, but there is a determined look in his set jaw.

"Not a problem," I add with a small smile, which is not returned. That was weird. I wonder what's up with Grumpy Cowboy; I ponder as I approach the dining hall for dinner.

Chapter Four

Brady

I have to give her credit; Adeline is good at
what she does. Angry campers and demanding
personalities don't phase her. Even bra-stealing dogs
don't get her frazzled. By the time I get there, she has
the situation under control, but since I am ultimately
in charge of all operations, I feel like I should show
my support.

As I'm rushing toward the source of the
commotion, I almost collide with a stunning woman
with wavy auburn hair. I quickly apologize for nearly
running into her, and her green eyes meet mine for
a brief second. I want to say something else, but the
words escape me. Small hands with ridiculously long
red painted fingernails wrap around my left bicep,

and I am pulled away from my focus on the woman.
I see her walking toward the dining hall.

I am not prepared for the force that is Barbara
Hirsch. Her hand is still firmly latched onto my arm
as she explains the entire situation in more detail than
necessary. I don't need to know about the specialty
lingerie store in Boca Raton, Florida, where her
bras are custom-made to her exact dimensions and
specifications.

As she speaks, I subtly pull my arm away from
her grasp, but it's like trying to escape the jaws of a
vice. Her words spill out in a breathy, flirtatious tone,
making me very uncomfortable. I am grateful when
Adeline interrupts her with a question about whether
the store has a website.

As I try to extricate myself from her grasp, Barbara
leans close to me. Her perfume is overpowering, and
I have to stifle a cough.

"I hope you don't mind my saying, but you're a
strapping young man," she says with a wink.

I clear my throat and force a smile. "Thank you,
ma'am."

Adeline shoots me an amused look, undoubtedly enjoying my discomfort. In return, I shoot her a glare, silently cursing her for abandoning me in my time of need.

Barbara continues to talk, her voice low and seductive. "Do you have a girlfriend, honey? You know, I could use a man like you in my life; someone strong and capable."

I resist the urge to roll my eyes. Dealing with cranky campers and lost bras is one thing, but fending off the advances of a frisky senior citizen is another.

Adeline must sense my unease because she steps in again, her voice professional. "So, Ms. Hirsch, dinner is almost ready. Would you like me to show you your bungalow so you can freshen up?"

"No, dear, I think I can find #6 Sagebrush on my own, thank you. I'll see you in a few minutes. Save me a seat, handsome," she adds as she gives my bicep one last squeeze and makes her way toward the bungalows. Addie and I go in the opposite direction toward the dining room.

"You handled that well," I said, letting out a sigh of relief. "I have never been objectified by a grandma before."

"Hey, it's all in a day's work. Besides, it's not every day we get to meet a real-life cougar."

"Ads, she puts the term Cougar to shame."

Shall we, or would you like to wait for your dinner companion?"

"Very funny."

First-night dinners with the campers are always lengthy events. Everyone is introduced, questions are answered, and way too much small talk is made for my liking. Addie has everything planned perfectly, so I can always count on a good steak on this first night. She is probably doing this for my benefit because she knows I am always happier and more amenable to mingling with the guests after a good meal, especially beef. Tonight's ribeyes were no exception, and I am fat and happy when the introductions start.

Addie introduces herself and the staff first, then presents me and a few of my brothers in attendance tonight. The campers introduce themselves as well. In addition to my new best girl, Barb, I learn that the smarmy forty-something man with her is her son Geoffrey. He seems to be a bit of a weasel as I watch him leering at the female guests as they introduce themselves.

The introductions drag on, and my mind wanders. I pick up on some of the subtle dynamics between the campers. Geoffrey, the weasel, seems to be trying to impress the younger female guests by making crass jokes and showing off his Rolex. Barbara Hirsch is now flirting with one of the men at her table. I hope this is not how things will go for the next three weeks. I swear under my breath.

My thoughts are interrupted by the next introduction - Dr. Michael Baker, DDS from Fresno, and his teenage daughter, Claire. He seems like a nice enough guy, a little nervous maybe, but genuine. His daughter, on the other hand, is a bundle of energy. She practically vibrates with excitement as she introduces herself.

"Hi, I'm Claire!" she exclaims, her eyes bright and friendly. "I'm a TikTok star! I have, like, ten thousand followers. I make mostly dance videos," she says, her cheeks flushing with pride. "But I also do some comedy sketches and stuff. It's really fun."

I can see how proud her father is of her. He beams at her, his eyes shining with affection. "She's always been a performer," he says, his voice fond. "I used to take her to all my dental conferences, and she would put on these little shows for the other dentists. She's got real talent."

Dr. Baker and his daughter Claire seem like a nice pair. I make a mental note to speak with Addie about setting up some activities for the younger guests during their stay.

"I'm Finley Prescott. I am a corporate attorney from Boston," is all she shares. I am intrigued by the woman I almost collided with earlier. The auburn beauty's name is Finley. She's much less talkative than

I would have expected. I thought attorneys liked to talk.

"Good evening, everyone. I'm Brad Chapman, and I am the lead Meteorologist at KOKL-TV in Tulsa. This is my son, Simon, he's fifteen, and my daughter, Sasha, she's twelve." This guy is seriously polished and accustomed to speaking in front of a group. His children, not so much.

"Hey," is all the boy offers as he barely looks up from his phone.

Sasha, on the opposite spectrum, explodes with her introduction. "Hi, I'm Sasha. I am super excited to be here. I love horses and can't wait to go on a trail ride. I am almost thirteen. My birthday is next week, and I'm super excited to be here. Oh, I already said that. Oops!" Her face flushes with embarrassment, and she quickly sits down.

The quiet attorney, seated next to her, gently pats her hand to try to console her.

The Chapmans appear a little disjointed; Brad is unsure how to relate to his teenagers; Simon clearly doesn't want to be here and looks bored out of his mind; Sasha appears desperate to get her father's attention.

"Hi, I'm Albert."

"And I'm Samuel."

"We own a floral design studio in Dallas, and we're here to celebrate our fortieth anniversary," they say in unison.

That gets a lot of awws and congratulations from the room.

And finally, there is the twenty-something couple, Max and Zoey Whitaker, computer programmer and nurse from Wichita, Kansas, who seem to be newlyweds. Max speaks for both of them, and they hold hands throughout the introduction.

Max, Zoey, Albert, and Sam appear to be the only ones currently enjoying themselves. The one wild card I can't seem to get a read on is our attorney, Finley Prescott. I can't tell if she wants to be here or not, and I wonder to myself why she's here by herself. I'll have to see if Addie knows more about her.

Addie tells everyone that tomorrow will be a day to get settled, pick their horses and gear, and get familiar with the ranch. She instructs them to get a good night's sleep and meet back in the dining room for breakfast between 6 and 8 am, which receives a few groans from the teenagers and Geoffrey. I can't say that I am surprised.

While everyone is having dessert, Addie makes the rounds to interact with each guest personally. She is genuinely in her element. On the other hand, I feel a strong need to retreat to my office. So, as soon as I can get her attention, I nod in that direction, which she confirms, and I escape.

"Why are you hiding out here?" I look up from my desk to see my brother Wyatt's imposing frame filling the doorway.

"I'm not hiding, just working on some financials. Why does everyone think I hide in my office?"

"Not sure what you're talking about, Brady. I just got here, remember."

"Yeah. Sorry. It's been a long day, I guess."

"It's all good. How's it going taking over for Dad?" He asks as he plops his large frame sideways across one of the chairs in my office. "I'm sure it's harder than it looks."

"You have no idea." I huff. "I knew it was a big job, but until his heart attack, I didn't know quite how big. Thankfully, he's still able to help a little. Mama's not letting him do too much these days, but I can still pick his brain when I need to. Not much of what he did is documented, so I'm just winging it some days, but it's all good. How are things in Houston?"

"Not too bad. I'm still trying to get us a better contract at the refinery end, but negotiations are going well."

"Awesome. Are you prepared for Dude Ranchers?" My tone is anything but pleased.

"Any single ladies lookin' for a cowboy to show them the ropes and give 'em a taste of the Wild West?" His eyes sparkle mischievously, and a confident grin spreads across his face.

"Not this group, brother!" I say possessively. I'm not sure why I say that. I don't even know if Finley is single, but I sure don't want Wyatt to be the one to show her the ropes.

"Down, boy!" Wyatt smirks at me like the Cheshire cat. "Not trying to infringe on your territory, man," he says, making me wonder what the heck just went down here.

"Sorry, not sure why I'm so worked up tonight."

"Don't sweat it. Addie said y'all needed my help for this session, and I'm having some work done on my condo, so here I am."

Wyatt doesn't have an uptight bone in his body. He is the most laid-back guy I have ever known. Nothing rattles him. If I didn't know better, I'd think we had different parents.

"A few of the boys are in Fort Worth for PBR next week, so we're a little short-handed."

My curiosity gets the better of me, and I add, "Won't Katerina miss you?"

"That, dear brother, is a story for another time." Wyatt stands to leave. " I'm beat, so I'll see you in the morning. You want me at the horse barn first thing?"

"That'd be great. Glad to have you back for a while. You going to see Mom and Dad?"

Wyatt nods without turning around. "Yeah. Then I'm gonna crash. See you in the mornin'."

With that, he disappears, and I am left to my thoughts again.

Chapter Five

Finley

I slept like a rock last night. I don't know if it's from exhaustion from the long trip, yesterday's fresh air, or the amazing mattress. I wake to a light scratching at the door, but since it is still dark outside, I hesitate to check and stay put in my cozy bed. It's only five-thirty a.m., so there is no rush to get to breakfast just yet. But then I hear the scratching again. It's probably just the wind, I tell myself. But when I hear it for the third time, I get up to peek out the window and slowly open the door.

"Bandit, what are you doing here?" The pup is excitedly sitting on my small porch with something in his mouth. "What have you got there?" He drops his gift at my feet, and I realize it is a fur slipper, probably rabbit fur. I find this kind of disturbing, but Bandit obviously is quite proud. I pet his head, and his tail wags furiously. " Silly boy. What am I supposed to do with only one slipper?" I ask him. He rubs his head on my legs, demanding more pets, licks my hand, and takes off down the path.

"Weird little dog," I say as I scoot the slipper out of the way but leave it on the porch. I step back inside to get ready for the day.

I start my coffee pot and head to the closet. I dress quickly in jeans, a tank with a shirt over it for layers, and my hiking boots. I wish I had thought to purchase some cowboy boots before the trip, but it was so rushed. Hopefully, these will be good enough. I don't want to be the first one to breakfast, so I take my journal and coffee out to one of the Adirondack chairs on my porch.

June 5

Andrew,

It's my first morning at the ranch, and I am in awe of the breathtaking landscape. The rolling hills and vast open sky bring a sense of peace I haven't experienced in a while. The ranch is bustling with activity, and I feel a glimmer of hope stirring within me.

As I sit on the porch of my bungalow, sipping my coffee, thoughts of you flood my mind. I can almost hear your laughter blending with the sounds of nature, and I can picture you enjoying this place as much as I am. The horses grazing in the meadow, the smell of fresh hay, and the gentle breeze on my face remind me of our adventures together.

Donna and Kaitlyn were right; coming here was a good idea. It's been so long since I allowed myself to fully appreciate something, and being surrounded by the beauty of nature helps ease the weight on my shoulders. I know you would be proud of me for taking this leap of faith and for embracing new experiences even in the midst of my grief.

Yesterday, I met some other guests, who are all such interesting people from different backgrounds. Families from California and Oklahoma are here on vacation: a couple celebrating their anniversary,

*newlyweds, and an odd mother-son duo from
Florida.*

*I had a good laugh just now, and I wish you were
here to share it with me. One of the dogs on the ranch
just brought me a slipper in his mouth, acting like he
had found a great treasure. It looks like rabbit fur.
I wonder which of the other guests is missing it.*

*I am excited to meet my horse today and hopefully
go on a short trail ride. Though I'm a little nervous,
too - let's hope I don't fall off!*

*I miss you daily, and your love will always be with
me wherever I go. Please continue to watch over me
as I navigate this new chapter in my life. You will
always have my heart.*

Yours always,

Finley

When I'm done writing, I turn off my porch light to
enjoy my first Texas sunrise. The quiet, peacefulness
of this place comforts me as I watch the pinks and
oranges rise from the horizon. My stomach growling
lets me know it's time to get moving. I finish off the

remaining coffee from my small pot and go in search of breakfast.

"Good morning, ma'am." I am greeted by an older-looking cowboy that I did not see yesterday. He's probably in his late sixties, but his tan, weathered skin might be deceiving me. He is holding the door for me as I approach the front porch. "Ladies first."

"Thank you. Good morning to you as well. Breakfast smells delicious, doesn't it?" I add.

"Sure does, but the wife's got me on a diet of oatmeal and egg white omelets, so you get you some of that bacon and hashbrowns for me," he laughs, and I laugh with him. Despite his imposing stature, probably six and a half feet, and muscular for his age, he seems like a large teddy bear with an infectious smile. "I'm Bill; nice to meet you."

"Finley," I reply as Bill holds the door open for me, and we proceed to the dining room, which has been converted into a breakfast buffet.

As we enter, I can smell the fresh coffee and bacon. My stomach grumbles even louder than before. Several people are here already, but I only recognize the grumpy-looking cowboy from last night and the woman who greeted me yesterday. A tall, muscular man in an apron emerges from the kitchen with a plate of food.

"Good morning, sir; where will you be sitting today? I see the lady has her coffee already. Would you like some as well?" he asks my companion.

"Luke, anywhere is fine, and yes, please, black with that pink sugar that my wife keeps for me."

"Finley, would you like to join me after you get your food?"

"I would love to. Thank you." I grab a plate and put a little bit of everything on it. I look around for Bill and find him sitting with the grumpy cowboy.

"May I join you?"

"Of course, Finley, this is my son, Brady, who you probably met last night," adds Bill as he pulls the chair next to him out for me.

"Nice to see you again," I say. I don't add that we didn't technically meet because I don't recall grumpy Cowboy speaking last night.

"New York Lawyer, right?" Brady gunts in response and goes back to his bacon and eggs.

"Boston, actually," I add.

Bill gives him a disapproving look. "So, Finley, what brings you to these parts? Bill asks.

I hesitate for a moment, not wanting to give away too much information about myself. "Just needed to get away from Boston for a while," I say, taking a forkful of hashbrowns. They are crispy and delicious.

"I understand why you recommended the hashbrowns, Bill. They are amazing."

"Yeah. I try to sneak them every once in a while, but somebody always rats me out to Betty," he says teasingly while looking over at his son.

Brady rolls his eyes at his father's comment and grumbles something unintelligible before taking a sip of his coffee. The dynamic between the two of them is amusing. Bill seems to be the jolly, mischievous one, while Brady is the brooding cowboy—quite the pair.

Bill turns back to me. "So, getting away from Boston, huh? Must be quite the change of pace for you."

I nod, appreciating Bill's attempt at small talk. "Yes, it's definitely a change."

Brady finally looks up at me, his piercing blue eyes meeting mine for the first time since I sat down.

"Nice to meet you, Boston. I'll probably see you in the barn a little later," says Brady as he stands to leave.

"Pop, no hashbrowns. Dr.'s orders," he pats the old man's shoulder as he grabs his hat from the adjacent chair and leaves.

"Darn, heart. I'm not as young as my mind still thinks it is," he says as he takes a bite of what looks like spinach, mushrooms, and egg whites. "What I wouldn't give for a little more youth."

I turn to Bill and ask, "So, how long have you lived here?"

"Oh, I've been living here all my life. This ranch has been passed down from generation to generation in my family; about a hundred and fifty years or so," he says with pride.

Bill and I chat while we finish our breakfasts. I learn that he and his wife, Betty, a former beauty queen, have seven children, most of whom live on the ranch and work for the family business in some way. I can't even imagine having that big of a family. I have two brothers, and that seemed like a lot growing up.

As we finish our breakfast, Bill stands with a bit of a struggle. "Well, Finley, I hate to leave such great company, but I have a little bit of work to do while they'll still let me. I'm sure we'll see each other again soon."

I smile at Bill and wonder how these two could be so familiar-looking but so opposite in personality. Unlike the older man, Grumpy Cowboy is a younger version of his handsome father but completely unapproachable. Oh, and what the heck is up with that nickname? Boston? Really?

My phone chimes with a text from Kaitlyn.

> Good morning. Are things better today?

> Much better thanks. Did you have the talk with Dr. Dull yet?

> Planning to tonight.

> Good luck.

> Thanks. I'll let you know how it goes.

I finish my coffee and glance at the familiar faces of my fellow ranchers at various tables in the large dining room. They are grouped by couples and families, and I am suddenly feeling like the fifth wheel. I hadn't noticed until now that I am the only one here alone. I take a deep breath and stand up from the table, determined not to let my nerves get the best of me. As I turn around, I nearly bump into the tall, muscular man who had brought Bill his coffee earlier.

"Oh, sorry about that," he says with a smile, his blue eyes twinkling. "I didn't mean to startle you, ma'am."

"It's okay," I say, feeling my cheeks heat up. "I'm just a bit jumpy this morning; I might have had a bit too much coffee."

"First time on a ranch?" he asks, leaning against the counter beside me.

"Yes. Is it that obvious?" I say, surprised that he guessed so quickly.

"I figured as much. You have that look about you," he says. "I'm Luke, by the way."

"Finley," I say, holding out my hand for him to shake.

"It's nice to meet you, Finley," he says, taking my hand. His grip is firm but not too strong. "So, what brings you out here?"

"Just needed a break from the city, I guess," I say, feeling a bit foolish for repeating this false reason.

"Well, you picked a good place to come," he says, gesturing around the dining room. "The folks here are all good people. You'll fit in just fine."

"Thanks," I say, feeling a bit more at ease. "I'll see you later."

"I'm making barbeque for lunch, so come back hungry," is his reply.

I start to go to the barn and realize that I left my hat in my room, so return to my bungalow instead. When I reach the porch, I notice I have another gift by my door. There is a second rabbit fur slipper laid out for

me. I can only guess that this one is also from
Bandit, but he is nowhere to be seen. I scoot
the slipper over where the first one is still sitting.
"Clever dog; quite strange though." I grab a
wide-brimmed hat and a water bottle from the
fridge and head to the horse barn.

I am greeted by four cowboys when I enter
the barn. Each one is a younger version of Bill,
my breakfast acquaintance. Wyatt, Cody, Carter,
and Sawyer Cavanaugh are all unrealistically
good-looking and friendly; their demeanor is more
like Bill's and not like their brother, whom I have
already met. I notice a small group gathered at the
far side of the barn. Grumpy Cowboy is talking
with the teenagers from last night. I would not
have recognized him if I hadn't just seen him a few
minutes ago. He smiles and interacts with the teens
like they are old friends, and he doesn't appear
to be grumpy at all. His body language says he's
completely relaxed here in the barn.

"Did it hurt?" I turn around and am surprised to
find a forty-ish man with way too much cologne.

"Did what hurt? I'm not sure what you're talking about," I say with a slight scowl. His excessive scent accosts my eyes and nose as I try to casually back away.

"When you fell from heaven. Did it hurt? You know, cuz you're an angel. Geoffrey Hirsch, Boca real estate broker at your service."

I can only manage a groan and a forced smile at his extremely old and overused pickup line. "Yes, I remember you from last night. I'm Finley."

"Right, I'd never forget a beauty like you. What do you say we ride together today?"

"Oh, I don't think I'm advanced enough to ride too far from the instructors. This is the first time I've ever done anything like this before."

Geoffrey leans in closer, invading my personal space even more. "Come on, I'll show you the ropes. It'll be fun." His breath is hot, and he reeks of coffee and cigarettes. I take another step back, feeling trapped between him and the wall.

"I appreciate the offer, but I think I'll stick to the lessons for now," I say, trying to keep my voice steady.

Geoffrey doesn't seem to take the hint. "I have a feeling you're a natural. I bet you could handle anything I throw at you," he says, winking at me.

I roll my eyes and try to move past him, but he steps in front of me. "Hey, where are you going? I thought we were just getting started," he scoffs.

I feel a presence to my left and turn to see Grumpy Cowboy standing there. "Everything okay here, Mrs. Prescott?" he asks, looking at Geoffrey sternly.

Geoffrey takes a step back, noticeably intimidated. "Well, I'll be around if you change your mind." He gives me a sleazy side glance and saunters off, mumbling something under his breath.

"Thank you. I really appreciate it."

He gives me an apologetic look. "No problem. You looked more than a little uncomfortable, and I don't like seeing people get pushed around. I'll try to keep an eye on that one." And with that, he walks towards the group of cowboys that greeted us.

Okay. That was weird. A girl could get whiplash from this guy. He appears to be so different when he's around me than when he's with the other guests. Maybe it's just me that makes him grumpy.

Adeline's voice rings out this morning, cheerful and inviting. "Good morning everyone. I hope ya'll slept well and are ready to meet your horses. Let me introduce you to my brothers and a few of our amazing ranch hands, who will be assisting you with your horses and gear today. Of course, you met my oldest brother, Brady, last night at dinner. He'll be around every day, but he's the one who keeps this whole place running, so we might not see him some days. This is my brother, Wyatt, and yes, he does look a little like that hunky Hemsworth brother, Chris, but he won't be winning any awards because he can't act. Cody here flew in from Nashville, where he and his band were working on their album. He'll be with us for a bit and may even play some music for us while he's here."

There is some applause from a few of the guests. I had no idea there was a celebrity in the barn.

"This is Carter; he and my baby brother Sawyer will be instructing you today as you get familiar with everything. They may even take the group out on a short trail ride later this afternoon once you have all gotten familiar with your horses. These guys, who are almost like family, are Jake, Lane, Chet, Hudson, and Clay ." She says, pointing to five more cowboys who have joined our group. Each of them nods or tips their hat as they are introduced. "Does anyone have any questions?"

"Will you be riding with us, beautiful? Everyone turns to see Geoffrey Hirsch wink at Adeline.

"No, sir, I will ensure that everything is running smoothly here and that lunch is ready when you get a break later." She takes a deep breath and puts on her best fake smile. "Well, I'm sure you'll have a great time with Carter and Sawyer. They're both excellent riders and will keep you safe. Now, let's get everyone paired up with their horses. We have some amazing animals that we're excited to introduce you to."

As everyone starts to move towards the horses, I catch a glimpse of Grumpy Cowboy watching me. He gives me a slight nod before turning back to help one of the guests. I wonder what his deal is. He's so different from earlier. Maybe he just had a bad morning. Or maybe he's one of those people who takes a while to warm up to others. Either way, I feel a little drawn to him.

Chet pairs me with a beautiful mare named Rosie. She's a chestnut with a long, flowing mane and a gentle disposition. I'm a little nervous as I approach her, but she seems to sense it and nuzzles my hand. I can feel myself relaxing as I start to pet her.

"Can I ride with you?" a timid Sasha approaches. "My dad and brother are having a bit of a thing right now," she says, pointing to a corner of the tack room where Brad and Simon appear to be arguing.

"Of course, sweetie. You can be my partner. Chet, is that ok with you?"

"You bet, Ma'am, I'd never say no to a lady," which elicits a giggle from Sasha.

Sasha's horse, Sugar, is a mostly white paint mare with light brown spots on her face and back with a honey-colored mane and tale. Chet helps her with Sugar's saddle.

As Sasha and I start to get ready for our first lesson. I notice Geoffrey hanging around again. He is supposed to be with his mom and Jake but keeps trying to talk to me. I do my best to ignore him. I haven't had to deal with guys like Geoffrey in a long time, and I don't want to start now. He's the type you find in the singles bars, which I avoid at all costs. I definitely don't want this guy to think that I'm even a little bit interested in him.

Chapter Six

Brady

The horse barn this morning is nothing short of organized chaos. Addie has my brothers and several of my Cowboys busy with the guests. Each group of two will be paired off with a cowboy to help them with introductions to the horses they will be using for their stay.

Lane has already gotten Albert and Sam's horses. They have Soldier and Pancho saddled, and they look comfortable with everything.

Brad and his son are actually talking as they work with Clay and their horses, Biscuit and Powder.

Claire is taking selfies with her horse Scout, but the horse doesn't seem to mind. Dr. Baker isn't as comfortable with his horse, Domino, or maybe any horse for that matter. He is standing several feet away as Hudson is trying to show him how to use the gear.

Jake approaches. "Quite the group we've got here today, huh? Where do these city people even find this stuff?" he says, gesturing to the overdressed woman approaching us in designer boots and jeans.

"I have no idea. But, it sure looks uncomfortable to me," I add as I realize the woman is Barbra Hirsch.

"Hey, handsome, which of these good-looking Cowboys is going to help me ride today?" Barbara croons, glancing back and forth between Jake and myself like she's picking out the best steak in the meat case.

"Good Morning, Mrs. Hirsch. We have selected a beautiful horse for you to ride. His name is Chief, and he is a gentle giant. Jake here, will be working with you and your son during your stay. He will assist you in getting your horses saddled so you can both learn to ride today." I say through gritted teeth, trying to keep my tone courteous.

Barbara giggles and gives Jake a coy look.

"Jake, Honey. It's Ms. Hirsch, but you can call me Barb. My husband Ira, God rest his soul, passed almost 15 years ago."

"I'm sorry to hear that, ma'am."

"Oh, you are such a gentleman," taking his arm as he leads her to the stall where Chief is waiting. "It's so refreshing to be around a real man." She adds, her hand grazing over his arm. I mouth an apology to him as he turns my way.

When I move to check on the next group, I hear Barbara. "Oh, you're such a charmer, aren't you, Jake? I'm sure you'll make a great husband for someone someday."

Jake is a hulk of a man with the patience of a saint. He's been with us for as long as I can remember, and I have only seen him lose his cool once. He broke a guy's nose at a rodeo in Abilene when a belligerent guy with a serious chip on his shoulder wouldn't leave a couple of young ladies alone. I'm sure that's why Addie put him with the Hirschs. Unfortunately, poor Jake has been saddled with both of the Hirschs for the

3-week session. The Ranch will surely be paying him a big fat bonus on his next check.

I watch the guests, all working with one of our staff, learn the basics of horse tack and basic commands. Some are stumbling around, trying to figure out how to hold their reins and adjust their stirrups. Others are more comfortable and are helping each other.

I enter the covered arena and I am filled with a sense of pride. Despite my dislike for the direction the ranch is taking, Addie is doing a great job. By the end of these three weeks, each camper will bond with their horse and some with each other. Cavanaugh Ranch hasn't been doing this long, but I have seen it happen time and time again. Each one of these campers will leave with long-lasting memories of their time here.

Suddenly, the sound of galloping hooves come barrelling toward me in a blur. Finley on Rosie and Sasha on Sugar race towards the rail at the edge of the arena. My motions are quick, practiced, and honed from years of ranching. Spinning on my feet, I start to rush toward the horses. Chet appears on Hickory, but before either of us can reach them, Sasha responds quickly, grabbing Finley's rains to calm the horse for her.

"Are you okay?" Sasha asks as she passes Finley the reins.

"I am. Thank you, Sasha. I don't know what happened. One second, I was just sitting on Rosie listening to Chet, and the next thing I know, I'm racing through the barn," Finley manages, though a bit shaken up.

"Need a hand there, Miss Prescott?" Geoffrey asks as he and Thunderbolt sidle up beside her, his dark eyes sparkling with mischief.

"Um, no, thank you, Mr. Hirsch," she stammers, trying to maintain her balance.

"Well, let me know if you need anything," Geoffrey continues, undeterred by her lack of interest.

Sasha speaks up, "I think she squeezed Rosie when she couldn't get her right foot into the stirrup properly, which made her ack up and go."

"I think you're right, Sasha," Chet praises as he leads Hickory and himself between Geoffrey and the two ladies. "Good observation,"

Geoffrey strides away from the pair toward his group, leaving Finley and Sasha alone for now.

"Finley, let's get you and Rosie better acquainted before we go on a short ride," he adds as he dismounts his horse to help Finley adjust her feet.

She glances around nervously, clearly unsure of how to proceed. I watch as she finally gets settled into the saddle, albeit with an expression suggesting she'd rather be anywhere else. Despite her obvious discomfort, the stubborn tilt of her chin tells me she isn't going to give up without a fight. I admire her tenacity, even if I don't understand why someone like her would choose to spend their vacation roughing it on our ranch.

"Everything all right here now? You ladies okay?" I inquire despite it being obvious they aren't.

"That was some quick maneuvering Sasha. Great job." Her response is a huge smile.

My gaze meets Finley's for a moment. Her green eyes lock onto mine. In return, she manages a tight-lipped smile before Chet interjects with a short, "I got this boss."

There is something in her eyes that I can't quite place, a mix of fear and determination that is both unsettling and attractive.

I pat Sugar and Rosie and check their bridles and bits while Chet adjusts the stirrup for Finley. I quietly whisper to Rosie to "take it easy on Finley" and hope the mare understands me.

I glance around the arena to ensure all the riders are accounted for and notice Geoffrey staring at Finley. My frustration with the whole dude ranch thing is only magnified by the likes of Geoffrey Hirsch. I don't understand how a man can be so clueless and self-absorbed to think that every woman they come across is interested in them. The flashy watch, the unwelcome advances, and the crass comments don't belong at this ranch. I am not a babysitter for spoiled playboys. Unfortunately, I think this guy has taken a liking to the quiet attorney, and every bone in my body feels the need to protect her for some reason.

Wyatt approaches. "Woah, that was a close one, huh? Is she all right?"

"Yeah, I think Chet's got it handled. I didn't think Rosie had it in her."

"Isn't that the horse you put little old ladies on?" Wyatt quips.

"Ladies, yes. Finley isn't little or old, brother."

"So it's Finley already, huh? First name basis with the LADY!" Wyatt drawls and singsongs the words as he waggles his finger in my face.

"You're Hilarious, Wyatt." I can feel my cheeks warming slightly. "Make yourself useful and go help Jake with Mrs. Hirsch."

Wyatt nods mockingly before walking away, still waggling his finger at me, with a huge smirk on his smug face.

About an hour into their arena lesson, the guests and their horses have found a good rhythm. Adeline approaches me with an offer. "Do you want to go with us for a quick ride?"

"Yeah, sure," I answer without thinking. I'm taken aback by my eagerness to join in with the dude ranchers.

"I thought you might say that." She says, gesturing towards my horse, Bandera, who is already saddled and waiting for me. "You can thank Wyatt. He thought you might like to get out of your office today."

With that, Adeline strides to the center of the arena and calls out loudly. "Are y'all ready to show what you've learned and take a short ride on the land?" The answer is a chorus of enthusiastic cheers.

Adeleine, riding Jolene, expertly leads the group single-file out of the arena. I take the rear to make sure there are no stragglers, and the wranglers ride with each of their groups.

We make our way across the sprawling land and I feel a sense of peace wash over me. Maybe Wyatt was right, perhaps I do need to get out of my office more often.

The guests are chattering excitedly, pointing out different things they see along the way. Adeline is leading the way, her horse seemingly knowing the path by heart.

The group continues their ride with laughter and conversation, soaking up the freshness of the open air.

As we crest a small hill, I notice Finley struggling to keep up with the rest of the group. I ride over to her and ask, "You doing all right there?"

She nods, though I can see the sweat beading on her forehead. "Just not very experienced with this kind of thing," she admits.

"Well, you're doing great," I reassure her with a smile. "Just take it slow and steady."

Adeline rides up beside us. "We have the best wranglers here; don't you just love him?" She says teasing.

Finley begins to relax into the rhythm of the ride. "I'll stay in the back of the pack with you," I tell her.

"Thank you. I think I'm getting the hang of it."

"Have you ridden a horse before today?" I ask.

"My mom has a picture of me on a pony when I was about 5, but I don't actually remember it, and I haven't ridden any since." A slight shade of pink on her cheeks.

"Nothing to be worried about. We take it for granted here, but I know not everyone has that luxury."

Adeline shared with me that Finely is a widow. She didn't have much detail, but it must be pretty recent since she was still wearing her rings when she arrived. Small talk is not my strong suit, but I want to learn more about her, so I keep talking.

"How was your trip to Texas? I'm assuming it was a pretty long one."

"Yes, it was about a four and a half hour flight and another two and a half from the airport to here."

"Yeah, that is quite a long time."

I don't know what else to ask her, so I just stay close.

I ride beside Finley for a while until I hear a loud, grating voice over the group.

My eyes search for the source of the commotion. Geoffrey, of course, has ridden up to Sasha's side and is trying to engage her and Claire in conversation. I can sense their discomfort, and I feel a sudden urge to come to their rescue. "I'll be right back," I tell Finley.

I urge Bandera forward until I'm riding beside Sasha. "Hey there," I call out to her, hoping to give her an escape from Geoffrey's attentions. "What do you think of the ranch so far?"

Sasha turns to me, a grateful smile on her face. "It's beautiful," she says. "I've never been anywhere quite like it."

"Geoffrey! Geoffrey, come take a picture with me," Barbara sing-songs from the front of the group.

"Well, Ladies, you'll have to excuse me. Duty calls." Geoffrey heads off for a photo op with his mother.

"Ew! That guy is the worst." Claire adds, and she and Sasha giggle.

"Thank you, Mr. Cavanaugh."

"I'll be behind you keeping an eye if you need me," I tell them, taking my place at the back with Finley again.

"I think you are going to be rescuing us from him for the next 3 weeks," Finley says when I reach her.

"Unfortunately, I think you might be right."

Adeline chimes in from the front of the line. "This is one of my favorite overlooks up ahead, folks. It's a great place to take a picture if you're interested." She looks over her shoulder with a smile.

When we reach the top of a ridge that overlooks a good portion of the land, Zoey Whitaker squeals, "Wow, this is amazing," her eyes widen in awe as she takes in the view.

"Sure is," I agree, feeling pride swell in my chest.

"It's almost like a painting," Albert says, his eyes scanning the horizon.

"I never knew such places existed." Dr. Baker adds.

"It's one of the reasons I love this ranch," I reply. "You can get lost in the beauty of it all."

Adeline nods in agreement. "It's why we do what we do. To share this with people and give them a chance to disconnect from their everyday lives and appreciate the world around them."

I look over at Finley and notice she is wiping a tear from her cheek. I wonder what brought that on and if she's okay. As we continue our ride, I keep a close eye on Finley. She seems to be lost in thought and occasionally wipes away another tear. I want to ask her if she's okay, but I don't want to pry.

The rest of the ride continues without incident, and we eventually make our way back to the ranch. As the guests dismount, I can see the look of satisfaction on their faces. I feel a sense of pride, knowing that we were able to give them an experience they won't soon forget.

Everyone starts to return to their cabins to freshen up for dinner as I catch up with Finley. "How was the ride?" I ask her.

She smiles. "It was amazing. Thank you for your help earlier. I never expected to enjoy it that much."

"I'm glad to hear it," I say with a smile. "Maybe you'll become a regular cowgirl before you know it."

Finley laughs. "I wouldn't go that far, but it was an interesting experience."

I watch her walk away, and I can't shake a feeling. I know I shouldn't get involved, but there's something about her that calls to me, something I can't quite explain.

I'm beginning to understand, maybe in part, why Addie asked me to join this ride: to see people connect with the land and appreciate its beauty.

Chapter Seven

Finley

June 6

Andrew,

Well, I had a bit of a scare with my horse yesterday, but I didn't fall off. So, thank you for watching over me. My riding partner, a 12-year-old girl from Oklahoma, had to save me. It was so embarrassing.

After learning the basics, we went on a short horseback ride around the ranch. The landscape is truly breathtaking, and the views of the sunset are amazing. At one point, we stopped at an overlook and I felt at peace for a moment, imagining you by my side, taking in the view. But then reality hit me, and I couldn't hold back the tears as I thought about how much you would have loved this place.

The people here are wonderful—well, all but one. You remember the obnoxious guy who runs the deli in North End, the one with the gold chains who hits on everything in a skirt. This guy is kind of like that, only he's here with his mother. Oh, and she is quite a character. They're from Florida, but the New York accents are a dead giveaway. I have a feeling that she will be keeping us all entertained.

I am going to grab a quick breakfast and go into town. It seems none of the jeans I brought from home are appropriate for horseback riding. I thought jeans were jeans, but apparently, I am wrong, and the chafing on my legs is proof of that. I am thinking about getting a pair of cowboy boots today, too. Wish me luck.

Oh. I almost forgot. That crazy dog brought me the other slipper. Got to run, sweetheart.

Love you always,
Finley

I set the pen down and close my journal just as my phone startles me.

Kaitlyn

Are you awake?

I call her and she answers on the first ring. "Hey, Fin. Sorry, I didn't call last night."

"That bad, huh?"

"No, not really. It actually went better than I expected, but I got called into surgery and had to leave early."

"So Ben took it well then?"

"Yeah. He said he thought that we were destined for a breakup but didn't want to be the one to initiate it. When I got the call from the hospital, he just packed up his meatloaf and hugged me goodbye. How are things there? Any handsome cowboys you want to tell me about?"

"Kaitlyn, it sounds like you're in the car. Shouldn't you be paying attention to the road?"

"I'm in an Uber since I didn't have my car last night. I'm on my way home to crash for a bit. Don't change the subject, Fin."

"Okay, yes. There are lots of handsome cowboys."

"Aaannd...are any of them on your radar?"

"I did have a moment with one of the ranch's owners yesterday, but he's kind of grumpy, and I don't think he likes being around me."

"What does that even mean, Fin?"

"He only seems grumpy when I'm around."

"That's funny. Maybe you remind him of someone."

"Kaity, I don't think I am ready for anything new yet."

"Leave yourself open to the possibility, Finley. You might be more ready than you think."

I don't say anything, and she adds. "I'm home, Fin. I need to hang up and pay this guy so I can go in and get some sleep. Don't close yourself off from the potential for something great. Andrew would want you to be happy again. Love you."

"I know. Love you too!"

"Ouch!" I wince as the denim of my jeans rubs against the sensitive skin on my inner thighs. It's only been a day on the ranch, and I already regret not investing in a better pair of pants for the occasion.

"Finley, you okay?" Barbara asks, worry etching her face.

"Fine, just these jeans," I mutter. "They're not made for this kind of work."

"Girl, you need to get yourself some proper cowboy gear," Zoey chuckles.

"I plan to go into town today," I sigh, rubbing my sore legs.

"Hey, the shuttle to town is supposed to be leaving after breakfast. You can hitch a ride to town to pick up some new pants," Zoey suggests.

"I'll be on it," I say gratefully, imagining the relief that sturdy ranch pants will bring.

I quickly finish breakfast and run to my bungalow to gather my wallet. I struggle with the safe for longer than I care to admit and rush out toward the driveway. I appear to be the only one waiting to go to town. Or, I just missed it.

"If you're waiting for the shuttle, you just missed it." a gruff voice interrupts my internal tirade.

I turn to see Brady Cavanaugh leaning against his dusty truck, one eyebrow raised in amusement.

"The ride to town already left?"

"That shuttle waits for no one. Need a ride?"

I hesitate for a moment - after all, he's not exactly Mr. Congeniality - but desperate times call for desperate measures.

"Sure," I reply, trying to sound nonchalant. "But only if it's not too much trouble."

"None at all. I have a meeting in town, so no trouble," he says, pushing off the truck and opening the passenger door for me. "Hop in."

I slide into the passenger seat of Brady's pickup truck, trying to avoid eye contact with him. I can feel his gaze on me as he starts the engine, but I keep my focus on the dashboard in front of me. The sound of the gravel crunching under the tires fills the silence between us.

"Good thing I was there to save the day," he says with a smirk. I can feel the heat rising to my cheeks, partly from embarrassment and partly from annoyance at his smug attitude.

"Thanks," I mutter, still avoiding his eyes. I notice how the sunlight highlights the rugged angles of his profile, casting shadows across his strong jawline. Despite myself, I'm drawn to the sight of him - though I'd never admit it out loud.

As we drive through the rugged terrain, I try to ignore the chafing sensation on my legs. Instead, I focus on Brady's strong hands on the steering wheel.

"What are you needing from town?"

"Some better jeans," I say.

"Ahh. Ranch pants, huh?" he asks after a while, glancing my way before returning his attention to the road.

"Yep," I reply, wishing I could sink into the worn leather seat and disappear. "These city jeans just aren't cutting it."

"Can't say I'm surprised," he smirks. "But don't worry, we'll get you fixed up at Benton's."

"Thanks," I mumble, unable to keep the blush from creeping up my cheeks. It's not every day that a grumpy but undeniably handsome cowboy comes to your rescue.

As we continue the drive into town, I can't shake the feeling that the universe has a funny sense of humor - throwing me together with Brady like this. But despite our differences, there's something about him that intrigues me. And who knows? Maybe by the end of the three weeks, I'll figure out what it is.

We drive in silence for a while, the tension between us thick enough to cut with a knife. It's strange how someone can be both infuriating and undeniably attractive at the same time.

"Nice weather we're having," I say, desperate to break the silence. The moment the words leave my mouth, I cringe at my awkwardness.

"Sure is," he replies, chuckling lightly. "You sure do know how to make conversation, Boston."

"Hey, I'm just trying to be polite," I shoot back, finally meeting his gaze. His eyes are a bright, clear blue that I could easily get lost in - if I weren't so focused on being annoyed with him. "But if you prefer silence, that's fine with me."

"Suit yourself," he shrugs, turning his attention back to the road.

Despite our mutual decision to keep the conversation to a minimum, the air between us is charged with an electric tension. I can't ignore the tiny, almost imperceptible sparks of attraction that seem to flicker in the air between us. The scent of his cologne drifts over, mingling with the fresh breeze coming through the slightly cracked window. It's a woodsy, manly scent, and it stirs something within me.

Kaitlyn's words echo in my mind, and my heart skips a beat each time his gaze meets mine like a silent conversation passing between us. His fingers tap lightly on the steering wheel, a rhythm that matches the racing of my pulse, and I can't help but wonder if he feels it, too.

"Almost there," Brady says after a while, pointing to a sign for Benton's Feed Store up ahead.

"Alright, let's get you those new pants," Brady says, holding the door open for me as we enter the store. The scent of leather and cedar fills my nostrils, and I feel a sense of excitement about my upcoming adventure on the cattle drive.

"Thanks," I reply, trying to sound nonchalant, even though my heart races every time I catch his eye. As much as I hate to admit it, something about Brady's rugged charm draws me in.

"Any idea what you're looking for?" he asks, leading me through aisles upon aisles of cowboy gear.

"Sturdy jeans that won't chafe while I'm riding," I say, twisting my hair nervously. "And maybe some boots?"

"Good choices," he nods approvingly. "I'll show you some options."

As we walk through the store, I steal glances at Brady's strong, calloused hands. We stop at a rack filled with jeans, and I notice him sizing me up before pulling out a few pairs for me to try.

"Here, these should do the trick," he says, handing me the jeans. "There's a dressing room over there."

"Thank you," I murmur, suddenly feeling self-conscious under his gaze.

While I try on the jeans, I hear Brady chatting with another customer nearby - an older gentleman who seems to know him well. I catch myself listening intently to their conversation.

"Yep, that old bull was a tricky one," he laughs in response to the man's question. "But we managed to get him back home safe and sound."

"Sounds like quite the adventure," the man replies. "How are you holding up now that your dad's retired?"

"It's been a challenge to take over the entire ranch. I'm not sure what I'm doing some days, but I'm doing my best. I'm happy to do it so Dad can finally take it easy."

"Not everyone is cut out for this kind of life, but your family has always been exceptional."

"Thank you, sir," Brady says humbly.

I eavesdrop on their conversation from my dressing room. I'm struck by the self-doubt he's hiding beneath that tough exterior. He may be a grumpy cowboy, but there's so much more to him than meets the eye.

"Hey, Boston," Brady calls from outside the dressing room door. "How are those jeans working out for you?"

"Great!" I answer, surprised by how well they fit. "I think I found a winner." I step out of the dressing room and do a little twirl. I catch him staring a bit with a slight blush on his face. I smile when I notice a small chink in his armor. "What do you think?"

"Those will do," is his reply, the grumpiness back in place.

I quickly change into my clothes and grab a second pair of jeans as he waits by the dressing room.

"Let's get you some real boots as well," he suggests, leading me to another aisle. Brady leads me to the boot section, eyes scanning the shelves for the perfect pair.

"Size seven?"

"Seven and a half, actually."

"Here," he says, handing me a pair of authentic cowboy boots. "Try these on."

"Thanks," I reply, sitting down and sliding my feet into the supple leather. They fit like a dream, making me feel even more comfortable and ready for the cattle drive.

"Those look good on you," Brady remarks, and I notice a hint of warmth in his voice.

"Thanks," I say again, feeling a little shy under his gaze. "I think I'm all set now."

"Great," he nods. "Glad to help."

"I'm going to the front to check out," I tell him as I proceed to the counter to pay for my new clothes.

As I am standing there getting my purchases rung up, the group from the ranch enters the doors of Benton's.

"There you are! We thought you changed your mind," Zoey says as she approaches.

Brady comes around the corner just as Barbara joins me at the counter. "Looks like she has a private shuttle," she says teasingly, winking at Brady.

"Just helpin' the lady out. She missed the shuttle, and I was heading to town anyway," Brady replies sheepishly, his gaze briefly meeting mine before he turns toward the door.

Just before he reaches to open it, he turns back. "You're in good hands now, Boston. I've still got that errand to run. I'll see you ladies back at the ranch later."

"Oh, girl. Now I know why that handsome cowboy didn't give me the time of day." Barbara says as she puts her arm across my shoulder. "I think he fancies you, my dear."

"Never thought I'd see the day Brady Cavanaugh willingly goes shopping," pipes in Cole with a huge smirk on his face.

"He was just helping me out." I insist, feeling my cheeks heat up slightly. "I missed my ride."

"Right!" they all say in unison.

"Did you find some pants that'll survive the cattle drive?" Zoey asks while stifling her giggles.

"Yep, and some boots, too," I reply, lifting my foot to show off my new purchase, feeling oddly proud of my transformation into a bona fide cowgirl.

"Nice! You two seem to have gotten along just fine without the rest of us," Barbara teases, her eyebrows waggling suggestively. "I wonder if they have any with some embellishments? I might get myself a new pair too," she adds as she grabs Zoey by the hand, dragging her towards the store's clothing section.

While I wait for the others to do their shopping, I wander around Benton's for a bit. I have never encountered a place quite like this. They have Western wear, thank goodness, and sell everything from plumbing supplies to baby chicks. What kind of weird universe have I fallen into?

Chapter Eight

Brady

An inexplicable feeling hits me as I leave Benton's and return to my truck. It's not just her looks, cuz she is definitely beautiful. I hate to admit it, but something about this city girl captures me in a way I didn't anticipate. I start the engine, and the well-known rumble of the diesel fills the air. I glance at my watch – just enough time to make it to my meeting with George Johnson, my attorney.

I overheard Cole's reference to shopping but chose not to respond. For one thing, being with Finley at Benton's is causing me almost to be late for my appointment; secondly, I am even more taken aback than anyone else by why I stayed instead of simply dropping her off. I shake my head in an attempt to discard whatever influence Boston has over me and drive to meet Mr. Johnson. Despite my efforts, images of her remain in my mind as I park the truck. I need to focus on whatever nonsense my ex-wife and her attorney have concocted now.

"Mornin George," I greet my attorney as I enter his office. "What's she demanding now?"

"Brady," he replies, offering a handshake. "Your ex-wife is claiming mineral rights to the property in question. She's trying to get a bigger slice of the pie."

"Mineral rights? You've got to be kidding me," I mutter, anger and frustration bubbling up inside me.

"After going through all the paperwork they filed, I can say there is no real legal basis for her claim." He explains coolly. "If we're lucky, the judge will just throw it out for what it is – a money grab."

"Good to hear," I say, my thoughts drifting back to Finley again. I need to get a grip on myself. There's no room for distractions right now – certainly not in the form of a woman who's just passing through town.

"Brady, are you listening?" George asks, snapping me out of my thoughts.

"Sorry, lost in thought. What were you saying?"

"Focus, Brady. We're discussing your family's land here," he reminds me, and I nod in agreement.

"Right, of course. George, what do you need from me?

"I've already drafted the counter documents. I need you to look over them and give me your signature if they are to your liking."

George passes the stack of documents across the table toward me. He directs me to the specific passages that need my approval. I focus on the wording and give him my approval. I sign the document and stand to leave. "George, do you think Amber has any chance of winning this claim?" I ask, hoping for some reassurance.

"Brady, I can't make you any guarantees, but I promise I will fight tooth and nail for your interests. We have a strong case, and I'm confident we can come out on top."

As I leave the attorney's office, I feel a strange mix of relief and frustration. I have a good feeling that George will be able to put an end to Amber's frivolous lawsuit, but this whole mess is just one more reason I regret marrying her in the first place. Maybe I shouldn't get too caught up on Finley. No more city women for me since I obviously don't know how to pick em.

Finley Prescott consumes my thoughts on my drive back to the ranch. That city lawyer from Boston has somehow worked her way into my everyday life since she arrived on my doorstep. I shouldn't even consider letting another woman into my thoughts, with the first still such a bitter reminder.

The sun hangs low in the sky, casting an orange glow on the sprawling fields as I pull up and exit my truck. There she is, pacing the front lawn like a restless lioness, phone pressed tightly to her ear.

Her jaw is clenched as she speaks firmly yet patiently into the phone. "Look, Jason, I need you to go through the contracts one more time and make sure everything's solid. We can't afford any loopholes." She pauses, listening intently to her colleague's response. "No, it's not too late. We can still withdraw from the merger if their board doesn't accept the terms. They were made aware of our deadline months ago." Right, end of August. Okay. Sounds good. Thanks"

She runs her fingers through her auburn hair as she looks to be contemplating her next move. "Donna has access to all my files. Have her check my notes before you respond. I don't want them trying to pull a fast one on us." Then she nods in agreement with whatever Jason says next before adding, "Good. Keep me updated, and we'll go over everything in detail when I'm back in Boston in a few weeks." Even though she's miles away from her office, Finley's dedication to her work appears unwavering. It's that kind of passion and intelligence that makes her so captivating.

When she ends the call, I hesitate a beat before approaching her. "Everything okay?" I ask, genuinely concerned.

Finley gives me a small smile as she puts the phone in her back pocket, "Just some legal matters I need to keep an eye on while I'm here. Unfortunately, the law never sleeps."

"Don't I know it," my voice full of sarcasm. "I've had my fair share of experience with legal matters," I admit, rubbing the back of my neck sheepishly. "Family business and all."

"Ah, yes. The glamorous life of a cattle ranching billionaire," she teases, trying to hide a grin.

"Hey, it's not all glamour and glitz," I defend playfully, unable to keep from smiling back. "There's plenty of hard work and dirt involved too."

"Speaking of which, will you be joining us on the cattle drive tomorrow?"

"As a matter of fact, I will. A couple of my guys participate in the rodeo so they are off the ranch for a few days. Y'all are stuck with me till they get back."

"I wouldn't call it stuck," she replies, looking a little pink in the cheeks. "Isn't it about time for dinner? I'm starving," she says, quickly changing the subject.

We enter the dining area together. "Wow, this looks amazing," Finley breathes in awe, her eyes scanning the room appreciatively.

"Out here on the ranch, we don't mess around when it comes to food," I chuckle, guiding her towards the buffet line. "Especially after a long day of working the cattle."

"Clearly," she agrees, her eyes lingering on the impressive spread of dishes before us. "I might have to roll myself out of here tonight."

"Trust me, you won't be the only one," I assure her, filling my plate with generous helpings of food.

"What is that you have there?" she asks.

"This here is chicken fried steak, a southern staple."

"Hmm. I've heard of it but never seen it in person. What is it exactly? Chicken? or steak?"

I laugh and give her the Wikipedia explanation. "It's actually a tenderized round steak that's coated in seasoned breading and then pan-fried."

"Why does a steak need breading?" she asks, still seemingly confused after my description.

"I'm not sure why it needs to be breaded; it just does. It's delicious, especially with the white gravy and mashed potatoes. Take a small one, and if you don't like it, I'll have Luke make you anything you want," I add, confident that she will like it.

"Anything? Really?" The mischievous look on her face gives away a more devious side of her. "Does Luke have any lobsters back in that kitchen?" Her hands are on her hips now, like she's won the game.

"No, but if that's what you want, I can have a lobster here in a few hours. Do I need to make a quick call?" Her surprise is evident, but she shakes her head.

"I'm sure this will be fine. I didn't think you were serious."

"Trust me," I tell her. "Luke could chicken fry an old saddle, and it would taste great."

We are both laughing and loading our plates when I see my sister Addie approaching, and I know she's up to something. Her blonde hair is pulled back in a loose ponytail, and her blue eyes are sparkling with mischief. She's wearing her favorite worn jeans and cowboy boots, the picture of a true Cavanaugh cowgirl.

"Hey, Brady," she says, sidling up beside me at the buffet table. "Mind if I join you two?"

"Not at all," is Finley's response before I have a chance to do so.

"Addie, don't start anything," I warn, my cheeks heating up as I glance at Finley.

"Start what?" Addie asks innocently, batting her eyelashes. "I just wanted to make sure you're treating our guest right."

"In fact, Brady's been very kind and welcoming," Finley interjects, giving me a warm smile. "He even gave me the Bradypedia explanation of this whole chicken fried steak thing," she says, gesturing to the buffet. "This isn't something I've ever experienced in Boston."

"See, Addie? I can be nice when I want to," I say defensively, shooting her a pointed look.

We join Albert, Sam, and Barbara at a table. The atmosphere is lively and energetic, filled with laughter and a bit of good-natured teasing. Despite her overt flirting earlier, Barbara seems to have mellowed out and is quite funny. She regales us with stories of her youth when she was a chorus girl on Broadway, and her humor is infectious. The way she embellishes each tale makes me laugh along with the group.

"I mean," Barbara says. "Have you ever seen someone tap dance in stilettos? It's not for the faint of heart!" We all chuckle as she continues with her anecdotes from the past.

The Franklin's tell a few stories of their experiences in their floral shop in the most bougie part of Dallas. They recount some of their more eccentric customers, including rock stars and politicians, and we roll with laughter at their stories.

"We nearly sent a magnificent bouquet of daffodils to the wife of a well-known celeb before realizing he meant them for his girlfriend," Albert interjects with a snicker.

"Oh, the stories we could tell," Sam adds.

We chat and joke around throughout the meal and I realize it's been a while since I've let myself live in the moment. Usually, I don't participate in the guests' nightly meals. This evening, for some reason, I felt the need to participate. Finley somehow puts me at ease, and I am drawn to her. There is something about her: her intelligence, her wit, her warmth. I have a strong desire to be wherever she is.

"I hope you saved some room for dessert," I ask as I head to the buffet.

"Of course! I always have room for dessert," she insists, her eyes shining up at me. "Especially if it's as amazing as this spread."

"Trust me, our peach cobbler is legendary," I say, grinning at her enthusiasm.

"Is that a fact?" Finley asks, raising an eyebrow.

"It absolutely is," I reply, my heart pounding with the thrill of our playful exchange. "This peach cobbler will make you forget all other cobblers that came before. I'll be right back."

"Hey, Brady," Addie calls out as she grabs my arm before I can walk away from the buffet back to the table. "Don't forget about the cattle drive tomorrow."

"Wouldn't dream of it," I reply with a grin. The thought of spending two days out on the open range and away from the chaos of life at the ranch is appealing, but more so because Finley will be joining us. It's the perfect opportunity to get to know her better.

"Good," Addie says, looking pleased. "I think you and Finley will have plenty of chances to talk and bond."

"Is that so?" I raise an eyebrow, trying to keep my expression neutral, but the anticipation bubbling inside me makes it difficult. The idea of spending time with Finley sends a thrill down my spine.

"Yep," Addie confirms with a mischievous smirk. "I may or may not have arranged for you two to share a tent."

"Addie!" I exclaim, both horrified and secretly grateful for her meddling. She just shrugs, her eyes twinkling with amusement.

"Relax, big brother. I'm kidding."

Chapter Nine

Finley

I'm awake before my alarm this morning. I am packed and ready, but my nerves and excitement have me pacing my bungalow. I pull my journal out of my bag. Maybe a little writing will calm me.

June 7

Andrew,

We leave for the cattle drive in a little bit. It's still dark outside, but I can't sleep from the excitement, so I'm packed and waiting. I'm not sure I'm truly ready, but we'll find out soon enough.

I got a couple of pairs of new jeans in town yesterday. I missed the shuttle and had to catch a ride with one of the ranch's owners. His name is Brady. I refer to him as grumpy cowboy, but only to myself. I'm not sure what to make of him. He's the typical cowboy stereotype - tall, rugged, with a perpetual scowl etched on his face. Despite his gruff exterior, there's a kindness in his eyes, and I'm curious about this Brady character.

Oh, Andrew, Kaitlyn thinks I should consider dating again. I don't know if I'm ready. I keep wondering what you would think of that idea. If the roles were reversed, I would want you to move on with your life and be happy again. I know you would want the same for me, but the thought of dating again is scary. I feel as if I'm betraying you by even considering the notion of moving forward. You were always the one who pushed me to grow, embrace change, and find happiness, and sometimes, I hear a whisper of your voice urging me to embrace life once again. Please give me a sign that you would be ok with this.

It's time to wrangle some cows. Keep a watch over me, please.

Love always,

Finley

It's still not even light out when my alarm finally lets me know it's time to go. I put the journal back in my bag, zip it up, and step outside to join the others.

Dawn barely cracks the horizon, casting a soft glow over the ranch as I grab a quick pastry and coffee from the dining room. The gravel crunches under my boots as I walk to the barn, the early morning chill nipping at my cheeks. Cowboys mill about, wrangling horses and loading supplies for the cattle drive. I spot Brady across the yard, his worn leather chaps and battered hat silhouetted in the soft dawn light. We briefly make eye contact and he winks at me.

Oh. Holy, I think to myself. Was that my sign, Andrew? - A wink from a cowboy.

"Alright, y'all," Brady says, his gruff voice somehow even more attractive this early in the morning. "We're moving the cows to a new pasture today. They've overgrazed their current field, so it's time for some fresh grass."

I glance around at the gathered group of cowboys and guests, all equally anxious and excited about the upcoming cattle drive. My city-slicker self has never done anything like this before, but that's what vacations are for, right? Experiencing new things. And maybe I'll get a chance to get to know the handsome cowboy who's caught my eye.

"One more thing, y'all, before we head out, I want to give you a warning. We might encounter some wildlife out there — particularly wild hogs and coyotes. They can be unpredictable, so it's best to keep your distance and stick together. If you see one, don't approach it. Just keep calm and let the wranglers handle it."

"Any questions?"

The group remains silent, exchanging wary glances.

"Ok, everybody," Brady continues, "Let's saddle up and get movin'."

We mount our horses, and I realize I'm twisting my hair nervously around my fingers. I know I'm far from being an experienced rider, and the thought of herding cattle across the ranch's vast expanse is both thrilling and terrifying.

"Hey, Boston," Brady calls out, riding up beside me. "You ready for this?"

Why do I find his strange nickname for me so endearing? It's not cute or sexy. It's just where I live. But I still blush when he uses it despite its generic origin.

"Ready as I'll ever be," I reply, trying to sound more confident than I feel. "But don't expect me to be a natural at this. Remember, I'm just a lawyer from Boston with a terrible sense of direction."

"Ah, don't worry," he chuckles, flashing a reassuring smile that makes me feel warm all over. "Just stick close, and you'll be fine."

Brady smiles at me and rides to the front of the group. "Alright folks, let's head 'em out!" he calls out. With a chorus of whoops and hollers, we set off. The cattle drive is underway as the sun peeks over the distant hills.

We begin at a leisurely pace. I ride beside Sasha and Barbara, taking in the sweeping vistas. The land unfurls for miles in every direction, painted in hues of amber and gold.

"Can you believe how beautiful it is out here?" Sasha sighs contentedly.

I nod, breathing in the crisp morning air. For the first time in ages, my shoulders feel loose, and the knot in my chest is unfurling. Out here, it's just me, the land, and the endless sky.

Up ahead, Brady expertly maneuvers his horse as he guides the herd. I find my eyes drawn to him again and again, taking in his confident posture and easy smile. Get it together, I scold myself, forcing my gaze elsewhere.

"I see you've been enjoying the view," Barbara teases as she rides closer to me.

I try to act like I don't know what she could possibly be referring to, but she just gives me a wink and speeds up to join Jake.

"She's funny," comments Sasha.

"Yes. Yes, she is."

The morning passes quickly. We stop to rest and water the horses around midday. As we gather around eating sandwiches, Chet outlines the plan for the evening.

"We'll set up camp near the creek north of here," he explains. "Get a fire going, throw some grub on..."

"Ooh, will we get to roast marshmallows?" Sasha interjects excitedly.

Chet chuckles. "I reckon we can rustle up some marshmallows for you, little lady."

My pulse quickens, thinking about cozying up around the campfire under a blanket of stars with Brady. Down girl, I tell myself. But I can't deny I'm looking forward to what the evening holds.

I smile to myself, already imagining the campfire glow lighting up Brady's handsome features. Focus, I remind myself, taking a deep breath.

"Everything ok over there, Boston?" Brady calls out, catching me staring.

I feel my cheeks flush. "Oh, uh, just thinking about how different this is from my usual routine," I say, scrambling for a response.

He grins. "Well, I'm real glad you decided to give ranch life a try."

My heart skips a beat at his words. Get a grip! I silently yell at myself.

"Alright, let's mount up," Brady says, pulling himself easily into the saddle with a grace that makes me envious.

I awkwardly hoist myself up onto my horse, Rosie, trying not to kick her in the process. Brady trots over and reaches down to adjust my stirrups for me.

"There, that should help," he says. "You're a natural."

"If by natural you mean naturally uncoordinated, then yes," I joke, eliciting a smile from him that makes my stomach do somersaults.

What is happening to me? I am not a flirt. I've never been like this around a man before. But there's just something about Brady that draws me in.

As the afternoon sun beats down on us, my eyes continuously drift to the cowboy riding in front of me. The way the sunlight brings out the golden tones in his hair, the bunch and release of his muscular shoulders as he guides the reins of his horse.

I take a deep breath and try to focus on the cattle drive. This is my first time participating in something like this, and I want to prove that I can handle myself out here and not fall off my horse because I'm staring at a man.

The herd lumbers along slowly, the cows shuffling their hooves on the dusty trail. One of the dogs, a border collie named Scout, darts back and forth behind them, nipping at their heels to keep them moving.

Suddenly, one of the cows breaks for it, bolting from the herd. Scout races after it, but the cow keeps running.

Brady and Wyatt spring into action, and their horses race forward. They overtake the cow in seconds, expertly maneuvering their horses to cut it off and turn it back towards the herd. I watch in awe at their skill.

"And that's how it's done!" Chet says with a grin.

"Wow, that was amazing!" I say, staring at Brady as he rides back to the group.

"All in a day's work, Boston," he says, tipping his hat at me.

I have to laugh at his over-the-top cowboy manners and his silly name for me. But I'm also impressed. The Cavanaugh brothers obviously know what they're doing out here.

Chet informs Sasha and me that he and Lane will go ahead of the herd to set up the camp before nightfall. "I think we'll be fine," I assure him confidently.

As we push forward, the terrain becomes more rugged. The trail narrows as it winds through a ravine, forcing us to ride single file. Doctor Baker seems nervous, but Brady calmly talks him through, keeping everyone relaxed.

Despite the challenges, there's a thrill to being out here, riding the open range together. And getting to see Brady in his element makes it even better. Coming on this cattle drive was a great idea!

"Alright, folks," Wyatt announces, pointing toward the cluster of tents in the clearing. "This is where we'll set up camp for the night." "Let's get these cows corralled and gear unloaded before it gets too dark."

The encampment is a welcome sight, a small oasis amidst the rugged terrain. Tents are pitched in a loose circle around a central fire pit, and the smell of something delicious wafts through the air. My stomach growls in anticipation as we dismount and begin to tend to our horses.

"Finally," complains Geoffrey, rubbing his sore backside. "I never thought I'd be so happy to sleep on the ground."

"Speak for yourself," Barbara chimes in, rolling her eyes playfully. "I could go for another few hours. Now, could one of you handsome men please help me off this horse?"

Sasha and I unload our things into one of the tents and join the others around the roaring fire where bowls of Texas chili await. The atmosphere is light and relaxed, probably because we are all exhausted. Everyone is trading stories and jokes as the stars begin to twinkle overhead.

Laughter and camaraderie fill the air, drawing us all closer together. It feels as if something magical is happening, and the bonds forged during this cattle drive will last long after we return to our everyday lives.

And as I steal glances at Brady throughout the evening, hope blooms in my chest that perhaps, just perhaps, our connection will prove to be something even more lasting than friendship.

I am curious about a conversation between Claire and Albert. They're discussing the finer points of s'mores making, with Zoe commenting on the merits of dark chocolate versus milk chocolate.

"Finley, what do you think?" Claire asks, catching my attention.

"Dark chocolate, definitely," I reply, earning an approving nod from Zoe. "It balances out the sweetness of the marshmallow."

"Agreed!" exclaims Zoe, and we all giggle as we share our sticky treats.

Claire announces that she and Sasha will finish off the Smores if everyone doesn't get them soon.

"Ah, to be young and carefree again," Barbara sighs wistfully, her eyes twinkling with memories. "I can't even look at that much sugar without it going straight to my thighs. You girls enjoy!"

I laugh as I wipe the sticky marshmallow from my fingers. My gaze drifts back to Brady, who is talking to some of the cowboys on the other side of the fire. He seems so at ease here, so comfortable in his element. I'm glad for whatever brought him to join us in this cattle drive. I know he has responsibilities on the ranch, but there seems to be more to him than meets the eye – more I'd like to see anyway.

I get ready for bed and wonder: Is this all too soon? There aren't any clear guidelines for what I'm experiencing; trust me, I've searched. I loved my Andrew deeply, and losing him so early was devastating. What timeline should I adhere to, and am I even prepared to consider someone else? These questions swirl in my mind as I rest my head on my cot.

I wake up in my tent; the sun is barely peeking over the horizon. Sasha is already up and elsewhere, so I dress quickly and step out. The morning is cool, and the smell of coffee and bacon mixed with hay and outdoors fills my nostrils. It is a welcome change from the city's exhaust fumes.

"Morning, Boston," Brady greets me, his gruff cowboy voice warm and comforting. He looks ruggedly handsome in his worn jeans, plaid shirt, and wide-brimmed hat. His usual scowl is replaced by a hint of a smile that sets my heart racing. "Coffee?" he says, handing me a cup. "Wyatt keeps a stash of creamer in one of the coolers if you need it."

"Yes, please."

"Brady thinks it makes him look more rugged to drink it black." Wyatt teases as he hands me a container of creamer. "I'd rather get teased about my 'girly coffee' than to drink it like that."

I doubt anyone in their right mind would think of Wyatt Cavanaugh as "Girly" about anything.

"I happen to like the taste of it without all the froof," Brady adds, looking slightly annoyed. "It has nothing to do with how I look."

"Whatever, Bro, creamer is a condiment, not froof. If you're gonna critique my refined palate, I'll leave you to your tar water and go check on the herd." And with that, Wyatt leaves Brady and I standing around the coffee pot.

"Did you sleep ok?" He asks. "Sometimes the cows can be loud and make it hard to sleep."

"If they were loud, I didn't hear a thing. I think I was asleep before my head hit the pillow."

"The outdoors and hard work will do that to you. Have you eaten?"

"Not yet."

"Well then, let's fix that," he says, leading me to a small wooden structure at the end of the campsite. The smell of food getting stronger as we make our way to the group gathered in camp chairs around small folding tables.

Chapter Ten

Brady

I admire Finley from across the campsite as the morning sunlight highlights her slender figure. My gaze lingers as she meticulously rinses her plate in the basin. A faint line of freckles is dusted across her nose, hinting at a life of sun-kissed adventures. Her green eyes, vibrant like jade stones, capture my attention. There's a spark hidden in their depths, and it sends my heart racing.

She is breathtaking. I let out a barely audible sigh as I take in the sight before me.

She looks up from her dish, and I quickly look away before she notices me watching her. I can't let myself get distracted out here today.

I am so lost in thought that I don't even realize breakfast is done until the sound of utensils scraping against plates snaps me out of my daydream. I take a final swig of coffee and push back my chair, eager to get back on my horse. We've got a full day's ride to get the herd to their new pasture. I sneak glances at her as the others are bustling about, packing up camp after breakfast. "Get it together, Cavanaugh," I scold myself as I pack my things in my horse's saddle bags.

Barbara sashays up next to Finley with a mischievous glint in her eye. Barbara's lips move a mile a minute as she leans over to chatter in her ear. Finley's eyes widen, and she glances back at me, pink staining her cheeks. I quickly avert my gaze, staring hard at the side of my horse.

Just in time to save me from further humiliation, Wyatt hollers for everyone to "mount up!" His commanding voice bellows through the campsite, and eager riders scramble to prepare their horses.

As we ride along, keeping the cattle moving steadily, I drift to the back of the group towards Finley. Her auburn hair blows in the breeze as she sits atop her horse like she's been doing this her whole life. We chat about the weather and the herd, nothing too deep. But I savor the soft tone of her voice, the way her nose crinkles when she laughs.

I spot two cows ambling off from the herd, so I square my shoulders and urge my horse into a trot. With precise movements, I maneuver through the sea of brown-and-white bodies, cutting and weaving around their lumbering forms as if I were in complete control. Out of the corner of my eye, I caught her watching me with admiration - at least, that's what I choose to believe - and I feel a wave of satisfaction wash over me.

After a quick lunch, I glance apprehensively at the sky. Storm clouds are looming closer, edging out the blue sky with an ominous shade of grey. Thunderheads are forming quickly to the north, and it won't be long before the rain starts coming down in sheets.

"We better pick up the pace," I call out to the group. "I want to get the herd past the creek before the sky opens up on us."

Everyone nods in agreement, and we urge our horses on faster. The cows, however, protest at being rushed along and let out a chorus of indignant moos. Fat raindrops start to fall, slowly at first, then picking up intensity, drumming loudly on the parched ground.

Finley rides up alongside me, wiping water from her eyes. Her hair is matted and wet against her cheeks. "Will the herd be okay in this storm?" she asks, voice tinged with concern.

"They'll fair alright," I reply. "As long as we keep 'em moving. We need to all get across the creek. It's higher ground on the north side. This side tends to flood when the creek rises, so I'm worried about us." A crack of lightning splits the sky as if on cue, followed by a boom of thunder that animals and people alike are hard-pressed not to flinch from. Our horses snort and sidestep nervously, their ears pressed back and eyes wide in fear, but they follow obediently as we urge them forward.

The sky continues to light up like fireworks from heaven. At one point, Finley's horse startles. Instinctively, my fingers grasp her arm firmly, keeping her steady in the saddle. Our gazes lock for what feels like an eternity before I release my hold on her. Her face is slightly pale but determined. I take a deep breath and look into her eyes to give her all the confidence I can muster. "You got this, Boston," I holler over the storm.

"We better hurry!" I frantically shout out to the group as the storm intensifies.

My heart feels like it's pounding out of my chest as I urge my horse through the heavy rain. My shirt clings to my back and shoulders, weighing me down. We are all soaked to the bone but determined to see the herd through. We ride in focused silence for a short time, coaxing the nervous cattle along.

The creek comes into view, its waters rising quickly due to the downpour.

I shouted orders to Cody and Sawyer above the roar of the rushing water, screaming for them to get our guests across as fast as possible. I know from experience that if the water rises much higher, there will be no crossing at all.

The rain is coming down in sheets, turning the creek into a churning torrent before my eyes.

I catch Finley's eye as the wranglers start herding guests toward my brothers and the safety of the other side. She looks scared but determined. I gesture for her to go across and she gives me a quick thumbs up before being swallowed in the commotion.

I shout to the guys to move the herd across faster. We've got maybe minutes before this flash flood swamps the valley.

It is absolute chaos: cows bellowing, guests shrieking, everyone sloshing through the mud, working to escape the rising water.

Somehow, in the mess, I lose sight of Finley. My horse shifts nervously beneath me as my eyes anxiously sweep the area to ensure everyone is accounted for.

I search the north bank, and all I see are cowboys, cattle, and all of the other guests - no Finely!

My heart stops when I finally spot her. She hasn't yet crossed and is further downstream than expected, still on the south side of the creek. I holler her name, but she doesn't seem to hear me. Fear grips my heart as I urge my horse forward to rescue her.

I steer Bandera in her direction, yelling to everyone else to keep going to the next encampment. I will get her and catch up.

I follow her gaze to see a tiny brown body tumbling helplessly in the current. One of the newborn calves is separated from its mother.

My heart clenches. There is no way that little thing is going to survive this alone.

"The calf!" She yells, not hesitating a second before jumping from her horse into the fast-moving water, swimming with every ounce of strength towards the little creature.

"Finley, no!" I cry in dismay, watching helplessly as she fights the powerful current.

What the hell is she thinking? She could get swept away!

Cursing, I nudge my horse back up the embankment and plunge in after her. My long limbs close the distance between us quickly.

The calf bobs in the water, crying desperately. I wrap my arms around Finley, pulling her back against me just as she reaches for the calf and pulls it to her protectively.

"I've got you both!" I shout over the roar of the water.

We crash into the shallows, landing in a tangled, muddy heap, but we're on solid ground. Safe and together.

Finley struggles to her feet, unharmed except for a few scrapes. I look up to see her beaming triumphantly. She presses the frightened calf against her chest as if it's a newborn child as it cries gratefully against her chest. It seems to understand our predicament and stills in her arms,

My heart swells with an unfamiliar warmth at the sight.

I stand and clear my throat. "We need to keep moving."

Without hesitation, Finley falls into step beside me as we move quickly through the mud. Thankfully, Bandera and Rosie stayed put on the south side of the creek and are there waiting for us as we carry the calf to higher ground. It seems that a little bit of luck is still on our side.

"Looks like we better find shelter and wait out this storm. That creek will only get worse until the rain lets up."

"There is an old encampment close by that I think we'll be able to use.

Over there," I point towards a clump of trees not too far away.

We approach, trudging through the muddy ground that sucks at our boots with each step. It becomes apparent that this encampment is in dire need of repair or demolition. The remnants of some wooden fencing lie scattered across the ground, and a dilapidated shack leans precariously to one side. Despite its disrepair, it's our only option—the storm is worsening, and we need to act fast. I make a mental note to add this mess to my massive to-do list.

I send a quick text to my brothers that Finley and I will have to wait out the storm and catch up to them as soon as we can. I receive a few thumbs-up emojis in reply.

"Looks like we'll have to make do," I say, sizing up the area. Finley looks at me nervously, her fingers twisting a strand of hair. I can tell she's worried, and truth be told, so am I. But we don't have any other choice. "I'll see what I can do to fix this place up."

Working quickly, I pull two tarps from my saddle bags and manage to patch up some of the holes in the shack's roof with one. It's far from perfect, but it should keep us dry. Finley helps me secure the horses and the calf under the second tarp.

"We made a pretty good team out here today."

"Seems that way, doesn't it?" I reply with a grin, and for a moment, I let myself imagine what it would be like to have this woman by my side in all situations, not just on a cattle drive.

"Let's hope the rest of this journey is a little less eventful," She jokes.

"Agreed," I say, our eyes meeting briefly before I return to securing the shelter.

"I thought you were a goner out there in the water."

"Honestly, I didn't think, I kind of just reacted. I saw that baby and just jumped in," she says.

"You scared me to death." Emotions swirl within me, from admiration to sorrow. What if I hadn't been able to save her? I hate to even think of it.

"It all worked out. You saved us both, Cowboy." She says, trying to lighten the mood.

"Thank you, Brady," she adds as we step inside the shack, both relieved to be out of the weather yet exhausted from our near-miss adventure. "I don't know what I would have done without you."

"You're welcome," My voice is strained. "We do make a really good team, Bos...I mean Finley."

Chapter Eleven

Finley

Rain lashes against the worn canvas of our makeshift shelter, drowning out everything but the rhythm of water on the fabric. Brady and I sit across from each other, legs crossed, our faces illuminated by the flickering glow of a small lantern.

We both reach for supplies from our saddle bags that I brought in.

"Peanut butter or chocolate chip?" I ask as I hold out two granola bars.

"Chocolate chip, of course. But are you sure you don't need them both? It's going to be a long night."

"Are you kidding? I have enough of them for a week. I get hangry very easily, so I always come prepared. Though, I think I misplaced my water bottle somewhere."

"Don't worry, I have extra water," he responds, holding up two metal bottles of water. "There's that teamwork again!"

We both laugh as our fingers brush briefly, discharging an electric shock that sends a shiver down my spine. Our eyes meet for a moment before we quickly eat our snack—conversation ceasing as if neither of us wants to break this newfound connection. I wonder if it's the electricity in the air from the storm or something else.

"Okay, let's play a game," I suggest when the silence between us has become too much. "How about...two truths and a lie?"

"Alright, Boston," he says, leaning forward with interest. He runs his fingers through his hair before continuing. "I'll go first."

"Hmmm, here goes." His voice is low and full of warmth, and I can feel my heart racing as I wait for him to continue.

"I've only been outside of Texas once," he begins confidently, " I rode my first horse when I was three...and I'm deathly afraid of spiders."

He looks embarrassed by this last one, and I smile, watching as his cheeks redden ever so slightly.

I think he's playing this one up to throw me off.

"Hmm. Texas is as big as some small countries, so that could be true. A three-year-old on a horse is young, but that's what you do here, right?" He only nods. "Spiders. I think spiders is your lie."

"Hey, those things are nasty," he protests, feigning indignation. "Sorry, Boston – that one was the truth. Your turn."

"Spiders?" I tease, watching as his cheeks redden ever so slightly. "Really?"

"Yep. You've never seen spiders till you see Texas Spiders! Your turn," he says again, trying to take the attention from himself.

"So, which is the lie then?"

"My dad taught me to ride when I was only two. That was the lie."

"My turn. Let's see…" I ponder and shake my head as I pause, considering my options. "Okay. I once won a hot dog eating contest, I speak fluent French, and I've never ridden a bike."

"Hot dog eating contest?" Brady grins, clearly amused. "I would've pegged you as more of a salad girl."

"Underestimate me at your peril, Cowboy," I warn, smirking back at him. "Now, guess."

"Alright. So maybe that one is a truth. I think the French is true as well. So, it's the bike thing," he says confidently.

"Wrong," I reply, thoroughly enjoying the look of shock on his face. "I've only ever eaten two hot dogs at most, but I seriously have never successfully ridden a bike. Sad, isn't it?"

Another slow grin spreads across his lips as he leaned towards me. "Guess I'll have to teach you sometime," he says, his eyes meeting mine and lingering there for what felt like an eternity. The atmosphere around us is filled with an unmistakable tension that has nothing to do with the raging storm outside.

I feel my cheeks grow warm as I open my mouth to respond, but before I can say a word, an ear-splitting clap of thunder rocks the room and makes me jump.

Brady gestures for me to move closer, and I nestle in his embrace, my body grateful for the warmth and security his presence provides. His breath tickles my ear as he speaks, and I'm filled with contentment that reaches down to my toes.

"Hey, Boston?" he murmurs. "Once this is all over, let's promise to keep in touch, okay?"

"Deal," I whisper back, my heart swelling at the thought of maintaining this newfound connection. In this moment, surrounded by darkness and uncertainty, it feels like the most important thing in the world.

He reaches for my hand, his warm fingers interlacing with mine. Sparks fly through me as I look up at him in awe.

"Finley," he says softly. "I don't know what happens when this is all over, but I want you to know that I'm glad I met you."

"Me too, Brady," his warm fingers intertwining with mine. The simple gesture sends sparks flying between us, and as the storm continues to rage outside, I am grateful for this unexpected adventure and the bond it's forged between us. It's as if I've known this man for years rather than days. Here, in Brady's arms, it feels like the safest place on earth. I silently thank Andrew for keeping us safe and the overwhelming sense of comfort that could only be his blessing.

The first thing I register as I wake is the solid warmth pressed against my back. Brady's arm is draped over my waist, his breath stirring the nape of my neck. My hair splayed across my face, but I can't bring myself to move. I am frozen, torn between lingering in this cozy cocoon and the flutter of panic in my chest at our sudden closeness.

"Mornin," he brushes the strands of hair from my face, his voice gravelly with sleep."

His eyes crinkle at the corners. "Sleep okay?"

"Surprisingly, yes." I bite my lip, hyperaware of his arm still curled around me. "You make an excellent pillow."

"Happy to be of service." Brady's smile falters as he takes in my bedhead and mud-streaked clothes. "You alright after last night?"

"I'm fine, thanks to you." I reach out to touch his hand, our fingers tangling together. "I don't know what I would've done if you hadn't come after me."

"Wild horses couldn't have kept me away." Brady brushes a stray curl from my face, his touch igniting a swarm of butterflies in my stomach.

We linger there a moment, gazes locked, until a plaintive moo interrupts us—the baby cow.

"Duty calls." With a reluctant sigh, Brady sits up, raking a hand through his tousled hair.

I follow, immediately missing his warmth as the morning chill prickles my skin. We dismantle our makeshift shelter in companionable silence. Outside, the world is a muddy mess, but the storm has passed.

"C'mon, buddy. You must be hungry. Let's get you back to your mama," I murmur, giving the calf an affectionate pat while fastening Brady's rope around his neck so we can keep him with us on the ride to find the rest of our group. His big brown eyes blink up at me, eliciting a smile. Maybe I'm getting the hang of this cowgirl thing after all.

As Brady helps me onto my horse, his rough hands linger briefly on my waist. A tingle runs up my spine that has nothing to do with the morning chill. I glance at his rugged features and quickly look away, warmth rising in my cheeks.

"Alright, cowboy, let's get out of here."

"What? Not pleased with the five-star accommodations, Boston?"

"Oh, it's everything I dreamed of and more." I gesture at our ramshackle surroundings. "Getting stranded in an abandoned cabin during a raging storm thoroughly completes the experience."

Brady swings into his saddle, and we ride to meet the others.

We catch up to the cattle drive by mid-morning. Barbara spots us first.

"Well, look what the cat dragged in!" she calls out.

"We were fixin' to send out a search party for you two," Wyatt adds, walking towards us.

I feel my cheeks flush as the other campers turn to look. Brady tips his hat, completely unfazed.

"Just a little rain delay, is all. No need to get your lasso in a knot, little brother."

"I'm going to get this little guy back to the herd so he can find his mama," Wyatt says, taking the calf's lead from me.

"Bye, Charlie. I'll come check on you later."

"She named the damn cow?" Wyatt laughs as he walks away with my new friend.

"So. Hmm." Barbara waggles her eyebrows at me suggestively as I dismount.

"You two sure look cozy this morning," she persists with a twinkle in her eye.

Before I can respond, Zoey walks up, giving Barbara a reproachful look. "Leave them be. We're just glad you made it back safe." She smiles warmly at Brady and me as Sasha runs up to hug me.

"Chet saved you some breakfast. I missed you last night. I didn't sleep so good cuz I was so worried you floated away in the water." Her words are a rambling string as she finally takes a breath and continues to hug me tight.

"Thank you, sweetie. I'm sure I don't smell so good, though. Have they disconnected the camp shower yet?"

"I don't care." Tears look like they are threatening to flow. "I don't think so. Your stuff is with mine. I put your bag in our tent last night in case you came back," she adds, giving me one last squeeze before leading me to the rest of the group.

As I enter the camp, I receive more relieved hugs from some of my new friends. My quick camp shower is renewing despite the cold water. And hopefully, after some real food, I'll feel like a new person.

I grab a bowl of warm cinnamon oatmeal and sit to enjoy breakfast. My thoughts drift to Brady, and I feel the need to journal.

> *June 9*
>
> *Andrew,*
>
> *Thank you for watching over us in the storm yesterday.*
>
> *I'm not sure yet, but I might have feelings for Brady. He is rugged and kind-hearted, and he possesses a gentle strength that draws me to him. It's too early to tell where this will go, but his presence brings me comfort and happiness.*
>
> *I find myself wondering what you would think of him. I know you would want me to be happy, to find joy in life again. I can almost hear your voice encouraging me to embrace this unexpected connection, to allow myself to explore these feelings without guilt.*
>
> *But I also worry—worry that opening my heart again might mean letting go of the love we shared. I*

miss you every day, Andrew, and I carry you with me. Yet, as I sit here under the Texas sky, I can't help but wonder if it's possible to honor your memory while also allowing myself to feel alive again.

For now, I'll take it one day at a time. I'll cherish the laughter, the warmth, and the moments of light that Brady brings into my life. Whatever happens, I promise to keep you close in my heart.

Love,

Finley

I pause, letting the warmth of the food seep into my bones, and the laughter of my new friends echoing around me fills me with a sense of belonging. Perhaps this is the start of something beautiful, a chance to embrace life again.

The herd trudges along under the baking afternoon sun. I wipe sweat from my brow and squint against the harsh light reflecting off the sea of cattle ahead. Brady rides up beside me.

"Hot enough for ya, Boston?"

I make a face. "It's like a sauna out here." How could the weather have changed so much from this morning?"

He grins, eyes crinkling at the corners. "Welcome to Texas, where we have four-hour seasons. Just wait until the real summer hits; this is practically brisk."

"Don't tell me that." I groan. "I might melt into a puddle."

"Well, we can't have that." Brady reaches into his saddlebag and hands me one of his water bottles. "Here. You keep this one. Don't want you evaporating on us."

"My hero." I take a long drink, letting the cool water soothe my parched throat.

We ride in comfortable silence for a while. Despite the heat, it's nice just being here together.

Up ahead, the point riders turn the herd toward a creek shining through the trees. Brady nods toward it.

"This is our destination, folks," Wyatt calls out from the front of the group. "We'll make camp here tonight and head back to the ranch in the morning."

Cheers ring out from many in the group.

"Let's get 'em all watered. "Even us puddles." Brady grins at me, tipping his hat.

I laugh and steer my horse after him, a lightness rising in my chest. Whatever this trip brings, I'm suddenly very glad I didn't miss it.

As the day winds down, the cattle settle in the new pasture as the sun dips low on the horizon. Brady and I unsaddle the horses side by side, sneaking glances when we think the other isn't looking.

"C'mon," he murmurs in my ear, sending further waves of electricity throughout me. "Let's watch the sunset."

We walk to a bluff overlooking the pasture. The sky is awash in pink and orange, the light dancing over the hills and trees.

Brady wraps his strong arms around me and kisses my temple. His touch sends shivers down my spine and sets my soul alight. "Is that ok?"

"Mmmhmm." is my answer as I turn and face him and press my lips to his, gentle at first, then eagerly intensifying the kiss as I melt into him.

Brady's other hand comes up to cup my face and I feel his lips turn up into a smile against mine. After a few more minutes, we reluctantly part, gazing into each other's eyes.

"That was...amazing." He whispers and slips an arm around me as we stand there, the promise of something more shimmering between us like stardust.

He takes my hand and leads me back to the campfire where everyone else is gathering for supper. The evening passes in a pleasant blur.

One by one, people drift off to bed until all that remains is Brady and I, watching the flames dance in the fire pit. He reaches out suddenly, taking my hands and drawing me closer.

"I'm so glad you came." He murmurs into my hair as he pulls me into an embrace. "It wouldn't have been the same without you."

I snuggle closer to him, breathing in his scent as we sit quietly for what feels like forever until the fire embers have died down and nothing is left but darkness and contentment around us.

"Come on," He says softly after a while, untangling himself from me gently but regretfully. "You should get some rest before tomorrow."

He stands up and holds out his hand to help me up, then walks me to my tent where he leaves me with a gentle kiss on my forehead before heading off to his tent down the line.

Sleep comes quickly as I experience a light feeling of something deep inside that has been missing for a while - peace.

Chapter Twelve

Finley

I am exhausted. Three days on horseback has taken its toll on my body, but my spirit feels light as a feather. After we got back yesterday, I got a hot shower and a warm, cozy bed, which were just what I needed. Despite sleeping through breakfast, I feel great.

Today, Brady and I are planning to have lunch, and he said he wants to take me out on one of the ATVs to see another part of the ranch.

Some of the group is going to the little church in Cramer tomorrow morning, but I'm not sure I will be part of that outing. I can't believe tomorrow is already Sunday. It doesn't feel like I have been here a week already.

I dress and hear the sound of an engine out front. Brady is waiting by the ATV to give me a ride to the dining hall.

"Do I need a helmet for that thing?" I ask, looking at the machine.

"When we get out in the rugged terrain, you will, but not for the ride to lunch.

We sit down for lunch, and it is evident that Brady can't contain his excitement. We finish our meal quickly, and I grab two waters on the way out.

The sun is high as we set out on the ATV, kicking up dust behind us as we race through the open fields of the ranch. The wind whips through my hair, causing me to hold it in one hand while I cling to one of the bars for stability with the other.

Brady grins at me. "Hold on tight," he says as he takes a sharp turn around a bend. The thrill of the ride is invigorating. The adrenaline rushing through my veins makes me feel so alive at this moment.

We reach a clearing overlooking a shimmering lake, and Brady cuts the engine.

"This is my favorite spot on the ranch," he adds, gazing out at the tranquil scene before us. "It's where I come to think, to be alone with my thoughts."

"It's beautiful."

"Yeah, it is. We used to come to that part of the lake below when we were kids to swim and later as teens to party, but now I just look at it from up here."

"You don't swim or party anymore?" I ask.

"Not for a long time." He looks a little sad.

We sit there in silence, taking in the serenity of our surroundings. I can picture a small Brady swimming and playing with his siblings. I can also picture the teen version of Brady, but not as clearly. He doesn't seem like the partying type, so that's a little more difficult.

After a moment, he turns to me, his gaze searching mine. "I've never brought anyone here before," he admits, his voice barely above a whisper. "But there's something about you... I feel like I can be myself around you."

"I'm glad you brought me here," I reach to place my hand on his arm.

Just then, Brady's phone chirps with a message. He checks his texts and lets out a sigh.

"I'm gonna have to cut this short. I am so sorry."

"Is everything okay?" I ask, concerned by the sudden change in his demeanor.

"Just ranch stuff. Got to keep adulting, I'm afraid."

"It's okay, Brady. I'm the only one on vacation. Duty calls, right? "

Brady smiles at me and starts up the ATV. We speed back towards the ranch, and as he pulls up in front of my bungalow and helps me out, he asks. "Will I see you at dinner?"

"You better."

Chapter Thirteen

Brady

I wake before the alarm.

Church has never been a regular part of my weekly routine since before college when my family used to go together. But this morning, for some reason, I feel the need to go to church.

I know Cole will drive anyone who wants to attend in the camp shuttle, but just in case there is an overflow of people, I park my truck next to his van. Even though I've already eaten, I make my way to the dining hall. Maybe I'll grab a coffee for the road is the excuse I tell myself.

I scan the room for Finley, hoping she will join us this morning. Just then, Cole announces that we are leaving, and I feel a pang of disappointment that I don't see her. Michael notices and approaches me, saying, "She's already outside."

A surge of relief washes over me as I step outside and see Finley engaged in deep conversation with Claire on the porch while the rest of us exit the building.

The Chapman family is already loading into the van, and the Whitaker's are not far behind. Finley and Michael's daughter, Claire, are already walking towards my truck, so I don't stop them.

Cole asks, "Is this everyone?" It's probably wise to double-check after leaving Finley behind the other day.

Albert informs us that Sam has a headache and is sleeping in.

"Barb told me that God forgives you when you're on vacation, so I guess that means she's sleeping in, too," quips Zoey as Max helps her into the van.

Michael speaks up amidst the bustle, "Who has room for me?"

"It looks like Claire and Finley are with me, so you're welcome to ride with us."

Michael takes the passenger seat since the ladies have already claimed the back seat. I catch glimpses of them watching something on Claire's phone from the rearview mirror.

"Good morning, everyone," I say, uncharacteristically breaking the silence as I put the truck in drive and follow the van into town.

"Good morning, Brady," Finley finally replies, catching my eye in the rearview mirror. "Claire has been sharing some of her social media posts with me, and they are fascinating. I must have gotten old. I had no idea there is so much going on besides Facebook and LinkedIn."

"If you're old, then I must be entering my Geezer phase," I joke, eliciting a laugh from everyone in the truck.

"Claire keeps me young, at least mentally," adds her dad. "I wish my knees and back felt the same."

We fall into a comfortable silence as we drive through the scenic country roads toward the small church in town. I glance at Finley in the rearview mirror and catch her eye again. She smiles, and I feel a warmth spreading through me. It's strange how just a simple smile from her can light up my whole morning.

We all pile out of the vehicles, and I notice Finley walking beside me. Her presence beside me feels comforting, and I want to keep her close.

When we enter the church, I see my two sisters saving pews for our group behind Mom and Dad.

"Oh My Gosh!!!" Claire exclaims as we approach, causing several heads to turn in our direction.

Michael shushes her, and we all look at her in confusion.

"I never put it together until now," she gasps. " Maddy Cav of Maddy and Josh is Maddy Cavanaugh. She is like Instagram Royalty. I am literally going to die."

"Well, please try to die quietly or wait until after church," Michael jokes, making us all snicker.

I look over at Finley. "I had no idea my sister was royalty. I guess that explains a lot."

Finley smiles, and we take our seats.

Halfway through the minister's sermon, I suddenly snap out of my daze and realize I have not been paying attention to a single word. My mind has been occupied with thoughts of the gorgeous woman sitting next to me and the desire to hold her hand. It's as if I've regressed to my teenage years and can't focus on anything else but the girl beside me. I steal a glance at Finley, who is listening intently to the sermon, her face serene and thoughtful. The urge to reach for her hand grows stronger, and without overthinking it, I slowly let my hand move closer to hers on the pew between us.

Just as our fingers are about to brush against each other, a sudden loud snore breaks the silence. We all turn to see old Ned, the grocer-head tilted back, fast asleep in the pew two rows behind us. Finley stifles a giggle, her eyes sparkling with amusement. I see his wife glare at him from the choir and stifle a laugh myself. The pastor, oblivious to the disruption, continues his sermon.

After the service ends, we all gather outside the church, exchanging pleasantries with the other churchgoers. Cole assures me that everyone is accounted for and It's okay to leave.

Once we're back in the truck and driving toward the ranch, Claire asks, "Mr. Cavanaugh, would you introduce me to your sister? Pretty please, with sugar on top?"

"I suppose I could be persuaded," I tease her.

"That would be so awesome. Thank you."

The atmosphere in the truck is light. Claire is gushing about meeting Maddy, and Finley is discussing a recent dental procedure with Michael.

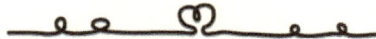

It's almost lunchtime when we park and unload. The sun beats down on us, and I feel beads of sweat form on my forehead.

"I think I'm going to change into something more casual before lunch," Finley announces. I offer to walk her to her cabin, and she nods in response. We stroll in comfortable silence until we reach her door.

"I'm glad I went. I had a nice time. I have to admit, I almost didn't go."

"Oh?" I raise an eyebrow, curious to hear more.

She takes a deep breath before continuing. "I've been struggling and blaming since Andrew's passing. I haven't been to a church since his funeral."

My heart goes out to her as she shares this vulnerable side of herself with me. "Wow, that's huge."

"I don't have any good reasons for not being a regular attendee," I add. "But I'm glad we both went today."

"Me too. Do you want to wait while I change or meet me at the dining hall?"

"I'd like to wait if that's alright."

"I'd like that. Come on in. There are water bottles in the fridge."

My eyes scan the cabin for the first time since the remodel. Addie has truly outdone herself with these bungalows. They are a perfect mix of modern comfort and rustic charm – Nothing like the old cowboy cabins they used to be. I am impressed with what my sister has created. I imagine all the families that will make memories in these spaces.

I grab two bottles, but Finley emerges from her ensuite in shorts and a light cotton tee before I can sit. She looks effortlessly beautiful.

"I should change as well; staying in these dress pants all day will be uncomfortable in this heat."

"You should definitely change if you want to be comfortable. But I have to say, you do clean up nicely, Cowboy."

A slight flush creeps up my neck at her compliment, and I clear my throat before replying, "I'll take that as a hint then." Her teasing tone makes me smile. It's been a long time since someone has made me feel this way.

I walk Finley to the dining hall and excuse myself to change.

Upon my return, I find Finley seated at one of the tables, taking small sips from her water bottle. Her eyes light up as she sees me, and a warm smile spreads across her face. I feel a rush of happiness at the sight of her.

"I waited for you so we could go through the line together."

A warm grin spreads across my face at her thoughtful gesture. We move quickly through the bustling lunch line, and I sneak glances at her. I wonder how this woman can fit so naturally into my world and make it feel like we have known each other for ages in such a short time?

We find a table near the window with a view of the ranch's sprawling fields. The chatter and laughter from the other guests create a pleasant background noise, but my attention is solely on Finley.

"What do you have planned for this afternoon?" I ask, eager to spend more time with her.

She ponders my question for a minute before asking with a mischievous glimmer in her eye, "Did you have something in mind, Cowboy?"

"Well, darlin', I have a little bit of Cowboy'n to do after chow, but I reckon we could take a little ride on horseback before supper if your willin.'" I am laying the twang on thick now.

"Sounds like a date."

"I should be done about three."

"Well, I reckon I'll just read by the pool until then." She giggles, also trying to put a Texas drawl on her words.

My heart races at the thought of spending the day with her, exploring the ranch, and getting to know her better. Time seems to stand still as we plan our afternoon.

When the clock nears three, I wrap up my tasks and ask Jake to saddle Rosie and Bandera.

As I walk towards the pool area, I catch a glimpse of Finley relaxing, a book in hand. Seeing her against the backdrop of the ranch's beauty takes my breath away. She looks up and waves as she spots me approaching, a smile lighting up her face.

Before I reach Finley, I notice my sister, Madison, at the pool. She is wearing the smallest bikini I have ever seen.

"Hey, Maddy, there is a dentist here looking for his floss. Did you steal it?"

"Very funny, old man. I'll have you know this is high fashion."

"I'm sure it is outside of West Texas, but you are going to give some guy a heart attack out here by the pool." I grab her towel on the adjacent chair and throw it over her.

"Whatever, Old Man!"

"There is a teenage girl, one of the guests, her name is Claire. She would love to meet you. Can I introduce her to you later? Apparently, she's one of your fans. She thinks you're some kind of Internet Queen."

"Of course, Brady. I am always available to my fans."

"I can see that, Mads. Just don't be too available and wear something less revealing. You're gonna kill somebody."

"Is that your lawyer, lady? She's gorgeous, Brady. Don't screw this up."

"She's not my anything, Mads." I leave out the word YET. "Got to run."

I walk toward Finley. She has an odd look on her face.

"Ready for that ride?" I ask as I reach her side.

"Sure, but do you always cover the guests with towels?"

"No, just sisters."

"Ahh," she replies, setting her book aside and putting on her boots. "Lead the way, Cowboy," she adds, gathering her things into a small string bag.

I offer her my hand, which she takes, a playful twinkle in her eye. We go to the stables, where Jake has readied our horses for an afternoon adventure.

I help her onto her horse and her eyes light up with excitement and nervousness as she adjusts herself in the saddle. I assure her that she looks like a natural up there, and her smile reassures me that she's ready for our ride.

With a nudge of my heels, my horse leads us out of the barn, and soon, we're trotting along familiar paths that wind through the picturesque ranch that I love so much. Finley follows close behind, her laughter filling the air as we navigate the winding trails together. The warm afternoon sun casts a golden glow over everything. The breeze tousles our hair, carrying with it a sense of freedom and joy that only comes from being out in nature.

We ride side by side, and the gentle sway of our horses' gait lulls us into a comfortable silence, occasionally interrupted by a comment or shared smile.

I steal glances at Finley. Something about her presence soothes me in a way I hadn't expected. Her easy laughter, genuine smile, and kind spirit have woven their way into my guarded heart.

Before long, we come to a hill overlooking the ranch, bathed in the sun's warm hues. I bring my horse to a stop, and Finley follows suit, the majestic view spreading out before us. She gazes out at the landscape, her eyes wide with wonder. The view of the tranquil open fields and distant mountains is breathtaking.

"This is incredible," her voice filled with awe.

"It's one of my favorite spots on the ranch," I admit, my gaze shifting from the view to settle on her. "I'm glad you're here to share it with me."

Finley turns to me, a soft smile on her lips. "I'm glad too, Brady."

Her use of my first name catches me off guard, but in a good way. It feels intimate and personal, like she's inviting me into a new level of connection. I am drawn to her in a way that excites and terrifies me.

As we sit there in companionable silence, the sun begins its slow descent toward the horizon, casting a warm glow over everything. The peacefulness of the moment wraps around us like a comforting blanket, easing any lingering tension between us.

We linger on the hilltop, letting the peacefulness of the moment envelop us. And as the sun starts its descent, casting a warm golden light over the land, I feel a sense of possibility and hope stir within me.

We make our way back to the stables as the sky is painted in hues of orange and pink. The fading light accentuates Finley's features, casting a soft glow around her. She catches my eye and smiles, a silent understanding passing between us.

Once we reach the stables, I dismount and offer her a hand down. Our fingers touch briefly, sending a jolt of electricity through me. I notice how her eyes sparkle in the last light of the day. The familiar sound of horses settling in for the night surrounds us, a comforting rhythm that matches the beating of my heart.

Everything feels different around her, softer and more alive.

Dinner with the group is a blur. My thoughts are still on the incredible ride we just shared. I watch Finley from across the dinner table, her easy laughter and bright eyes drawing me in. The chatter around us fades into the background as I realize how much I enjoy her company.

After the meal, as everyone starts to disperse, I feel a hand gently brush against mine.

"Walk me home?" Finley asks softly.

We step outside into the cool evening air. The sky is a canvas of stars, twinkling above us like diamonds scattered across velvet. I turn to Finley, who is looking up at the night sky with wonder in her eyes.

"Beautiful, isn't it?" I say, matching her gaze at the stars above.

"Absolutely stunning," she breathes out, a smile playing on her lips.

We walk towards her bungalow, and a comfortable silence settles between us, filled with unspoken words and shared moments. When we reach the front porch, I turn to face her, wanting to prolong this moment a little longer. "Thank you for sharing this day with me," I say, my voice softer than intended.

Finley looks up at me, her gaze meeting mine with a warmth that fills me up from the inside out. "I should be thanking you, Brady. Today has been... amazing."

Her words hang in the air between us, heavy with unspoken emotions and possibilities. I lean in closer, unable to resist the magnetic pull between us. And then, as if drawn by an invisible force, our lips meet in a kiss.

In that fleeting moment, time seems to stand still as we explore the tentative connection that has been brewing between us since the moment we met. And as we pull away, breathless and wide-eyed, I know this is just the beginning of something beautiful and unexpected.

Finley smiles at me, a soft blush dusting her cheeks as she reaches for my hand. "I don't want this day to end," she admits as a small yawn escapes her lips.

"Me either, but how about we make a plan for tomorrow? Another ride, perhaps?"

Finley's eyes light up at the suggestion, excitement dancing in her gaze. "I'd love that," she says, her voice filled with genuine enthusiasm.

"Good night, Finley."

"Good night, Brady," Finley replies, her smile lingering as she turns to unlock the door. After she steps inside, I stand there for a moment, watching the door close behind her.

When I finally settle into bed, the image of Finley's smile and the feel of her hand in mine fill my thoughts. The unexpected connection we shared today has stirred something deep within me, awakening emotions I thought long buried beneath the rugged exterior I've always worn like armor.

I close my eyes, letting the memories of our ride and our tender kiss wash over me like a gentle wave. In that moment, I know that my world has shifted, irrevocably changed, by the presence of this spirited woman who has found her way into my heart in ways I never thought possible.

Chapter Fourteen

Finley

After Brady walks me to my door I am floating on air. I am exhausted but not ready for sleep just yet.

I decide to indulge in the luxurious bathtub that is calling me. I grab my journal and pour myself a glass of red wine while I wait for the tub to fill. The scent of lavender and vanilla fills the air, calming my senses and inviting me to relax.

I realize I haven't checked my phone since this morning, which surprises me. I see two messages from Kaitlyn, one from earlier in the day and one from a few hours ago.

Dr. Dull stopped by to pick up a few of his things. Super awkward.

You must be having too much fun, or you lost your phone again.!!!

I quickly reply, unable to contain my excitement.

I kissed him!

WHO? Grumpy Cowboy?

LOL, His name is Brady.

Woo-Hoo!

Don't get too excited. It was just one kiss. Well, actually, two.

Woo Hoo X2!!

Feeling a bit uncertain about where things are heading with Brady, I confide.

I'm not sure this is more than a sweet distraction.

There are still 2 weeks left of your trip and endless possibilities.

I'll keep you posted.

You better. I am living vicariously through you for now.

That's too much pressure. Got to run; my tub is probably overflowing.

The moment I sink into the warm water, all my worries melt away. The bath salts provided are more luxurious than anything I would typically splurge on for myself. I lean back, close my eyes, and let out a content sigh. This is the perfect way to end a perfect day.

Sleep comes quickly.

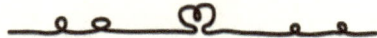

The next morning, I wake up feeling refreshed and eager to start the day. As I sip my coffee and gaze out at the sprawling ranch from the cozy cabin, I can't help but think about Brady. The memory of his soft kisses and rugged charm lingers in my mind, sending a flutter through my stomach.

My journal sits on my bedside table, making me feel a sliver of guilt. I reached for it, but my hand hesitates briefly before finally grasping the leather cover. I open it to add my thoughts for today and realize the pen is missing.

I look on the floor and all around the table. I grab a pen from the desk so I can write. I'll look for that pen more thoroughly later.

June 11
Andrew,
Brady convinced me to go to church with him yesterday, and I'm glad I did. I don't think I'm mad at God anymore. The minister talked about

letting go of anger. I didn't realize until today that I wasn't just sad; I was angry too. I have been blaming him for taking you away from me for so long that I haven't been able to find happiness in anything. I think I may be getting past that now. Being on this ranch in nature every day has been amazing. I feel strangely at home despite the weirdness of my location.

I love you and miss you.

Always,

Finley

When I finish, I place the journal back on the bedside table and look down behind it. The pen is nowhere to be seen. That is odd; maybe I left it on the porch the other day.

I head to breakfast and wonder about the fate of my favorite pen. Maybe housekeeping moved it. I will have to ask later.

Chapter Fifteen

Finley

After a late morning yoga, I join Zoey and Barbara at a rustic wooden table in the cozy ranch kitchen. They are sitting with Brady's sister, Addie, drinking coffee. The smell of warm bread invites me to join them.

"Finley, here." Zoey smiles widely, lifting a small jar filled with a bright red jam. "You must try this. It's made right here on the ranch. It is so delicious that I am going to smuggle some in my luggage and take it home with me."

I eagerly accept a cup of coffee from Addie and pull up a chair.

I sit down, and Zoey passes me the jar. It looks like it's made from a berry – or maybe a combination of several different kinds.

I take a slice of bread and spoon some jam onto my plate.

"If it's as good as you say, I might never leave this place." I joke, taking a bite.

"Oh my gosh. That is delicious!"

"That's the spirit! Embrace the ranch life, girl." Zoey says, pointing to a bit of jam on my chin.

Addie, the subtle observer, chimes in, "You seem at home here, Finley."

I feel a warmth in my chest, knowing that it's true. Despite the initial strangeness of being on a ranch in the middle of nowhere, I have found a sense of peace and community that I didn't know I was missing.

Since returning from the cattle drive, Brady has been busy managing the ranch during the day. We've shared dinners in the dining room, and he's shown me every corner of the ranch on ATVs or horseback. Most afternoons, I spend time bonding with my fellow campers.

It's a new experience for me; I don't think I've ever just relaxed like this with a group of women. I have female friends, of course, but this experience feels different—so wonderfully casual and effortlessly comfortable. It's as if we've known each other for years.

I savor this moment, feeling grateful for the easy camaraderie that is developing between us.

"What do y'all think of the ranch so far?" Addie asks between sips of her coffee.

"So amazing," Zoey gushes. "I am so glad Max and I came. We have been working so hard. We needed something like this!"

"Same here," I admit, taking a bite of my bread slathered in the heavenly jam. "Zoey was right – this stuff is life-changing." I give her a grateful smile, and she winks back at me.

Adie laughs. "Well, there's a lot more of the ranch to explore if you have the time. We have a lake on the property that's perfect for swimming or fishing and lots of hiking trails with incredible views. " I smile at this, having seen the lake firsthand.

"There are new babies in the goat barn." She grabs a notebook from her back pocket as if to double-check her list.

"Oh, and I almost forgot. My brother Cody and his band will be playing on Friday night at Over Yonder in Cramer. We're planning to take y'all if you want.

"The what?" I ask, looking at her perplexed.

"It's a honky-tonk," she clarifies, as though it should have been obvious. We must still look confused, so she keeps explaining.

"It's a local bar, kind of a dive bar, actually. But it's got a dance floor, and great bands play every weekend. It's a country music staple in this part of the world."

Barbara's face transforms as if she has just heard the magical words 'bar' and 'dance floor.'

Her eyes widen, and her face lights up with excitement. Or as excited as her Botox will allow her to look. "Ohh. I can't wait to get my groove thing on!"

Her enthusiasm rivals a small child on Christmas morning. That woman never ceases to amaze me.

After coffee, I walk to the barn where the goats are
housed.

"Did you come to meet some of the newest
members of the ranch family?" I am greeted by a
fifty-something lady in an apron bottle feeding the
tiniest baby goat I have ever seen.

"Come on in. I'm Loretta, and this here's
Peanut," she coos, nodding at the small goat in her
arms.

As soon as I push open the gate, I am surrounded
by baby goats bleating for attention and affection.
Their furry heads barely come up to my knees.

"They're so small and cute. Where are their
mamas?" I bend down to pet as many as possible as
they nudge each other for my attention. Their fur
is surprisingly soft under my hands.

"The mamas are out grazing, but these babies don't
do so good in the hot sun all day. We keep them
in here during mid-day. Plus, I think it gives the
mama goats a break for a bit. They are pretty active,

like school-aged children. I think that's why they call them kids.

"Why are you bottle-feeding this sweet little one?" I pet his head, and I think I'm in love.

"Gerty had twins, and since this one is the smaller of the two, he keeps getting shoved by his sister when he tries to nurse. See that bigger black goat over by the gate? That's her. I've been calling her Queenie."

"Do you want to feed him?"

"I'd love to."

I take the baby from her, and immediately, he starts to cry. Loretta sticks the bottle in his mouth, and he calms back down, drinking hungrily.

"Have a seat," Loretta opens a metal folding chair for me. "If you sit on the ground or one of these hay bales, you will be surrounded by these little guys."

"I'll be right back." She walks toward what looks like a supply closet, followed by about two dozen baby goats. It is just the cutest thing.

I cradle Peanut's soft, warm body in my arms and set his empty bottle on the fence post behind me. As

I look up, Brady's gaze meets mine, a gentle smile on his lips.

"You look pretty comfortable with that little guy." His eyes never leave mine.

"Yeah, I've always loved animals. Especially baby ones."

Brady nods. "I can tell. You have a way with them. First Charlie, now this baby." He takes a step closer and reaches out to pet Peanut. I feel a shiver run down my spine as his rough fingers brush against mine.

"His name is Peanut."

"That suits him. Did you name him?"

"No, I think Loretta did."

He crouches down beside me, his body only inches away from mine. His scent is a mixture of something woodsy and spicey and oh-so distracting.

"They seem to like you," he says, his voice low and smooth.

His eyes, a piercing shade of blue, lock onto mine, igniting a flutter in my belly. His tousled hair catches the sunlight, and I am even more distracted by his handsome, rugged features. There's a silent tension between us, almost electric. I try to maintain my composure, but his proximity is sending my heart racing.

The sound of a bleating goat gets my attention. I look up to see Loretta standing there, an amused expression on her face.

"Afternoon, Miss Loretta. I came by to see if the guys fixed that break in the goat fence and to grab your supply order."

Loretta's eyes are playful; she glances from Brady to me. A knowing grin finds its way onto her lips. "Now, Brady, you could have just called me. You didn't need to come all the way over here to check on things," her words are teasing.

"I'll run and grab that list real quick."

"I better get back to work," he says after Loretta returns with the list. I'll see you at dinner, Boston."

"I haven't seen that man in this barn for six months." Loretta's words startle me as I watch Brady leave the barn.

"I'm sorry. What do you mean?"

She chuckles as she teases me. "His office has a straight-line view of this barn. He was looking for you, sweetie. That man is smitten!"

Chapter Sixteen

Brady

The scent of hay and baby goats still lingers on my shirt as I return from the barn to my office. That woman has gotten under my skin like no other has since...well, in a long time. When she smiles, it's like the sun breaking through the clouds after days of rain. And when she laughs, I want to haul off and do something ridiculous just to hear it again.

I'd gone down to the barn on the pretense of checking the fence, but Loretta had seen right through me. She knew I just wanted an excuse to see Finley again. And she'd teased me about it, too. Am I that obvious?

Maybe so. There's just something about Finley that draws me in—that makes me want to open up parts of myself I'd locked away. I don't know if I'm ready for that, but I'll see her at dinner tonight, so maybe I'll find out.

I try my best to focus on work for the next few hours, but the darn clock doesn't seem to be moving fast enough. Despite my distracted thoughts, I managed to get a few things done. When my alarm finally lets me know it's a half hour before dinner, I pack it in for the day. I have time for a quick shower to wash off the day's dust before meeting her.

As the hot water washes over me, I think about that kiss she initiated on the cattle drive and how she smiled shyly at me afterward. Did it mean as much to her as it did to me? Or was it just a fleeting moment that she regrets? I know the kiss on her porch was mutual, but I'm dying to know if she is feeling what I'm feeling. Our flirtatious banter over the past few days tells me she feels something, too, but I need to be sure.

Loretta noticed the sparks between us; her comment about me coming all that way to the barn today is proof she sees what I've been trying hard not to admit to myself.

I catch my reflection in the mirror as I towel off. The scowl lines on my forehead have softened some since Finley arrived. It's only been a week, but somehow, this city girl has brought light back to the long days on the ranch. I shake my head. I never thought I'd go moon-eyed over a woman again, yet here I am.

I pull on a clean shirt and brush off my hat before hurrying to the dining hall.

I push through the swinging doors into the dining hall, scanning the long tables until I spot her. Finley is already seated, looking effortlessly beautiful in a simple sundress. She glances up from her plate and smiles.

Yeah, I'm in trouble here.

I grab a plate and join her. "Howdy, ma'am. Fancy meeting you here."

She laughs, light and easy. "Well, aren't you charming?"

I slide into the seat across from her. "So, how was the rest of your day with those crazy goats?"

"It was great!" Her eyes shine with enthusiasm. "I helped Loretta trim some of their hooves and made sure all the babies got cuddles."

As Finley talks about the animals, I mostly just watch her face—how it animates when she talks about something she cares about—how her nose crinkles when she smiles.

We chat easily over dinner, from ranch happenings to stories of our childhoods. The more I learn about this remarkable woman, the more intrigued I become. Underneath her polished exterior, I'm starting to glimpse a kindred spirit—someone who knows what it means to feel alone even when surrounded by people.

Maybe I'm not ready to let someone new into my most vulnerable parts. But I'm sure willing to give it a try with this woman. She just might be worth the risk.

"So what did you do after you left?" She pauses before taking a bite of her salad.

I chuckle. "Not nearly as much as I probably should have. You see, I seem to be a bit distracted by this beautiful lawyer I met a while back."

She looks surprised but smiles playfully and nods as if wanting more details.

"I did what needed to get done so that the ranch doesn't fall apart at the seams -- then I hustled to get myself all gussied up in time to meet her for dinner."

I am trying to let her know how I feel in a playful way in case I'm completely off track with how this is going.

I suggest we take a walk after dinner to enjoy the warm evening air.

Finley and I walk in silence just as the sun is beginning to set, casting a warm golden glow over the ranch. She seems different somehow as we stroll - not quite as lighthearted as before. I notice her fiddling with her empty ring finger.

The more time I spend with her, the more I realize how little I truly know about her life before now.

"Tell me about him," I finally ask.

"Andrew?"

"Was that your husband's name? Addie told me a little about your first day here, but I didn't want to push to you talk about it."

She looks like she is about to cry. "You don't have to tell me if you aren't ready."

"No, I think it's time. He's been gone over a year now."

We sit on the steps of the storage shed, and she takes a steadying breath before she starts.

"Andrew was an amateur pilot. He'd had his license for at least 15 years and was taking a routine flight back from visiting his mom in Maine, where she was staying for the fall. The plane went down over the coast." She reaches into her pocket, pulls out a tissue, blots the corner of her eyes, and keeps going. "I was supposed to be on that flight too, but I had a contract I needed to draft and stayed home instead."

"You can stop if you need to."

"No, I'm good," she sniffs and wipes her eyes again.

"It was determined that his plane had mechanical problems. He was unconscious when they found him, and he was taken by MedFlite helicopter to Boston General Hospital. That's where I spent the next six months of my life, at the bedside of my comatose 34-year-old husband. His broken body healed, but he never regained consciousness. Ultimately, it was a blood clot that finally killed him almost six months to the day of the accident." She finishes, focusing on the wadded tissue in her hand.

I place my hand over hers, and she looks up at me.

"That was over a year ago, and I am just now beginning to live again."

"Thank you for sharing that with me." I squeeze her hand gently. "I can't imagine what you've been through. It takes incredible strength to keep going after something like that."

Finley offers me a small, sad smile. "I don't know about strength. Some days, it's just putting one foot in front of the other and hoping for the best."

We sit in companionable silence for a moment; the only sound is the soft chirping of crickets as night descends around us. The sky is painted with hues of pink and orange, a stunning backdrop to our somber conversation.

"I'm sorry if that brought up painful memories," I say finally, breaking the quiet between us.

"No, no," she rushes to reassure me. "It feels good to talk about him."

After she opens up about her life in Boston and her struggles since losing her husband, I'm without words. It's heavy stuff.

I was planning on asking her to join me at the dance hall on Friday, picturing us laughing and dancing together under the stars, hoping to take our relationship to the next level—an actual date. But now, with Finley's vulnerability laid bare in front of me, it seems wrong - almost predatory. Instead of focusing on my desires, I try to think of what she needs right now. Maybe she only needs someone to listen: to understand. Dare I say – a friend.

I offer her a gentle smile. "Thank you for trusting me with your story, Finley. It means a lot to me."

She nods, grateful but exhausted from reliving those painful memories. "I'm sorry. I didn't mean to bring the mood down."

She stands up suddenly and shakes out her legs. "I think my butt is numb from sitting on these hard steps."

I laugh but wonder if she is simply trying to change the direction of our conversation.

"Let's walk some more," I suggest.

She reaches out, and I take her delicate hand in mine. The sparks that shoot up my arm make me feel more alive than ever before. I suddenly understand what people write in those sappy love songs – this feeling is indescribable and so powerful. Yet, at the same time, it feels like a betrayal even to entertain those feelings when she is hurting so much. At this moment, nothing else matters but being here with her.

"Thank you for listening."

"Finley, you don't have to thank me."

She smiles, a genuine warmth in her eyes.

In the quiet moments that follow, we continue our walk through the ranch, hand in hand.

We find our way to the skeet shooting range as we walk. "What is this place?" she asks.

"It's the shooting range."

"Have you ever been skeet shooting before?"

She shakes her head, causing a cascade of auburn hair to spill over her face. "No, I can't say that I have ever have. Is it difficult?"

"Not too bad once you get the hang of it."

"Do you teach it here?"

"I don't usually give the lessons, but I suppose I could be persuaded to-just this once."

"I'd like that very much."

My heart leaps at her words. She wants to spend more time with me! "It sounds like it is part of the whole ranch package," she teases. "I should get my money's worth and give it a try, don't you think?"

"It's getting a little too dark tonight, but let's try tomorrow after breakfast?"

She smiles, her nose crinkling adorably, and my stomach does a flip-flop for some reason.

A small yawn escapes her lips, and she rubs her beautiful green eyes. I glance at my watch.

"Well, we should get going; I've got an early morning."

I cannot imagine the grief she feels, as I have never lost someone as close as a spouse. But still, I can see the effort - how hard she is working to move forward and live her life again. Maybe, just maybe, I can be a part of that journey.

Since she shared so much, I should probably tell her about my miserable attempt at marriage, but the embarrassment of that epic failure is just too much right now. I don't want her to think less of me for giving up.

We hold hands as I walk her back to her bungalow. I want to tell her how proud I am of her and how strong she is. I worry that it will sound condescending, so I haven't said anything just yet.

"Well, I guess this is goodnight," She whispers wistfully.

"Yeah...goodnight." My throat tightens, making my words sound strained. I rub the back of my neck, and I suddenly feel shy. "So, I'll see you in the morning.

We stand there awkwardly for a moment, both reluctant to part ways. Before I can overthink it, I lean in and lightly kiss her forehead. Her eyes widen, and she inhales sharply with surprise but doesn't pull away.

"Sweet dreams, Boston," I murmur.

A warm blush blossoms on her face, making her all the more stunning. "You too, Brady."

As she disappears inside, I am left alone with only the sound of my heartbeat ringing in my ears. But instead of feeling lonely, I feel alive, and a slow grin spreads across my face.

Chapter Seventeen

Finley

I wake up in my bungalow, feeling a warmth in my chest that I haven't experienced in a long time. The sun streams through the curtains, casting a golden glow over the cozy room. I stretch lazily in the comfy king-sized bed, remnants of my dream fading as I recall last night with Brady. His smile, those dimples, the way he looked at me while I poured out my heart. A tingle runs through me. Can this really be happening?

June 13
Andrew,
Last night, Brady and I shared a quiet moment under the starry night sky. I told him all about you

and what we had. He understands that my heart carries the weight of your loss.

I feel guilty about these newfound feelings as if I'm betraying our love. But I also can't deny the spark of hope that Brady brings into my life. I hope you understand.

I will always love you,
Finley

"What does everyone have planned for today?" I ask as I join Albert, Sam, Barbara, and Claire at breakfast.

"I've got to meet Simon at the horse barn in a few minutes. He's gonna help me with one of my videos."

"What's your topic of the day, my dear, "Barbara inquires.

"Well, I'm not 100 that it is going to work, so I don't want to jinx it."

"Well, good luck with whatever it is. Sam and I are planning to help out with some of the fencing for a bit after breakfast. Apparently, a little goat keeps breaking through one of the pens," Albert explains.

I laugh, "That's probably Queenie if I had to guess."

"Familiar with the goats by name already," Barb teases.

"Just a few memorable ones."

"What do you have planned, Barb?"

"I'll probably spend some time with Geoffrey. He seems to like sitting by the pool, which is no different from his routine at home. Then, I plan to go to town for a mani-pedi. Anyone else interested?"

"I'd love to. I guess it depends on what time you go. I have a skeet shooting lesson after breakfast.

"I was thinking maybe after lunch, but I'll let you know."

"Sounds good. I'm off to the shooting range this morning. Wish me luck."

Claire and I gather our things and leave together.

"That Mr. Brady is really cute for an "Old" guy. But don't tell him I said so."

"He's not that old, Claire. And, I will not be telling him that you think he's old."

"For me, he's ancient. But for you, he's just right."

"Thanks, Goldilocks. Good luck with your video," I tell her as we part ways outside.

Butterflies begin swirling in my stomach as I near my destination. Brady is already at the shooting range when I arrive, leaning against the fence, looking as rugged and handsome as ever in his worn jeans and plaid shirt.

"Morning, Boston," he says, tipping his hat at me. "Ready for your lesson?"

"Totally!" I answer, even though I'm secretly terrified. I raise an eyebrow. "Are you sure you have time to give me a private lesson?"

"I made time for you this morning."

"Aww. Thanks."

"I'm not going to be available much the next two or three days unfortunately. I have about a hundred horses on their way here that need to be evaluated, which will take quite a bit of time."

"If you don't have time for this, we can reschedule."

"No, no. I want to be here with you. The horses are still in transit. I'll get a message when they are close, so let's make the most of the time we have."

"Thanks for making an exception for me," I say, touched by his gesture but a little bummed by what he just said. "I promise not to be too much of a disaster."

He leads me over to the shooting station, his hand lightly grazing my back. I shiver at his touch.

"Trust me, you'll do great." He winks playfully, and my heart does a little somersault.

Brady hands me protective earmuffs and glasses. His fingers brush mine, and a spark shoots up my arm. I fumble to get the gear on, nerves and excitement churning inside me.

He patiently shows me how to hold the shotgun properly, his strong hands guiding mine into position. "We're gonna do a practice one first, no ammo, so that you know how to hold the gun and pull the trigger at the same time. Just focus, breathe, and pull the trigger when you're ready," he instructs.

As I watch Brady prepare the equipment, I feel special knowing that he's taking the time to teach me himself. He explains the basics, helping me get a feel for the shotgun.

"Okay, this time, the gun is loaded."

It makes me a little nervous, but I keep myself calm.

"You're just gonna shoot the gun, no target yet. You will let you feel how the gun reacts when it's fired. Are you ready?"

"I think so."

"Just point it up a little more; there you go," his hands guide mine as he helps me adjust my stance. His proximity sends shivers down my spine, and I struggle to focus on his instructions.

"Like this?" I ask, looking up at him for confirmation.

"Exactly like that," he answers, his voice low and warm. "You're a natural, Finley."

"I'm gonna let go. Fire when you're ready."

I squint my eyes a little and picture a target. When I fire, the shotgun kicks hard against my shoulder.

"Owe. That was stronger than I was expecting."

"Are you hurt?" Brady asks as he puts his hand on my shoulder.

"No, it just startled me how much it packs a punch,"

"But I think I'm ready for the real thing now."

"It takes some getting used to. You did great, though. Just remember to lean into it a bit more next time, and you'll feel less of a kickback," Brady reassures me with a warm smile.

"On the count of three, I'll release a clay pigeon, and you'll try to hit it."

"Okay," I agree nervously, my heart pounding as I wait for his signal. "One...two...three!" I try to concentrate as the first clay target launches into the air. And I completely miss.

"Don't worry, you'll get it," Brady says. He steps up close behind me,

"Just tweak your hips like this..." he says, his hand grazing my waist. My breath hitches at his touch. He notices and meets my gaze. The air between us feels charged.

I'm hyper-aware of his hard, muscular frame pressed against my back, his breath tickling my neck. My heart races, and I'm sure he can hear it pounding.

"Try again," he says. The next clay pigeon soars through the sky, and I follow its path with my eyes, taking a deep breath before pulling the trigger. To my amazement, I hit it, sending pieces of clay flying in every direction.

"I did it!" I cry, thrilled.

"Atta girl," Brady wraps me in an awkward hug while I struggle to hold the shotgun.

He steps back quickly, realizing his mistake. "Sorry about that. Forgot about the shotgun for a moment. You did great!"

"Thanks to your expert coaching,"

Our flirtation continues throughout the lesson, filling the space between us with electricity. Each time our eyes meet or our fingers brush against each other, I feel a thrill of excitement at our growing connection. I feel myself falling for this complex, rugged cowboy. And I think, just maybe, he's falling for me too.

The sun overhead tells me we should probably wrap this up so Brady can return to work. Just then, his phone chimes, and he looks at the message.

"I have a load of potential horses about to arrive. I will be out of pocket for the rest of today and probably most of tomorrow while we evaluate them.

I am sorry, Finley. I wish I could have rescheduled this, but the breeder has a schedule I don't control."

"I understand," I say, trying to hide my disappointment. "I will find something to do until then. This ranch is so big, I'm sure I won't run out of things to explore."

Brady smiles warmly at me. "I'll make it up to you when I'm free again."

Brady kisses me on the cheek and gives me an apologetic smile before heading towards the stables. I watch him walk away, feeling a twinge of sadness at the sudden end of our time together.

My mind buzzes with thoughts of Brady as I walk to the lodge. The way he had looked at me, the gentle touch of his hand on my waist, the thrill of hitting that clay pigeon under his guidance. It all felt like a dream, too perfect to be real.

Lost in my reverie, I almost bump into Max, who is walking toward the shooting range with a fancy digital camera in hand.

"Have you seen my wife lately? I have some amazing shots of the landscape that I think will look great in my office at home."

"I haven't, but I'm about to get some lunch. Do you want to join me and see if Zoey is at the dining hall?"

Max looks at his watch. "Sure. I haven't been paying attention to the time. I've been out here for hours. This place has a way of making you forget about everything else. Let's go find her."

We walk together towards the lodge, chatting about the beauty of the ranch and the peacefulness of the surroundings. Max shows me a few photos he has taken on his camera, each more stunning than the last.

When we get to the dining hall, it is bustling with lunchtime activity. The smell of something spicy fills the air.

Max and I scan the room, looking for his wife among the crowd.

"There she is," Max says, pointing towards a table near the back of the room engrossed in a book.

We make our way over to her table, and as we get closer, I can see that she is completely absorbed in her reading, her brow furrowed in concentration.

"Hey, sweetheart," Max says as we reach her table.

She looks up from her book, a smile lighting up her face. "Max! Finley!

"I've been enjoying some quiet time with my book," she says, gesturing to the novel. "What have you two been up to?"

I filled her in on my shooting lesson with Brady and how I had hit several clay pigeons under his guidance. She listens intently, nodding along with my story.

Max pulls out a chair. "I have some beautiful photos of the ranch." He begins showing his wife the amazing photographs he just took.

"Oh babe, these are just what you wanted for that blah empty wall in the office."

"I know, right."

"Hey, Luke told me it's Taco Tuesday when I sat down to read earlier." Zoey says." It smells like lunch is ready."

"Yum. Tacos sound perfect."

Max nods in agreement. "Tacos do sound delicious. Let's go grab some before they're all gone."

Chapter Eighteen

Brady

I leave Finley at the shooting range, and my mood has soured by the time I reach my office. I grab the files the breeder sent on the new horses and leave to meet Jake and Sawyer at my truck.

On my way to the truck, I hear music coming from the barn. I make a detour to check it out.

"That's "Popular" from the musical Wicked. I love that song." Sasha's voice carries across the space.

When I look over at the pen, Claire and Scout are swaying in sync with the music; the horse is dancing around with Claire atop his back. She swings her hair, and Scout does the same with his mane. They turn in circles a few times one way and then the other. As soon as the song ends, the pair pause, then stick their tongues out at the same time. Simon is capturing this whole scene on a phone. "Did you get it this time? That was awesome. Good boy." She wraps her arms around Scout's neck and kisses him on his head.

"Yeah, I got it," Simon says in awe. "How'd you get him to do that?"

Claire smiles roguishly as she dismounts from the horse's back and takes the phone from Simon.

"Just call me the horse whisperer," she laughs, looking into the phone's lens as she speaks. My followers expect something amazing, and I aim to please."

As Claire pockets the phone, Scout nudges her, seemingly wanting more attention. She giggles and pulls a carrot from her pocket, offering it to the playful horse. Scout takes the carrot and munches on it contentedly.

Simon watches in admiration, enchanted by the girl or the horse. My money is on the girl.

I don't know why this whole scene annoys me so much. They're just kids having fun, and Scout probably loves the attention.

I watch for a moment longer, feeling a pang of jealousy at the easy camaraderie of these kids. They look so carefree, so full of joy in each other's company.

But as I turn to leave, Sasha spots me and waves.

"Hey, Mr. Brady!"

Claire calls out, walking over with Scout in tow. "Did you catch our little dance routine?"

I nod, trying to muster up a smile. "Yeah, I saw. Impressive moves."

Simon adds, "Yeah, it's pretty cool what she can get him to do."

There's a warmth in Simon's voice that catches my attention. It's clear he admires Claire's talent and connection with the horses. And that is more words than I have heard that kid utter since he arrived.

Claire's eyes narrow as she studies my expression. "Is everything okay? You seem... off."

"I'm good," I say, straightening up. "I'd better get going. Work to do."

They all wave as I leave the barn.

Refocusing on the day's responsibilities, I reach my truck and find Jake and Sawyer waiting for me. They both look excited, eager to see the new horses arriving any minute.

I hand Sawyer the files, outlining the plan for evaluating the new horses. He studies the documents intently, jotting down notes on a notepad.

"You okay, boss?" Jake asks with a concerned look.

"He's probably just annoyed that he has to be with us instead of his new lady friend."

Sawyer's not wrong. I do wish I were with Finley, but the earlier incident in the barn left me feeling down, reminding me that life isn't as carefree for me as it is for the kids there. I still need to talk to Finley about my own baggage, but the time doesn't ever seem right. Bringing up an ex-wife isn't going to be easy.

I take a moment to collect my thoughts before answering Jake. "I'm good; just have a lot on my mind. Let's get started on this evaluation, okay?"

When we finally reach the stables, I see the trailers already parked outside, and I can hear the whinnies and snorts of unfamiliar horses. The excitement in the air is palpable as we approach the trailer and prepare to unload the new arrivals.

One by one, the horses are led out of the trailer, their coats gleaming in the sunlight. They are a mix of colors and sizes, each more magnificent than the last. Jake and Sawyer are like kids in a candy store, oohing and aahing over each horse as it steps onto solid ground.

I watch Jake and Sawyer begin assessing each horse for conformation and temperament, and I feel a surge of excitement. This is what I live for - the thrill of working with these incredible animals, building a strong team, and creating something truly special.

Some of these beautiful creatures will soon be a part of our ranch, and this reminds me that there is always room for new beginnings and fresh connections. I watch the horses interact with each other and my team and feel a sense of hope.

Chapter Nineteen

Finley

The past three days have been a blur. I can hardly believe how quickly this trip is passing. There has been a whirlwind of activities to keep me busy. I find a sense of peace and comfort in the predictable rhythm of camp life, where each day offers new adventures and familiar faces-except one.

After tacos on Tuesday, Barb and I ventured into town for some much-needed pampering with manicures and pedicures. She had the staff in stitches. That woman is such a character. I thought she would be a nightmare when I met her that first day, but she has proven that first impressions aren't always accurate.

Her personality is unapologetically big and loud, and she is brash in her presentation. I think that comes from her years in the spotlight. But once you peel back the layers of her boisterous exterior, you find a heart of gold. Deep down, Barb is a genuinely lovely person, full of warmth and kindness.

She's the kind of person who, when you least expect it, shares a story about how she once tried to moonwalk her way out of a speeding ticket—and actually succeeded because the officer couldn't stop laughing.

She is a treasure with the remarkable ability to remind me that joy can come from unexpected connections.

We celebrated Sasha's thirteenth birthday. The ranch did it up big for her: Cake, balloons, and her favorite food for dinner. I would have thought pizza, but she wanted chicken piccata. She was the center of attention, and she looked so happy.

Wednesday morning, Zoey, Claire and I met Addie for yoga. It was peaceful watching the sun rise over the ranch.

Zoey and I have spent quite a bit of time together over the past few days. She has become my confidant and friend, encouraging me to step out of my comfort zone and see the beauty in the simple life of the ranch. And truth be told, it's starting to grow on me.

Later, I joined Sasha and Albert in making jam from fresh berries picked on the ranch.

I spent the afternoon lounging by the pool, immersing myself in a novel and exchanging stories with fellow campers. I was surprised to see that Geoffery wasn't in his usual spot. Hopefully, he has found something more interesting to do with his time.

Thursday, we spent time at the lake. I found myself frequently checking the bluff to see if Brady was up in his thinking spot. But no luck. I'm starting to miss him, and that worries me.

Some of our group tried their luck at fishing while the kids splashed in the chilly water. I opted to stay on the shore and spent the afternoon in the company of Michael, Sam, and Barb, engaged in lively conversation.

After dinner, over homemade ice cream made by Sasha and her dad, Zoey, Barb, and I sit on the porch and watch the sunset.

"Are you okay, Finley?"

"Oh, yeah. I'm good."

"Finley, you don't have to pretend with us." Zoey's voice carries a warmth that wraps around me like a comforting blanket. "We're all here for you, whatever you're going through."

Barb nods in agreement, her usual jovial expression replaced by one of genuine concern. "You can talk to us, honey. We're becoming like family here."

It's time to confront the thoughts plaguing me since I arrived at the ranch.

"Our time here is surreal. The weeks seem like years, but in reality, we only have another week here before we all have to go home to another life."

Barb listens intently, her expression a mixture of empathy and understanding. Zoey squeezes my hand gently, offering silent encouragement.

"Maybe you should consider staying here longer," Zoey adds. "See where things lead with Brady."

"I couldn't possibly stay; I have so much responsibility back in Boston. Things with Brady are so new, and I'm still so broken; I don't know if I'm ready to make that kind of commitment yet."

"You don't need to make that kind of decision tonight." Zoey's words calm me slightly.

Barb reaches over and places a hand on my shoulder, her touch warm and comforting. "You've been through a lot, Finley. It's okay to take your time, to heal at your own pace. I was much older when I lost my Ira, but I know what it's like to carry that weight with you every day. Just remember, healing doesn't have a timeline."

"Maybe Brady isn't your next Mr. Right; Maybe just Mr. Right Now!" Barb's levity makes me smile.

She stands from her chair and starts down the steps.

"You know, dear," Barb says after a thoughtful pause, "sometimes it takes a change of scenery to see things in a new light. And sometimes, it takes meeting new people to help us understand ourselves better."

Barb excuses herself with a knowing smile, leaving Zoey and me alone on the porch.

"She is a wise sage under all that glitter."

"She really is."

"It's okay to take things one step at a time, Finley. You don't have to have all the answers now. Just follow your heart and trust that everything will fall into place when the time is right."

"Thanks, Zoey."

"Any time."

Zoey's gaze is fixed on the horizon, where the last hints of daylight are slowly fading away.

"Max is probably going to send out a search party for me soon, so I'm going to go to our bungalow. Want to walk with me?"

"No, I think I'm gonna sit here for a little while longer. Thanks."

"No problem. Goodnight. See you in the morning."

I take their words to heart as I sit alone in the silence, the porch light casting long shadows. A part of me longs for the simplicity and warmth of this place, where time seems to stand still, but reality calls, too.

The following morning, I dress quickly and go to the dining hall, where Zoey, Max, Albert, Sam, and Claire are already seated for breakfast. The smell of bacon and freshly brewed coffee fills the air as they animatedly discuss their plans for the day.

"Finley! Come join us!" Zoey calls out, waving me over to their table.

I slide in between her and Claire. "How did the TikTok at the barn go? Do you have ideas for today?"

Claire's eyes light up. "It was AWESOME! I finally posted it this morning. I had to edit out some of the weird barn noises." Her confidence amazes me. I was never that sure of myself at seventeen.

"Today on the agenda is a line dancing tutorial! I'm so psyched for the Honkey Tonk tonight. My followers are gonna love it!"

I started following her last week, and it's pretty impressive. She's been sharing her adventures at the ranch on TikTok and appears eager to show her followers a good time.

I smile as everyone chatters enthusiastically about the evening ahead. The dance has brought such lively anticipation to this group. My thoughts drift to Brady. There was a message in my bungalow last night when I got back.

> **Missin' you, Boston.**
> **Save me a dance tomorrow night.**
> **-B**

Our flirty banter is like a drug, and I've missed it. The thought of seeing him outside of our usual ranch setting, perhaps even sharing a dance with him, sends a thrill down my spine. I quickly remind myself not to get too carried away. After all, I'm only here for one more week. I remember Barb's words from last night, though. Mr. Right Now.

"Finley? Earth to Finley!" Zoey snaps her fingers in front of my face, jolting me out of my daydream. "You've got that dreamy look in your eyes again. Are you thinking about a certain cowboy?"

"Oh, stop," I say, waving my hand dismissively but unable to hide my grin. My cheeks flush as they laugh good-naturedly, their teasing bringing me back to the present moment.

"Mmhmm," Sam says with a smirk.

"I had iced tea with his mom on the porch yesterday. She says he hasn't smiled this much in over a year," Albert adds.

"He does seem less grumpy than when we met him," Claire observes.

I feel my cheeks flush. "Maybe."

"Yeah, last night he even cracked a smile at one of my jokes!" Sam exclaims. "A real, genuine smile - I thought I was seeing things."

"Leave the poor girl alone," Max chuckles.

"You saw him last night?" I ask with a tinge of disappointment in my voice.

"Just for a second. He was writing a note on your porch."

"Well, whatever magic you're working on him, keep it up!" Sam says. "I think we'd all love to see more of the smiling, friendly version of Brady."

"Here, here!" Albert says, raising his juice glass in a toast. "To Finley, the Brady-whisperer!"

Everyone laughs and clinks their glasses together.

"Alright, let's change the subject, Zoey adds. "I can't wait to dress up and cut loose tonight."

"Me too," Sam sighs dreamily. "I can't wait to two-step with my Albie."

Albert blushes. "Oh, Sam."

"Don't let him fool you. Once this man gets on the dance floor, good luck getting him to leave tonight!" Sam responds enthusiastically.

"Speaking of tonight," Zoey says, grinning as she mischievously swipes a piece of bacon from Max's plate. "What is everyone going to wear tonight?"

Her question sparks an enthusiastic conversation about everyone's clothing choices for the evening. Max and Albert engage in a friendly debate over which style of western shirt is most appropriate – plaid or solid. Sam is the only one who planned for a party and proudly announces that he brought the perfect pearl snap shirt for the occasion.

"I have no idea!" I admit. "I didn't exactly pack for a honky tonk."

"We should go shopping this afternoon," Sam suggests. "There are a couple of cute boutiques in town."

"On that note, I'm out of here," Albert says jokingly as he stands and gives Sam a quick kiss on his cheek. "I trust you to pick something fabulous for me, but you know how I feel about shopping. I'd rather go to the dentist." He looks at Claire, and we all laugh. "Just don't tell your dad I said that."

"Yeah, he gets that root canal joke all the time. But shopping! ABSOLUTELY!" Claire responds enthusiastically. " I need to find something flashy. Maybe with fringe or sequins. This is going to be epic!"

"In that case, you should raid Barbara's suitcase, Claire." Max also gets up and kisses his wife, and we all snicker knowingly. "I'm off to learn how to weld fences this morning. I'll see you later, sweetheart. I trust you to keep the flash to a minimum for me, please."

"You be the belle of the ball, honey. I'm just your accessory." Their newlywed glow makes me miss having someone special.

"Of course, my sweet, subtle man."

I secretly wonder what outlandish outfit Barb will pull off tonight.

"I'll take care of booking the shuttle," Sam adds with the authority of a man on a mission. "Be back here at eleven, everyone."

"Sounds like a plan." I grin, my excitement building.

I'm stopped in my tracks by the handsome cowboy with an empty coffee cup coming in the door.

Brady sees me, and his face lights up. "I was hoping to catch you here this morning."

"Hi," I manage to reply.

"Did you get my note? When I stopped by last night, I had hoped you'd be in your bungalow."

"I did. I'm sad I missed you."

Our conversation is awkward, filled with pauses.

"So..." Brady drawls after a moment. "I hope I didn't assume too much. Adeline has the group heading into town tonight for some honky tonkin'. I really hope you're planning to join them?"

"I sure am," I say with a smile. "Zoey already roped me into shopping this afternoon for an outfit."

"Great to hear," Brady replies, a hint of relief in his voice.

I walk with him to the coffee pot.

"I'll see you tonight then." He adds as he puts the lid on the travel cup and gives me a quick hug. He starts out the door and turns. "I've got a full day in the office today, so I'll have to meet you there."

I nod as I watch him go. I can't deny my growing feelings for the gruff cowboy. But the nagging thought of my imminent return to Boston dampens my mood.

I have a few minutes before shopping, so I walk to check on the baby goats. Their playful antics always make me smile, and it's just what I need to clear my mind before tonight's dance.

When I enter the barn, the baby goats rush over, bleating and bouncing around my feet. I give them each a scratch behind the ears as two of them start to head-butt each other.

"Good morning. There's enough love to go around," I say, stroking their soft coats.

One tries to nibble on my shirt sleeve, its tiny tail wagging eagerly. I gently tug the fabric away and stroke its soft head instead.

As I move through the barn, the baby goats follow me in an adorable trail, vying for my attention.

I spot Queenie up on a hay bale triumphantly, surveying her kingdom. "Hey there, little girl," I say, amused by her regal pose. "You're quite the climber, aren't you?"

She looks at me as if to say, 'Of course, I am,' before leaping off the hay bale and bounding over to me. I laugh and reach out to pet her. Her soft fur and innocent eyes have a way of melting away any worries or doubts I might have.

She nudges my hand, looking for treats.

"Sorry, girl, I don't have anything for you today."

I'm leaning down to pet a sleepy Peanut curled up in the straw when I hear footsteps behind me. I turn to see Zoey and Sam entering the barn.

"There you are!" Zoey exclaims. "We've been looking for you everywhere. It's time for shopping."

I stand and brush the straw from my jeans. "Is it that time already?"

"Yep, and we have an important mission to accomplish," Sam says. "Finding the perfect outfits for tonight!"

Zoey nods eagerly. "I want to look hot but not too flashy, you know?"

"You could be in a burlap sack and still look hot," Sam adds.

I smile as we exit the barn, the baby goats trying to follow until I gently close the door.

"I have no idea what to wear," I confess. "Western fashion has never been my forte."

"That's why Sam and I are here to help," Zoey assures me.

"How about sundresses? Seems fitting for a dance hall. Maybe we'll find you some cute floral or denim number." Sam's enthusiasm is contagious. "Alright, ladies, let's get moving. We've got shopping to do!"

Anticipation builds inside me as we walk to the shuttle. I feel grateful for my new friends and can't wait to find the perfect dress. With their guidance, I just might manage to impress a certain cowboy tonight.

We return from our shopping excursion loaded with bags and excitement. After a quick lunch in the dining hall, Zoey and I head to our bungalows to start getting ready.

Something colorful catches my eye as I walk up the steps to my porch. I stop short, surprised to see Bandit lying there happily chewing on something sparkly.

"Bandit! What have you got there?" Zoey exclaims, trying to suppress a giggle.

He gives us an unrepentant doggy grin and goes back to chewing. I pick up what looks like a bedazzled scarf and notice an embroidered "B" on the end.

"This must be Barbara's," I say. "Oh, Bandit, what are we going to do with you?"

Zoey laughs when she sees the scarf. "That dog sure knows how to find treasure. Barb's gonna have a fit when she sees this."

I have to laugh too. Bandit looks so proud of his pilfered prize. It's hard to be mad at that adorable furry face.

Zoey steps away and grabs a towel from her bungalow. She takes the scarf from me and wraps it in the towel.

"Thanks for thinking of us, buddy, but I think we'll stick to something a bit less...sparkly," she tells him, shaking her head in amusement.

"Of all the treasures you could've found, you just had to pick this one, didn't you?" I pat his head affectionately.

"Alright, you little thief, let's get this back to Barb," she says to the dog as she leads him toward Barbara's bungalow.

As Zoey leads Bandit away, I return to my bungalow, smiling. That dog sure knows how to lighten the mood.

I start laying out my new outfit, and anticipation bubbles inside me. I bought a cute floral dress and red cowboy boots for tonight. Brady's smile and deep voice keep floating through my mind. I am excited about the dance tonight. I can't wait to see him again.

Chapter Twenty

Brady

The pounding bass vibrates through my boots as I step into the smoky haze of Over Yonder. Neon signs flash above the crowded dance floor, where couples twirl in time to the country tunes. I scan the sea of big hair and cowboy hats, looking for a glimpse of Finley. I know she should be here with the dude ranch guests. Addie texted me when they left, but I don't see her yet.

"Brady!" I hear my name and see Logan and Duncan waving me to the bar. I change my course and weave through the crowd to join them. They're both already nursing their drinks, and it doesn't take long for me to order a cold beer from the bartender.

"Good to see you, man," Logan says, clapping me on the shoulder as I settle onto the stool beside him. "It's been too long."

"So what brings you out tonight?" Duncan asks, sipping his beer. "Don't you have cows to herd or somethin'?"

"Ranch work keeps me busy," I reply, sipping my beer. "But I couldn't miss my brother's gig tonight." Out of the corner of my eye, I'm still trying to spot Finley, but my attention remains on my friends for now.

"Seriously though, man, you seem a little off tonight," Logan comments, his light-hearted demeanor shifting to one of concern. "What's going on?"

"Anything you want to talk about?" Duncan asks, genuine concern in his voice.

"Oh ho ho." Logan elbows me with a knowing look. "There's a lady involved. Who's the lucky gal?"

"Nothing, really," I lie, taking another sip of my drink in an effort to avoid their probing gazes. But I should've known better than to try and hide anything from these two, especially concerning matters of the heart.

"Come on, Brady," Duncan chimes in, his eyes narrowing in suspicion. "We've known you long enough to recognize when something's bothering you. Just spill it."

"Alright, fine," I relent, letting out a heavy sigh. "There's this woman..."

"Ah, that explains it," Logan says, grinning. "So, who is she? Anyone we know?"

I take a slow sip of beer to buy myself a moment. Do I want to get into this with Logan and Duncan? Then again, they know me better than anyone. Maybe talking it through would help me sort out this tangle of emotions around Finley.

I set down the bottle with a thud. "Her name's Finley. Finley Prescott..." I confess, feeling my face heat up at the mere mention of her name. "She's from Boston and has been staying at the ranch for a while. She's widowed, and I... I can't get her out of my thoughts."

Logan raises an eyebrow. "Don't tell me the great Brady Cavanaugh's got himself twitterpated over some city girl."

"She's not just some city girl." I bristle. "Finley's...different. Classy, you know?"

Duncan nods slowly, a knowing smile creeping across his face. "Yep, he's smitten, alright."

"Ah, shut it." I wave them off, my face growing warm.

"No shame in it." Logan claps me on the shoulder. "Ally's the best thing that ever happened to me. About time you let yourself feel something real for a woman. Especially after 'She Who Shall Not Be Named'."

I chew my lip, watching the couples swaying on the dancefloor. My heart kicks when I spot a flash of auburn hair. But it's not Finley. Where is she?

"So what's the problem?" Duncan asks.

I let out a heavy sigh, the weight of my worries pressing down on me again. "She's only here temporarily. And she's still grieving her husband." I shake my head. "I just don't know if getting tangled up in something that's got no future is smart."

My friends exchange a look. Logan squeezes my shoulder. "Listen, man, you can't predict the future. Sometimes you gotta take a leap of faith."

"Wow," Duncan whistles, an amused smirk tugging at his lips. "I never thought I'd see the day when Brady Cavanaugh falls head over heels for someone. But hey, good for you, man!"

"Yeah," Logan agrees, clapping me on the back. "Just take it slow and see what happens. You never know; she might be the one to finally crack that tough cowboy exterior of yours."

"She's only here for another week, man."

"Well then. Don't waste another minute. Find her and dance with her!"

I nod slowly, letting Logan's words sink in. He's right - I can't let the future rob me of something that feels so right in the present.

As I am contemplating Logan and Duncan's sound advice, the honky tonk's door swings open, and a group of people from the dude ranch filters in.

My gaze immediately locks on Finley, her auburn hair shimmering like fire under the dim lights. She's wearing a denim jacket over a floral sundress that floats around her knees as she walks. Her auburn hair is down in soft waves, and she's got a glow to her cheeks I haven't seen before. She looks so carefree, so happy, and she looks every bit as striking as the first time I laid eyes on her.

"Speak of the devil," I murmur under my breath, unable to tear my eyes away from her. Logan and Duncan follow my gaze, their expressions curious but unrecognizing.

"Which one is she?" Duncan asks, squinting at the group.

"The beautiful woman with the auburn hair," I reply, nodding towards Finley.

"Ah, I see," Logan says, grinning. "Well, she sure is a looker."

"Watch it," I warn playfully, nudging him with my elbow.

"Relax," he chuckles, holding up his hands in surrender. "I'm a happily married man, remember?"

While we continue our conversation, I keep an eye on Finley as she moves further into the honky tonk.

I slide off the barstool, my eyes never leaving Finley as I start weaving through the crowd. I watch her tuck a strand of hair behind her ear.

Just then, Barbara grabs Finley's arm, pulling her towards the dance floor.

They join a group that is being taught how to line dance by one of the locals. I smile and turn back to the bar. I watch her concentrate on the steps, her nose crinkling adorably in determination.

"Man, you've got it bad," Duncan observes, noticing my preoccupation.

"Can you blame me?" I ask, still watching Finley. "She's incredible."

"Go dance with her," Logan suggests, giving me an encouraging nudge. "You don't want to spend the whole night just staring at her from across the room, do you?"

"Maybe in a minute," I reply, hesitating. "let her finish with the line dancing first."

"Suit yourself," Duncan says in amusement. "But just remember what I told you earlier - trust your heart."

I admire Finley's persistence and grace as she continues to learn the dance. She stumbles a few times, laughing and brushing it off like it's nothing, and it only makes me fall for her more. It's clear that beneath her strong, analytical exterior lies a fun-loving spirit, and I'm eager to get to know her better.

"Alright, I'm going in," I announce finally, my resolve strengthening. Logan and Duncan exchange knowing glances, offering me words of encouragement as I go to find Finley.

When her eyes meet mine across the crowded bar, a smile spreads across her face, making my knees weak.

"Go get her, cowboy." Duncan claps me on the back. Duncan and Logan clink their bottles together behind me as I make my way across the room to the dance floor as the song winds down.

I take a deep breath and ignore the butterflies in my stomach. Barbara gives me a wink and nudges Finley in my direction before disappearing into the crowd.

"Hey."

"Hey, yourself. I believe you promised me a dance."

Finley bites her lip, looking unsure. "Oh, I don't know...I thought I could dance, but I feel like I have two left feet tonight. Did you see me trying to line dance?"

I don't admit that I have been watching her since the moment she stepped into the bar. I smile and hold out my hand. After a moment, she takes it, her palm soft against mine. "Alright, but go easy on me."

"Don't worry, I've got you," I say, leading her onto the dance floor as the next song starts. I put one hand on her waist, gently guiding her steps. "Just follow my lead."

I am only distantly aware of the whoops and laughter from my friends and the dude ranchers behind us. All my senses are full of her—the feel of her hand light on my arm, the sway of her hips as she walks. The rest of the bar fades away until it's just us, and the realization sinks deep into my bones.

I am in so much trouble here.

I guide her through the basic steps, keeping it simple. She stumbles a few times but laughs it off.

"See, I told you I was hopeless," she says.

"You're doing just fine," I assure her. "Just relax and feel the rhythm."

As the song continues, she starts to get the hang of it, moving fluidly with me across the floor. Her eyes are bright, and she has the most beautiful smile. Holding her in my arms feels right in a way I've never known before.

"I'm glad you made it!" Finley's face lights up as she looks at me.

"I even beat you here."

Finley looks up at me, trusting. My heart swells. I focus on the beat of the music, keeping us moving in sync. With every turn, Finley relaxes, leaning into me, her eyes bright.

Maybe she feels this too - this spark between us. All my doubt fades away as we dance. I don't want this song to end.

When the song does end, she smiles. "Okay, I think I'm getting the hang of this country dancing thing."

"What do you say we keep practicing then?" I ask.

The music kicks up into a lively two-step, and I guide her into the steps. She's a quick study, moving easily with me after only a few turns. Her eyes stay locked on mine, full of laughter and something more—a new awareness between us.

We drift closer together with each spin and twirl until our clasped hands are pressed between our chests. The rest of the bar fades away until there's only the two of us, caught up in the steps and the music.

Finley steps closer and slides her arms around my neck when the band slows into a romantic ballad. My pulse quickens at her touch. I pull her near, our bodies swaying gently to the melody.

"Tonight has been wonderful, Brady," she says softly, meeting my gaze. "Thank you."

"I should be thanking you," I reply. "I can't remember the last time I've enjoyed myself this much."

And her eyes, those gorgeous green eyes I could drown in. They see me—really see me—in a way no one has before.

It scares the hell out of me and thrills me right down to my bones.

We dance and dance, her cheeks flushed; she's never looked more beautiful.

As Finley and I sway to the music, I catch a glimpse of Geoffrey Hirsh stumbling over to us, drink in hand.

"Mind if I cut in?" he slurs, grabbing Finley's arm. She recoils, noticeably uncomfortable.

"I think you've had enough for one night," I say firmly, stepping between them. "Why don't you let me get you a ride back to the ranch?"

"Oh, come on, I'm just trying to have a little fun with the pretty lady," Geoffrey protests, leering at Finley.

My protective instincts flare. There's no way I'm letting this drunk playboy anywhere near her.

"Fun's over," I say sharply. "Let's go."

I take Geoffrey's arm and start leading him firmly toward the exit. He tries to pull away, spilling his drink in the process.

"Get your hands off me!" he yells, getting the attention of the other patrons. This guy is out of control.

He starts to push past me, but I block his path with an arm.

"I don't think so, Geoffrey. You're in no shape to be dancing with anyone tonight."

Geoffrey's face hardens, the drunken affability gone. "Don't tell me what to do."

He tries again to get around me. I shove him back, harder this time.

"Go sleep it off, Geoffrey," I say through gritted teeth. "Don't make me tell you again."

For a moment, we stand there, locked in a challenge. Then Geoffrey sags against the bar with a scowl.

"Fine. Have it your way."

I nod to one of the ranch hands nearby.

"Make sure Mr. Hirsh gets back to his bungalow."

As Geoffrey is led away, still cursing me under his breath, the tension leaves my shoulders. Crisis averted. I glance back at Finley and feel a surge of protectiveness.

"I need something to drink. How 'bout you?"

Finley nods, and I lead her to the bar.

As we wait for the bartender, my friends approach with their wives.

"Brady, aren't you going to introduce us to your lovely dance partner?" Duncan says with a raised brow.

"Everyone, this is Finley. She's staying at the ranch for a few weeks," I say and continue to make the remaining introductions.

"Pleasure to meet you all," Finley says sweetly.

"Likewise," Logan replies. "Our boy here looked a little lonely before you got here."

I shoot him a look, and he just laughs.

"When are you going to give me that bid on the remaining bungalows?" I throw at him, trying to change the subject.

"I'll swing by your place first thing Monday morning."

Finley touches my arm gently. "I should get back to my table. Zoey was supposed to order me a drink earlier, but I almost forgot about it. Thank you for the dances, Brady."

"Anytime." She walks away, and I stare after her, already longing for the next chance to hold her in my arms again.

I watch Finley go through the crowded bar to the table where the other dude ranch guests sit. Even from across the room, I can't take my eyes off her.

"So that's the girl, huh?" Logan says, elbowing me in the ribs. "The one to make you forget 'She Who Must Not Be Named.'"

I rub my side and scowl at him. "What are you talking about?"

"Oh, come on, we saw how you were looking at her on the dance floor," Duncan chimes in with a grin. "You've got it bad."

I feel my cheeks flush and take a swig of my beer. Logan and Duncan exchange knowing looks.

"It's okay to admit it, man. She seems great," Logan says.

I sigh, setting down my bottle. "Yeah, she's...something else. We just met a few weeks ago when her group got to the ranch, but there's this connection between us already. It's kind of crazy."

Duncan smiles and pats my shoulder. "That's how it was when I first met Avery. When you know, you know." He puts his arm around his wife and hands her water bottle. The two of them exchange a look of such tenderness that I feel a pang of envy.

I nod slowly. "The thing is, she's only here for another week. Then it's back to Boston for her." I run a hand through my hair in frustration. "I don't know if she'd ever consider giving someone like me a real shot."

"I thought I was only here for a temp job, but look at me. I'm a Cramer girl for life now," Avery adds, adoringly patting her slightly pregnant belly.

Logan raises his beer. "You'll never know unless you give it a try. What've you got to lose?"

I consider his words. As unexpected as it is, he's right - this thing with Finley feels too good to let go without a fight. I have to at least try.

I find Finley at the table with Sam and Albert, sipping what looks like a margarita. As I approach, she smiles. "It's really warm in here. Would you like to walk outside with me for a minute?"

I nod eagerly, grateful for the opportunity to be alone with her. I lead her toward the back door, which opens to a large patio with picnic tables. We step out into the cool night air, the stars twinkling above us.

"I'm so glad I met you, Brady. I didn't know what to expect coming out here, but you've made it so special."

"You too," I reply, my voice full of emotion. "I don't open up to many people, but with you, it's easy."

She tilts her chin to look at me, green eyes searching mine. "I feel the same way. Like I can tell you anything."

My heart swells. Without thinking, I lean in, brushing my lips against hers in the lightest of kisses. She responds instantly, gripping me tightly and returning the kiss with a fervor I hadn't expected. Our lips move in perfect synchronization, and I am lost in this moment, feeling a connection so powerful that it's almost unbearable. When we break apart, she stares at me with such intensity.

"Wow. That was..." Finley starts to say.

"Magical," I finish, my voice barely above a whisper.

She nods slowly before leaning back in, pressing her lips against mine again. We remain there for what feels like an eternity, enjoying each other's presence and reveling in the electricity between us.

When we pull away again, Finley grins, her green eyes shining brighter than the stars above us. "Mmm hmm. Completely magical."

We stand there for a moment, foreheads touching, lost in our private little world. The noisy bar fades away until all I see and feel is her.

I know then that this is only the beginning for us. We have something real, and I'll be damned if I let her slip away when she leaves the ranch.

But that's a worry for another day. Right now, all that matters is her in my arms under the starry Texas sky.

Chapter Twenty-One

Finley

The lingering melodies of some unknown country song still echo in my mind as I slowly open my eyes. I'm back in my quaint little bungalow at the ranch.

Brady's face flashes in my mind, the intensity in his blue eyes as we twirl across the barn floor. I can still feel the heat of his palm pressed against my back, the tickle of his breath against my cheek as he leaned in close. The ghost of his lips lingers on mine.

I brush my fingertips across my mouth, my heart fluttering at the memory. Dancing with Brady last night felt like finding a missing piece of myself I didn't know was gone. The gruff cowboy who bristles at human connection dancing, his guard lowered, his true self revealed.

I stretch and yawn as the early morning sunlight filters through the curtains. My muscles are pleasantly sore from all the dancing. I roll over and catch a glimpse of my dress from last night strewn haphazardly across the back of a chair.

I smile, remembering how I'd danced like nobody was watching, my earlier inhibitions swept away by the lively music. Brady's strong arms held me close to his as he spun me around the dance floor – it was a magical evening.

I dance to the bathroom to shower and glimpse myself in the mirror - flushed cheeks, mussed hair, eyes bright with a newfound joy. Brady has awakened something in me that I thought was long gone.

After dressing in jeans and a T-shirt, I step outside into the warm morning air. I spot Sasha and Claire across the way, chatting animatedly as they walk towards the main lodge.

"Good morning!" I call out to them with a wave.

"Finley!" Sasha exclaims as they walk over. "You look happy today."

Claire smirks knowingly. "Probably has something to do with a certain cowboy."

I feel my cheeks grow warm. "Maybe," I say, unable to keep the giddiness from my voice.

"You should talk, Claire. You danced with my brother!"

"Yeah, so. Simon's not that bad," she responds. "My followers thought he was pretty nice eye candy. And speaking of eye candy, how is your 'Cute Old Dude'?"

"Double Eww, Claire. Simon's my stinky brother and Brady is like your dad's age! Anyway, Finley, Sam taught me how to two-step, and I got to try to teach my dad. He's pretty terrible, but he kept saying he hasn't danced since forever. I just think he doesn't have any rhythm. Oh, and you missed Barbara dancing with some 30-year-old guy. It was so weird."

"I have video even I won't post," interrupts Claire.

Sasha takes a second to breathe before continuing her story. "I've never been to a bar before. We don't have places like this in Tulsa, or at least not that I've ever been. I had so much fun."

We continue on the path together, the girls filling me in on all I missed after leaving the dance. I'm only half listening, my thoughts still back to being in Brady's arms.

The mouthwatering aroma of freshly cooked bacon and waffles fills the air when we enter the dining hall. My stomach rumbles, reminding me I'm famished after last night's revelries.

I spot Zoey and Sam seated at a table, so the girls and I grab our plates to join them.

"Well, don't you look radiant this morning," Zoey says, winking.

I smile, letting my joy shine through.

I glance around the dining hall, taking in the other guests nursing their morning coffees. My eyes land on Geoffrey, seated alone at a table near us. He's slumped in his chair, head in his hands, looking utterly miserable.

"Did he have a rough night?" Sam whispers, having followed my gaze.

I nod, recalling Geoffrey's drunk antics on the dance floor. He'd made quite the spectacle of himself before being escorted home.

As if on cue, the dining hall doors burst open, and in sweeps Barbara. Her brightly colored caftan billows around her as she makes a beeline for her son.

"Geoffrey, darling!" she exclaims loudly, placing a perfectly manicured hand on her son's shoulder. "You look positively dreadful!"

Geoffrey winces at the shrill sound of her voice. "Not so loud, Mother," he groans.

"Well, that's what you get for drinking like a fish," Barbara chides. She reaches into her oversized handbag and pulls out a bottle of aspirin, shaking two into his palm. "Take these, it'll help."

Geoffrey tosses the pills back obediently. "I'm never drinking again," he vows, dropping his head back into his hands.

Barbara laughs in a way that only mothers can, a mix of amusement and exasperation. "Oh posh, don't be so melodramatic, my dear. You say that every time! Chin up; the day is young!"

"Mother, please," Geoffrey whimpers. "Can we not do this right now? I feel like a herd of cattle is stamping through my brain."

"Geoffrey, darling, I think you owe a certain someone an apology for your antics last night."

"Ugh, don't remind me," he groans, rubbing his temples. "Was it that bad?"

"Aw, come on now. You know I love you," she coos, ruffling his hair playfully. "But really, you should know better than to drink so much. You're not exactly a spring chicken anymore."

"Thanks for the reminder, Mother," he mutters sarcastically, taking a deep swig of his coffee.

"Tell you what," Barbara says, grinning mischievously. "Next time, I'll keep a closer eye on you, maybe even cut you off after your third drink."

"Third drink?" Geoffrey exclaims, feigning shock. "What kind of lightweight do you think I am?"

"Darling, trust me. At your age, three drinks will be more than enough to keep you dancing all night long," she quips, winking at him.

She hums a cheerful tune as she saunters away, leaving a miserable Geoffrey in her wake.

She stops by our table on her way to the door. "Now, I hope you all had as much fun last night as I did – but not as much as my Geoffrey," she says, shaking the aspirin bottle. "Anyone else need some?" And remember, there's always another party around the corner!"

"No, thanks, Barbara," Zoey replies, chuckling at her enthusiasm.

"Anytime, sweetheart! Now, if you'll excuse me, I have a massage appointment to get to. See you all later!" Barbara gives us a little wave and sashays from the dining hall, leaving Geoffrey to nurse his hangover in peace.

He glances over at our table, and I catch his eye briefly before he looks away, clearly embarrassed. Despite his reckless behavior last night, I feel a tiny pang of sympathy for him.

My breakfast companions depart to various activities, leaving me alone at the table.

Geoffrey takes a deep breath and pushes himself up from the table. I watch as he slowly makes his way over to me, looking uncharacteristically nervous.

"Finley, can I have a word?" he asks quietly.

I regard him cooly, gesturing to the empty seat across from me. He sits down, clasping his hands on the table.

"I need to apologize for my behavior last night," he begins sincerely. "I undoubtedly had way too much to drink and acted like a fool. It was unacceptable, and I'm deeply sorry if I made you feel uncomfortable in any way."

He meets my gaze, his eyes filled with remorse. I'm struck by his humility - this is a side of Geoffrey I haven't seen before.

"I appreciate you apologizing," I reply after a moment. "Let's just put it behind us and move forward, alright?"

Relief floods his face, and he nods quickly. "Of course. Thank you, Finley."

He stands, looking lighter than before. As he turns to leave, I call out to him.

"Geoffrey?"

He glances back.

"Drink some water next time," I say with a small smile.

The corner of his mouth quirks up, and he ducks his head, abashed but amused. Without another word, he departs, leaving me to finish my breakfast in peace.

Chapter Twenty-Two

Brady

I should be up already, but the events of last night replayed in my mind all night – dancing with Finley, my arms around her waist as we moved across the dance floor. When I close my eyes I can replay the kiss in the moonlight and feel the same rush of desire course through my veins. The beat of the music still lingers in my ears as I stare at the ceiling in my room.

I throw off the sheets and get dressed, eager to see her smiling face across the breakfast table. It takes me a while to get to the dining hall; it seems everyone has a question or a greeting for me this morning.

Finally, I take the porch stairs two at a time and burst into the dining hall. The room is already bustling when I arrive, the clinking of silverware and murmur of voices filling the cavernous room. I spot Finley at a back table by herself, sipping a cup of coffee.

I weave between the crowded tables, but Geoffrey saunters over before I reach the table. I tense up, ready to intervene if he tries anything inappropriate.

To my surprise, he stops in front of Finley with his hands in his pockets, shifting awkwardly. I can't hear what he's saying, but it's clear that she wants him to sit down, so I move slowly, not wanting to interrupt.

It looks like he is apologizing. The guy looks miserable, and for good reason.

I see Finley study him for a moment before nodding. I assume she is accepting his apology.

I stifle a laugh when she tells him to "drink some water next time" as he's turning to leave.

With a remorseful glance at me, he slinks away. Maybe the arrogant playboy has learned his lesson after all.

Finley glances up and meets my gaze, offering a weak smile.

"Morning. Are you okay?"

"Better now. Did you hear any of that?"

"I heard enough. I think he'll be leaving you alone from now on."

"Let's hope so."

"I'm still gonna keep an eye on him, though."

"Did you sleep well last night?" she asks, clearly ready to be done talking about Geoffrey. "With all that music replaying in my head? I was up half the night!"

We share a smile, the memories of last night swirling between us. I want to capture this feeling and keep it bottled up forever.

I clear my throat and rub my palms on my jeans. "So, I was wondering if you'd like to have dinner with me tomorrow night?"

Finley arches her brow. "But don't we eat dinner together every night anyway?"

"Well, yeah, with the whole group," I say. "But I meant just the two of us. A proper date." There's a flutter in my chest as I await her reply.

"I'd love to!" Her eyes dance bright. "Should I dress up?"

"Just wear your boots. I'll pick you up at your cabin around six."

She raises an eyebrow, and I feel embarrassed heat crawl through my cheeks as she teases, "Just my boots, Cowboy? Don't you think that's a bit risqué?"

My face only gets redder, as if the temperature of the room is rising. "Um, no, not at all...that is not what I meant!" I stammer out hastily.

"Boots are just a must-have for your outfit! Umm...you know what? Just wear whatever you feel comfortable in. "So...I'll pick you up at your bungalow at 6?" I'm not sure why that sounded like a question. I do not doubt that this woman is interested in me, but she has me flustered, which is so not me.

"Six is perfect." She leans in, biting her lip. "Can I get a hint about where we're going?"

"Nope. My lips are sealed."

She pretends to pout. "No fair."

I brush a strand of hair from her face, my thumb lingering on her cheek. "Don't worry, you'll find out soon enough."

Finley's eyes sparkle with curiosity as she tries again to get more information out of me about our date. I grin but remain silent, relishing in the playful teasing.

"Come on, just a little hint," she pleads, grabbing my arm. "I won't be able to concentrate on anything else unless you give me something!"

"Alright, alright. One small hint." I lean in close, my voice lowering. "Wear pants you can ride in."

"Ride? As in horses?"

I tap my nose secretively. "That's all you get for now."

She smacks my shoulder in mock annoyance. "You're killing me here!"

I laugh and squeeze her hand. "It'll be worth the wait, I promise."

I arrive at Finley's bungalow right at 6 p.m. with a bouquet of wildflowers. She opens the door, her eyes lighting up when she sees the flowers.

"For you, m'lady," I say with an exaggerated bow, eliciting a smile as I present them to her.

"Why thank you, kind sir," she replies in a silly, noble accent. Her smile softens as she inhales the flowers' sweet scent. "They're beautiful, Brady."

"Not as beautiful as you," I say, noticing how the sunlight illuminates her hair.

She blushes at the compliment. "Such a charmer."

I grin and offer my arm. "Your chariot awaits." Our horses, Bandera and Rosie, are already saddled up and ready to go; I have a wicker picnic basket and a blanket on the back of mine.

I help her into the saddle, and we set off at a leisurely pace; the only sound is the soft clop of hooves and the rustle of grass.

I lead us along a winding trail that takes us up into the foothills, the ranch and its buildings growing smaller below us.

Soon, we're riding side by side into the countryside. The rolling green hills stretch out before us, a sea of green dotted with wildflowers. A warm breeze rustles through the trees.

The sky is a perfect shade of blue, marred only by a few wispy clouds. A hawk circles lazily on an updraft high above.

I glance over at Finley often as we ride, drinking in how the sunset lights up her face. The warm hues bring out the different shades of copper and gold in her hair. A contented smile plays on her lips. Finley closes her eyes and takes a deep breath.

"It's so beautiful and peaceful out here."

"Yes, it is."

I point out the old Cavanaugh homestead in the distance, a weathered cabin nestled at the base of the hills. "My great-great-grandfather, I've forgotten how many greats go before that, built that when he first settled this land in the 1860s," I tell Finley. "It's been abandoned for decades, but we keep it standing for the history."

I gesture to a small, fenced-off cemetery under a canopy of trees up ahead. "That's the old Cavanaugh family graveyard. It's where some of the first settlers in this valley are buried."

"Wow, I'd love to see it!" Her eyes light up, ever curious.

We dismount, and I lead her between the weathered tombstones. I pause by the largest one, engraved with the name 'Malachi Cavanaugh.'

"This here is the grandfather I was talking about," I explain. "The one who started all this."

Finley traces her fingers reverently over the chiseled letters. "Incredible. Your family history is all right here."

I nod, swelling with pride over my ancestors. I tell her some stories of the colorful characters resting beneath our feet.

We continue our ride through the countryside unhurried, the rolling hills and open pastures stretching out before us. As we go, I point out more recent landmarks - my favorite hunting spot as a boy, the old oak tree I used to climb. Finley listens with interest, asking questions that show her curiosity to learn more about me.

I'm usually a private person, but something about her makes me want to open up. I find myself telling stories from my childhood that I've never shared before. Like when I fell into the creek chasing after a frog and showed up sopping wet for dinner. Or when I snuck out to go night fishing and got grounded for a week. Finley laughs at my adventures, her eyes twinkling.

Eventually, we reach a bluff overlooking the ranch. I halt and dismount, then help Finley down. "I thought we could have a late dinner up here," I say, pulling the blanket and wicker basket from my saddle.

"Brady Cavanaugh, you hopeless romantic!" Finley teases.

"I hope you're hungry," I say, unpacking the basket. I reveal an assortment of meats, cheeses, fresh bread, fruit, and a bottle of wine from Duncan's cellar.

Ooh! Charcuterie! This looks amazing, Brady. I'm impressed. Did you make this yourself?"

"So what's this CHAR-CU-TER-IE board I packed?" I ask teasingly. "Don't think I've ever made one of those before."

Finley laughs. "It's just a fancy way of saying meat and cheese platter. But this-" she gestures at the spread "-is an amazing charcuterie board."

"Why thank you, ma'am," I tip my hat playfully. "I aim to impress."

"Consider me impressed, cowboy," Finley says, her eyes dancing.

"Well, I can't take all the credit. Mary Ellen helped with the food. But I did pick the wine and the spot."

"It's perfect," she says, eyes shining. She leans over and kisses my cheek.

"Just don't ask me to identify any of these fancy meats and cheeses," I joke. "As long as it tastes good, I don't need to know what it's called," I say with a grin, popping a grape into my mouth.

I pour a glass of wine on each of us. The velvety liquid glints ruby-red in the moonlight.

"To us," I say, holding up my glass.

"To new beginnings," Finley echoes. We clink glasses and drink.

We continue talking as we enjoy the food and wine. The conversation flows easily between us, with no awkward pauses or lulls. I tell more stories about growing up on the ranch and the antics I used to get into with my brothers. She talks a little about her parents and her brothers. I learned what it is like to be a big-shot lawyer, and she regales me with tales of her city life in Boston.

We savor the delicious food and the tranquil surroundings as the early golden hues of the sunset envelop us. For a moment, nothing else matters except this perfect shared experience. I'm falling hard for this woman, and I have a feeling she might be falling for me as well.

I stand and offer Finley my hand. "Care to dance, m'lady?" I ask.

"There's no music," Finley points out, even as she lets me pull her to her feet.

"We'll make our own," I reply, twirling her into my arms.

We sway together beneath the emerging stars, no music necessary. Finley rests her head on my shoulder and sighs contentedly. I don't ever want this moment to end.

I gently tilt Finley's chin up to look into her eyes, beautiful green eyes that sparkle whenever I look at her. Slowly, I lean in, giving her time to pull away if she wants. When my lips meet hers, it's like coming home.

The kiss begins as a gentle brush of lips, soft and tentative, like the first spring breeze. Her lips are warm and inviting, and I can feel the tender hesitance in her touch. We linger there, exploring the sensation, as if we have all the time in the world. The world around us fades away, leaving only the sweet connection between us.

As our lips move together, the kiss deepens, growing more fervent and passionate. It's as if the floodgates of our emotions have burst open, and we're swept away in the current. Her lips part slightly, and I feel the warmth of her breath mingling with mine. The taste of her is intoxicating, a blend of sweetness and the electric thrill of something new yet familiar.

Finley wraps her arms around my neck, pulling me closer, and I can feel the urgency in her touch.

Her fingers weave into my hair, anchoring me to the moment. I respond by drawing her even closer, feeling the warmth of her body against mine, unable to get enough of her. Our kiss is a dance, a silent promise, and every second we linger feels like a beautiful eternity.

We kiss until we're both breathless, our hearts racing and our minds spinning in the aftermath of what feels like magic. When we finally break apart, we're both grinning like fools.

"Wow," she whispers.

"Wow, is right." I brush a stray hair back from her face.

"I'm falling for you, Finley Prescott."

She smiles, eyes shining. "I'm falling for you too, Brady Cavanaugh."

We share another long, slow kiss as the sun sinks below the horizon, bathing us in the vibrant hues of sunset. Right here, right now, everything is perfect.

We stare up at the vast expanse of the sky in a comfortable silence. I feel Finley shiver slightly as a cool breeze drifts by.

"Cold?" I ask.

"A little," she admits.

I grab a small blanket from the saddlebag on my horse. Returning, I wrap it around Finley's shoulders.

"My hero," Finley says, her voice laced with warmth, a wide grin spreading across her face. She nestles closer to my side, her body fitting perfectly against mine as if it were always meant to be there. I lean down to press a gentle kiss on the crown of her head, inhaling deeply the sweet, floral aroma of her shampoo.

"Thank you for this incredible evening, Brady. It's been absolutely perfect."

"It has. We should probably get back before it's too dark to see."

The night air is cool and still. Crickets chirp softly in the distance. Finley squeezes my hand before we ride back as if she can read my thoughts. No words are needed; I'm the happiest I've been in a long, long time.

Chapter Twenty-Three

Finley

The sun is descending to the horizon, casting an enchanting glow through the trees as Brady and I walk hand-in-hand toward the main house. We returned our horses to the barn after our romantic evening, and now, with full stomachs and full hearts, we meander back along the dusty path. The warm breeze plays with my hair, causing it to catch on my eyelashes.

"Beautiful night, huh?" Brady's deep voice resonates as he brushes the hair off my face, sending tingles through me.

"Very," I agree, noticing how the moonlight brings out the rugged contours of his face, making him even more handsome than usual.

As we near the house, however, the tranquil atmosphere is shattered by the sound of raised voices. We exchange puzzled glances before quickening our pace, curiosity and concern driving us forward.

"Brady! You need to tell them to let me in!" a shrill female voice calls out as we round the corner of the house.

Standing on the porch are several of Brady's siblings – their arms crossed defensively – a tall, blonde woman dressed in designer clothes that scream 'high maintenance' is yelling towards the door. Her body language is tense and confrontational, hands on hips as she glares at Brady's siblings, who stand firmly in her path. Next to her is a smug-looking man in an expensive suit. The woman is attractive, but her look is severe, with her hair pulled back into a high ponytail that swings with each vehement gesture she makes. The woman folds her arms and shifts her weight onto one hip, tapping her foot impatiently.

"Brady isn't here right now. Screaming his name at the house isn't going to change that, Amber," Brady's brother, Cody, says in a harsh tone.

"Where is my husband?" she demands, her eyes narrowing as she looks around. When they land on Brady, she sneers and makes a humph sound toward Cody.

"Amber," Brady sighs, releasing my hand as he steps forward. "What the hell are you doing here?"

"Discussing our financial arrangement," she replies, her gaze flicking over to me for a moment before returning to Brady. "Now, can you please tell your siblings to let me in? This marital matter isn't any of their business."

"Fine," Brady relents, waving a hand at his siblings, who reluctantly stepped aside to let Amber and the man into the house.

He gives me an apologetic look but doesn't say a word.

As they disappear inside, I stand there wondering about this woman who refers to Brady as her husband. Who is she, and why is she here? I'm not sure if I should stay or walk back to my bungalow.

My curiosity gets the better of me, and I follow Brady as he leads us into the living room, where

Amber and the man sit on one of the couches. I stand awkwardly by the door as Brady sits across from them.

"Alright, Amber," he says, his voice tense. "Last week, you claimed you have mineral rights, which we all know is BS! What is it that you want now?"

"It's very simple, Brady, even for you," she scoffs. "I want more money. My brother Chip has been doing some checking. You have been holding out on me. With all the windmills that y'all have added to the property, I'm being cheated! And I want my share of that piece of income stream. Howard, give him the document."

"As Mrs. Cavanaugh's attorney, I can assure you that we have a valid claim here."

"Hell no!" Brady states firmly. "You already got your settlement, Amber. We agreed on that amount before we parted ways."

"Like I told you then, Brady, it isn't enough," she argues, leaning forward in her chair. "But now, with what Chip has discovered about those windmills, you owe me even more."

Brady grits his teeth, "You've already gotten more than you deserve. Whatever we get from our land is none of your concern. Our arrangement has been settled."

"Brady, don't be unreasonable," Amber persists, her attorney nodding along beside her. "I'm only asking for two million dollars – or my share of the wind revenue in perpetuity." She looks at her lawyer as if to make sure she said that right. He nods at her.

"Two million?!" I gasp, my hand flying to my mouth in shock. All eyes turn to me, and I feel my cheeks growing warm under their scrutiny.

"Who is this?" Amber asks, a sneer curling her lips as she looks me up and down. "Your new little plaything?"

"Amber," Brady warns, his voice low and dangerous. "Watch it."

"Fine," she huffs. "But I still expect my demands to be met."

"Your demands are outrageous, Amber," Brady shoots back. "You're not getting anything more from me. We've been through this before."

"Then I guess we'll have to let the courts decide," she threatens, standing up and smoothing her skirt. "Good luck, Brady. You'll need it."

As she storms out of the room, followed by her attorney, I stand there with my heart pounding out of my chest. My thoughts race as I try to process everything that has just happened. Is Brady married to this woman? Is he just separated? Do they have children? How could he not have told me? The hurt that twists in my gut is almost unbearable.

"Finley," Brady says, stepping towards me. "I can explain – I..."

"Save it," I interrupt, holding up a hand to stop him. "I shared everything: Andrew, my grief, everything. You couldn't squeeze in a second to say. Oh. By the way, I'm married. I don't want to hear it right now, Brady. I just... I need some time to think."

With that, I turn on my heels and leave him standing in the living room. My shock and hurt battle for dominance within me, and all I know is that I need some space to sort through my emotions.

Once outside, I take a deep breath, trying to calm my racing heart. The sun has set, but the moon is so bright that the ranch has a glow. Tonight, the beauty of the landscape does nothing to soothe my frayed nerves. Instead, I feel a mix of betrayal and confusion coursing through me, leaving me dazed and unsure of what to do next.

I take another deep breath and start walking further away from the main house, needing to put as much distance between Brady and myself as possible. The moon allows me to see my way along a well-trodden path. I can feel the tension start to leave my body with each step I take, my breathing steadying as I inhale the fresh, crisp air.

As I continue on the path, my mind drifts back to Brady and the turmoil of emotions. I refuse to be the 'other woman' even if he is married to that monster. Part of me wants to believe that there's a reasonable explanation for everything, but another part struggles to reconcile what I've seen with my own eyes. He never told me he was married.

A small voice in my mind reminds me that love is never simple. And while I haven't fully admitted it yet, I know I'm falling for Brady. That realization only makes the entire situation more painful and confusing.

Chapter Twenty-Four

Brady

I clench my jaw as I watch her silhouette fade.

"Brady, what do you need?" Wyatt is at my side.

"I don't know yet. I need to find Finley – I need to explain."

"Go talk to her then," he says, urging me on.

I can't believe she just walked away like that. I know I'm the one in the wrong here, but the moment my ex-wife showed up, my brain went haywire. I want to explain, to tell Finley I am sorry, but she vanished without a word. I need to find her, talk to her, and make sure she's okay. With an uneasy feeling gnawing at my gut, I rush to Finley's bungalow.

"Brady?" I hear Zoey's voice behind me as I bang on Finley's door. She walks out of her bungalow, wiping her hands on a towel. "I saw Finley go for her walk on the path, the one she usually takes in the morning."

"Damn it." I run a hand through my hair, frustration mounting. "She could be anywhere by now. Thanks."

With a few of my wranglers gathered, we saddle up our horses and take off along the trail Finley usually walks. My heart pounds in my chest, a mix of fear and frustration coursing through me. Is she okay? How can I fix this mess?

Chapter Twenty-Five

Finley

"Alright, Finley," I say aloud, giving myself a mental pep talk. "You're a smart, capable woman who has faced far worse than this. You'll get through this."

I continue along the trail, appreciating the beauty of nature and the peace it offers on such a clear night. As I round a bend, a breathtaking view unfolds before me.

Yet, something feels off. An uneasy tension hangs in the air as if the land is mirroring my emotions. The occasional rustling noises behind me begin to unnerve me, prompting me to return to my bungalow.

I turn to retrace my steps, and I hear a guttural snort coming from nearby.

"Please," I pray silently, "don't let that be what I think it is."

But my hopes are dashed when a feral hog emerges from the underbrush, its beady eyes locked on me. Panic sets in, and I frantically search for something to defend myself with. I spot a thick branch lying a few feet away and manage to grab it. Gripping the makeshift weapon tightly, I prepare to face the aggressive animal.

"Back off, buddy!" I yell, attempting to sound more confident than I feel. The hog snorts again, its tusks gleaming menacingly as it edges closer. Its hooves scrape against the ground, kicking up dirt and rocks, and I can see the powerful muscles beneath its mottled hide.

"Okay, Finley," I think, "you're a city lawyer who's faced intimidating opponents before, right? You can handle this."

As the hog charges forward, I swing the branch with all my strength, making contact. It squeals in pain and fury, momentarily dazed but not defeated. I'm shaking as adrenaline courses through my veins.

"Come on, you ugly beast," I taunt, trying to keep the fear from my voice. "Is that all you've got?"

The hog recovers quickly, its beady eyes narrowing with anger as it prepares for another attack. My heart races, and I know I can't keep this up for long. Desperation sets in as I realize I must get out of here - and fast.

In a desperate attempt to distance myself from the feral hog, I take off running. But my haste proves to be my undoing as I misstep on an uneven patch of ground. The sharp pain that shoots through my left ankle is too much to bear, and I crumple to the ground with a cry.

"Damn it," I hiss through gritted teeth, clutching at my injured ankle. Panic rises in my chest as the feral hog continues its approach, snorting and grunting. I can see the cruel glint in its eyes as it seems to revel in my vulnerability.

"Get away from me!" I shout, scrambling backward on my hands and knees, trying to ignore the throbbing pain. I know I need to keep moving, but each movement sends fresh waves of agony coursing through my leg.

"Think, Finley, think!" I scold myself, my mind frantically searching for a way out of this dire situation. My fingers graze over a small rock, and without hesitation, I snatch it up and hurl it at the beast. The rock clips the side of the hog, only serving to enrage it further.

"Great, now you've done it," I chastise myself as the hog charges toward me again. In a desperate bid for safety, I spot another rock within reach - larger this time - and muster all my strength to throw it. The impact is enough to halt its charge momentarily, but I know it won't be deterred for long.

"Come on, Finley, you're smarter than a hog!" I tell myself, forcing my body to crawl away despite the pain radiating from my ankle. My heart pounds in my ears, drowning out everything else as I focus solely on putting as much distance as possible between myself and the determined hog.

"Help!" I yell again, my voice hoarse from desperation. "Please, somebody help me!"

"Oh, Andrew, please don't let me be killed by this hog. I'm sorry that I haven't written in days. Please, please make it go away."

When I think all hope is lost, a flash of movement catches my eye. Bandit appears from seemingly out of nowhere. He darts back and forth, barking furiously to distract the feral hog. And it works – the hog seems more interested in Bandit than me for a short time. The distraction gives me a brief respite, allowing me to drag myself toward a nearby tree. With a surge of adrenaline, I grab a low-hanging branch and hoist myself up into the tree, leaving the furious hog snorting and snapping its jaws below.

As I sit in the tree, silently thanking it for being my savior, Bandit continues barking at the hog. He is risking his life to save mine.

"Go, Bandit!" I cheer him on as he leads the feral beast away from my tree, giving me a glimmer of hope that I might make it out of this mess alive.

"Thank you, Bandit. Thank you, Andrew," I whisper gratefully, tears streaming down my face as I lean against the tree's rough bark. My ankle throbs incessantly, but it seems the danger has been temporarily abated. Bandit and the hog are both gone.

As the minutes tick by, my relief at escaping the hog turns to concern. What if it decides to wait me out? What if night falls and I'm still stuck in this tree, cold and alone? My heart races with anxiety, and I realize I am twisting my hair around my fingers once again.

"Come on, Finley," I whisper to myself. "Don't let fear get the better of you. You've been through worse."

"Brady, I wish you were here," I murmur, a tear slipping down my cheek. "I should have listened to your side of the story before running off like this."

As the adrenaline fades, the pain in my twisted ankle surges, making me wince. There's no way I can walk on it, let alone run if the hog decides to return. So, despite the lingering fear, I remain perched in my leafy refuge, praying for rescue.

Minutes pass like hours, each second punctuated by the throbbing of my ankle and the frantic pounding of my heart. I try to steady my breathing, focusing on the sunlight filtering through the leaves above me. But deep down, I know I can no longer ignore the truth: I need help.

And then, as if in answer to my silent plea, I hear the distant sound of gunshots.

Relief washes over me but is quickly replaced by worry for Bandit. Fearful thoughts race through my mind – what if he's been hurt? What if those gunshots were meant for him?

"Please, let Bandit be okay," I whisper, twisting my hair around my fingers, my eyes scanning the woods for any sign of the brave dog.

Suddenly, I spot movement in the distance. Bandit emerges from the trees, unharmed and wagging his tail proudly. My relief is palpable, and I let out a shaky laugh. "You're amazing, Bandit."

But it's not just Bandit who has come to my rescue. Brady and a few cowboys appear on horseback, their faces etched with concern as they approach my makeshift treehouse.

Chapter Twenty-Six

Brady

"Spread out!" I yell to the others, and we split up, covering different sections of the trail.

"Finley!" I shout, my voice echoing through the trees. "Where are you?"

As we ride deeper into the trees, I think about everything I need to say to her. How much she means to me, how I've been hiding parts of myself from her. I need to be honest and vulnerable with her, regardless of how terrifying that may be.

"Brady! Over here!" One of my wranglers calls out, bringing me back to the present.

"Did you find her?" I ask, urging my horse in his direction.

"Tracks," he says, pointing to the ground. "Looks like someone's been walking along here."

"Let's follow them," I decide, hoping they lead us to Finley.

The tracks wind further into the woods, and my worry for Finley grows with each passing moment. What if she's lost? Hurt? I can't bear the thought of anything happening to her.

"Finley!" I shout again, my voice desperate now. "Please, where are you?"

Just as I round a corner, Bandit comes barreling at us with a wild hog on his tail. The men and I instinctively pull out our guns. We shoot into the air, the loud bangs echoing through the forest. The hog screeches to a halt, startled by the noise, and turns to retreat into the underbrush. Bandit barks triumphantly, wagging his tail as he leads us further down the path.

"Good boy, Bandit," I praise as we follow him, my heart pounding even harder now. "You're leading us right to her, aren't you?"

It takes a while, but we finally reach Finley. She is perched in a small scrub tree, her face flushed and eyes wide with fear.

"Finley!" I call out.

"Brady! You found me," she says, her voice trembling. "I thought I would be that pig's dinner for sure.

Our eyes lock onto each other. "Are you all right?"

"Other than a twisted ankle and a bruised ego, I'm fine," She replies, trying to sound nonchalant despite the tears in her eyes.

"Thank God," I murmur, relief flooding my body. "Hold on, we'll get you down from there."

I get her out of the tree and realize she can't put any weight on her left leg.

"Let's get you back and have Doc Weaver take a look at that ankle," I say as I put her on my horse and climb on behind her.

"Brady, did you kill that pig?" she asks.

"No, we just shot into the air to scare it before it got a taste of Bandit. It's probably hiding in the brush somewhere."

With my arms wrapped around her, she leans back into my chest as I lead Bandera back to the ranch. A warmth washes over me that I haven't felt in years. It's a feeling of home, of rightness, of comfort.

"It is just a sprain, Finley," Doc informs us. Finley is sitting on the exam table, leaning against my chest as he examines her leg. "I want you to wear this brace whenever you are up and about for a few days. Ice the ankle on the way back to the ranch and then take it off for twenty minutes before repeating. Take a couple of Advil every four to six hours, but I wrote you a prescription for something a little stronger if that doesn't work. Call my office in a few days, and I can come out and see you, or you can come back in if you can get someone to drive you."

"Thank you, Doctor Weaver. I am so sorry to have disturbed your evening," Finley says, looking somewhat relieved.

"Not a problem at all, young lady. You got me out of watching 'The Batchelor' with the Mrs."

"Not a fan, Doc?" I ask.

"Not even a little, but Merna loves it. All those Ashley's and Rob's. I can't even keep up." Doc says with an exasperated breath. "But when Merna's happy, I'm happy. Young man, when you've been married for as long as we have, you find yourself doing things you never would have thought." He almost looks wistful as he talks about his wife. "Well, Brady, I'll have Stephanie send you the invoice in the morning."

"Thank you again, Doc. Have a good rest of your night," I say as I help Finley off the table and grab her ice packs and prescription.

"Do you want me to carry you back out, or do you want to try out that brace?" I ask, hoping she'll let me carry her.

"I'm going to take it slow and try out the brace while we're still here," she says.

Once we get to the truck and I open the door for her, it is evident that she will not be able to climb up into my big dually pickup.

"Do you mind?" she asks timidly.

"Not at all; this is all my fault anyway." I set the things in my hands on the center console and lift her bridal style.

"How do you figure? I'm the one who ran away and was almost eaten by Pumba."

"Pumba? You named the pig?" I ask, confused. "Anyway, I am the sole reason you needed to take that walk in the first place."

As I hold onto her, I realize this is the moment. It's time to lay myself bare before her, no matter how hard it may be.

"Finley, there's something I need to tell you," I begin, my voice shaky. "I haven't been completely honest with you about my past."

"Brady, please put me in the truck first so we can talk there." I gently set her in the passenger seat and start to grab the seatbelt.

"I got this, thanks," she says.

I go around and get into the driver's seat. I start the engine but don't pull out of the clinic parking lot.

She remains silent, waiting for me to continue.

"Finley, before you came into my life, I briefly married Amber. But now, thankfully, she's my ex-wife – she betrayed me. She only wanted me for my money. Since then, I've struggled to trust people and let anyone new in. But you..." I pause, swallowing hard. "You're different, Finley. You've broken through my walls. I'm sorry I didn't bring up that I was married. I'm not married anymore and haven't been for about three years. I try to never think about it, so I didn't bring it up. I should have told you when you told me about Andrew, but my marriage was such a disaster compared to how you described yours. I was embarrassed that I was so bad at it. After that, it never felt like the right time. I never meant to hide it from you."

Finley's face softens, and she gently touches my cheek. "Oh, Brady," she murmurs, her eyes filled with empathy. "I'm so sorry you went through that. We should all be loved for who we are, not what we have. But thank you for trusting me enough to tell me."

"Thank you for being worth the risk," I reply, my heart swelling for this incredible woman.

And then, without another word, I lean in and kiss her – a passionate, soul-bearing kiss that speaks volumes about the depth of our connection. We might not know what the future holds, especially with Finley set to return to Boston soon, but one thing is certain: there is something about her that I don't want to lose, and I will find a way to make it work, no matter the distance.

Chapter Twenty-Seven

Finley

I sit up in bed, and the sun's light filters through the curtains, casting a soft glow in my cozy bungalow. I stretch, shaking off the remnants of sleep and the ache in my muscles from last night's encounter with the hog.

The soreness is a small price to pay for the optimism I feel this morning. My ankle will be in an orthopedic boot for a while as a reminder of the chaos. I smile as I remember Bandit charging in to save me. It feels like a scene straight out of a movie, and I can almost hear Andrew's laughter in my mind, encouraging me to embrace the absurdity of it all.

I glance at the leather-bound journal on my bedside table, and that continuous tug of guilt hits me.

Should I be writing about Brady? Shouldn't I still be mourning Andrew? But then I remember how Brady made me feel last night—the connection we shared, the way he held me close, and how he finally opened up and shared his story. It's okay to feel joy, I remind myself. It's OK to let new experiences in.

I take a deep breath and reach for the journal, flipping it open to a fresh page. The words come easily as I pour out my thoughts.

June 19

Andrew,

This morning feels different. I woke up with a lightness in my heart that I haven't felt in a long time. The last few nights have been incredible, filled with fun, dancing, and starlit walks.

But as I sit here, I also reflect on the chaos that led up to this moment—the scare with the wild hog and how Bandit came to my rescue. I know you were watching over me, maybe even sending that brave little dog to save me when I needed it most.

I feel a freeness to live life again. I'm grateful for this moment of clarity now that I realize I

*can still laugh and feel alive, even in the midst
of uncertainty. This storm in my life is passing,
and yesterday's harrowing experience feels like a
metaphor for my life; after the chaos, there's beauty
to be found.*

*I'm determined to find that beauty today and
enjoy this new chapter. With my orthopedic boot,
I might not be able to move as freely, but I won't
let that stop me from exploring this ranch and
the friendships I'm forming. I want to be open to
whatever comes next, even if it's scary.*

*Thank you for watching over me, Andrew, and
sending me Bandit when I needed a guardian. I
love you and miss you every day.*

Forever yours,

Finley

I slip on the orthopedic boot and one of my tennis shoes. The height feels more balanced than when I wore my cowboy boots last night, which means my cowgirl days are on pause for now. As I adjust the straps, I am grateful for my pedicure session with Barb a few days ago. My bright pink toenail polish peeks out cheerfully from beneath the boot, a vibrant contrast to the drab black Velcro, and it brings a smile to my face despite the circumstances.

I don't have anything planned for today now that I can't ride Rosie anymore. I plan to have a leisurely breakfast and relax. There is a note taped to my door as I step out to leave.

> *I left you one of the gators. The keys are in it. It doesn't have a clutch, so you should be able to drive it with only one foot. It's yours for the duration.*
>
> *-B*

I turn to see what must be the Gator. The little green vehicle looks like a cross between an ATV and a golf cart. I'm not sure I need to drive everywhere, but it was very sweet of Brady to have this for me.

As it turns out, the Gator is fun to drive. I zip to the dining hall in no time.

As soon as I walk in, Barb greets me at the door and guides me to a table, keeping hold of my arm the entire time.

"We've been so worried about you, dear," she says as she helps me sit down. "We heard you had an awful scare."

Albert and Sam arrive with plates of food and place them in front of me. "We saw you drive up on that little machine and thought we'd save you the trouble of struggling through the line," Albert says, giving my shoulders a side hug before returning to his seat.

"You really worried us, young lady," Sam adds as he sits.

Michael pours coffee from the carafe on the table and places it in front of me.

"Wow! Thank you, everyone."

"Now that we see you're alive and unmaimed, take a few bites and tell us what happened," Zoey adds, always the straightforward one.

The story of my incident last night has them all asking a ton of questions, all at the same time.

Did the hog bite you? Were you scared? Did you take any pictures of it? Is your ankle broken?

I take a deep breath, preparing to recount the events of the previous night. "Thank you all for your concern," I begin, trying to address their questions one by one.

"No, the hog didn't bite me, thankfully. Bandit managed to chase it off before it got too close," I explain, relief evident in my voice.

"I was definitely scared when I saw that huge creature charging towards me, but Bandit was my hero," I continue, smiling at the memory of the brave little dog coming to my rescue.

"As for pictures," I shake my head apologetically. "I was too focused on getting to safety to even think about taking a photo," I admit sheepishly.

"And about my ankle," I pause, looking down at the orthopedic boot. "It's not broken, just a bad sprain. But I'll be fine with some rest."

I sip my coffee before continuing, "It was a scary experience, but I'm just grateful to be here with all of you today."

The group listens intently as I recount the details of the encounter with the hog, their expressions ranging from concern to amazement. Once I finish telling my

story, there is a moment of silence before Barb breaks
it with a warm smile.

"Well, we're glad you're safe and sound now," she
says reassuringly.

"Let us know if you need anything," Max adds.

"Thanks, you guys."

"Absolutely. We're all part of your ranch family
now," adds Sam.

I am grateful for my new friends' genuine concern
for my well-being.

I drive over to Brady's office. He called to tell me he
has something to show me.

When I hobble inside, it's nothing like I imagined.
Although his office is located in a barn, it doesn't
resemble one at all.

The walls are lined with bookshelves filled with
leather-bound books, giving the space a warm and
inviting feel. A large oak desk sits in the center of the
room, papers neatly organized, and a colorful array
of sticky notes stuck to his monitor adds a splash

of color. I glance around, impressed by the cozy yet sophisticated atmosphere.

Brady welcomes me at the door with a kiss. "Good morning, Finley. I'm glad you could make it," he greets me warmly.

"I watched you whip in her a minute ago. It looks like you're enjoying yourself on that Gator."

"Zippy and I are doing great. She's a lot of fun to drive."

"Zippy?"

"Gator is too masculine. She needed a better name."

"Well, you can call it anything you want."

"Your office is lovely. Not at all what I expected."

"What were you expecting?"

"I'm not sure, but this is not it."

Brady gestures for me to take a seat in one of the plush armchairs across from his desk.

"I have to check on something real quick. Do you need a water or something?"

"No, I'm good."

"I'll be back in two minutes. Make yourself at home."

When Brady leaves, I pick up a large leather-bound album.

The pages are filled with black-and-white images of cowboys and cowgirls riding horses, tending to cattle, and engaging in various ranch activities. The pictures are very old and well-preserved. As I flip through the album, the photographs become more current, and I am aware that I am looking at history.

Brady returns and stops at my chair. "I love that thing."

"It's fascinating," I say as I flip to a color picture of three shirtless little boys and a small calf. I can bet that the one on the right is a young Brady.

Brady laughs as he looks at the picture over my shoulder. "Yep, that's me on the right. We were quite the troublemakers back then," he reminisces.

"Are the other boys your brothers?"

"The one on the far left is Logan Davis, who you met at the bar the other night. We've known each other since we were in grade school. That little guy in the middle, with white-blonde hair, is Wyatt."

"Oh, my gosh. He's so little."

"Yep, little Wyatt. Can't say that anymore. He's like a tree."

"This is a beautiful book, Brady. Did someone make it for you?"

"Actually...I did."

I look at him, surprised by his answer. "You made this?"

Brady nods, a hint of pride in his eyes.

"It started as a project for my seventh-grade Texas History class, and it's grown over the years. I wanted a way to preserve the history of this ranch."

I flip through more pages, each one telling a story of its own through these frozen moments captured in time. Cowboys around a campfire, children learning to ride horses, families coming together for branding day—it's all here.

"This is beautiful," I say, genuinely impressed.

"Thank you. This ranch is more than just a piece of land to me. It's a legacy, a home, a part of who I am."

I look up from the album to meet his gaze, and in that moment, I see the depth of his connection to this place reflected in his eyes.

"So," he says after a moment, breaking the spell. "I have something else to show you."

He leads me out to Zippy. "Do you mind if I drive?" he asks.

"Not at all."

Brady takes me to a barn quite a bit farther away.

"This is where we're boarding the new horses that came in the other day."

He opens the large barn doors, and a chorus of nickers greets us as we step inside. The smell of hay and animals fills the air, and I feel a rush of excitement at the sight before me. The stalls are filled with horses of various colors and sizes.

"These are some of our newest additions," Brady says proudly, gesturing towards a majestic black stallion in the corner stall. "That's Midnight, a purebred Friesian. And over here," he continues, leading me to another stall, "this beauty is Ruby, a spirited chestnut mare."

"She looks a bit like Rosie," I add.

"They do have similar coloring," he confirms. "But Ruby's got a bit more fire in her."

I reach out to stroke Ruby's soft nose; she snorts playfully and nuzzles my hand. I feel an instant connection with the spirited mare.

"You're gonna make Rosie jealous," Brady teases.

"Not if I can't ride anymore, I'm not."

"You should be able to ride again. You might just have to use one of the mounting blocks instead of the stirrups."

"I would love to ride again before I have to go back to Boston."

"Speaking of back, we should get back to my office. Lunch has probably been delivered."

We return to Brady's office and enjoy a delicious lunch. We talk more about the horses and our plans for the next few days. I leave him to get some work done and agree to meet him again for dinner tonight.

Chapter Twenty-Eight

Brady

Finley and I are seated at a small, round table in the bustling dining hall. She tells me about her morning with the baby goats when I see my sister, Maddy, making a beeline towards us.

"I swear they are like tiny tornados!"

"Yeah, Brady can be quite the little tornado sometimes," Maddy interrupts.

"She was talking about the baby goats, Mads."

"I figured it was something like that, but if I can't give you crap, who can?"

"I'm Madison, by the way. You must be the gorgeous lawyer he's been talking about."

"Mads, this is Finley Prescott."

Finley smiles warmly at Maddy. "It's nice to meet you, Madison."

Maddy turns around, looking for someone. I spot my mother. "Mom!" Maddy calls out over her shoulder, "He's over here."

Mom's eyes light up as she approaches, her smile broadening.

"Mom, this is Finley Prescott. Finley, this is my mother, Betty," I stammer, trying to keep my voice steady. Why am I so nervous for her to meet everyone?

"Hello, dear," she greets Finley with a gentle hug. "It's lovely to finally meet you. Brady has told us all about you. How is your ankle doing?"

"It's getting better, thank you. Brady has been taking good care of me," Finley replies with a grateful smile.

"I'm glad to hear that," my mother replies, taking a seat at the table.

"Brady, would you please go get me an iced tea?"

"Sure, would you like anything else? Mads?"

"No thanks," they both say.

"I'll be right back, but don't spill all my secrets while I'm gone," I tease as I walk towards the drink station.

I return to the table with the iced tea for my mother and a fresh lemonade for Finley. Maddy is in the middle of recounting a particularly embarrassing childhood story, and Finley is laughing so hard tears are streaming down her face.

"Ah, you're back just in time," Maddy exclaims. "I was getting to the best part!"

I shake my head as I retake my seat. "Oh no, what have you been telling her?"

"Just some classic Brady stories," Maddy replies with a mischievous glint in her eye.

Finley wipes away her tears, still giggling. "Your sister is something else, Brady."

"That's one way to put it," I agree, shooting a playful glare at Maddy.

When she finishes her tea, my mother excuses herself to attend to some business, leaving Maddy, Finley, and me at the table.

"I hope to see you again before you leave, my dear."

Finley smiles warmly at my mother's words. "I would love that. Thank you for making me feel so welcome here."

"Well, you two love birds, I've got some new products to look at, so I'll catch you later," Maddy says, standing up. "It was nice meeting you, Finley."

"Likewise, Maddy. Thanks for the stories!"

Once we're alone, I turn to Finley. "I hope my family isn't overwhelming you."

"Not at all. They're wonderful."

"I'm glad you think so. My sister can be a handful at times."

"She seems fun. And your mother is lovely."

"She is. She's the heart of this ranch."

She reaches across the table to take my hand in hers, "I'm glad I got to meet them."

Chapter Twenty-Nine

Finley

After wrapping up his work for the day, Brady finds me in the lodge's game room. We are trying to spend as much time together as possible before my inevitable return to Boston in five days. The space is packed with a variety of entertainment - books, games, movies, and puzzles. Brady enters as I am perusing the back cover of a murder mystery.

"Is that one of my Larry McMurtry's?" He asks as he embraces me.

"No. Not unless he's a female medical examiner."

"Not even close. He writes westerns. Have you heard of Lonesome Dove?"

"I have actually. My dad has some old VHS tapes that he loves. I remember watching them with him when I was a little girl. I don't hate Westerns, but they aren't my go-to. I personally love mysteries and thrillers."

"I would have guessed you were a Romance reader. But it sounds like your dad and I are going to get along just fine."

"I do like a good romance, but nothing too cheesy. I'll read just about anything as long as it's interesting. And my dad is a pretty easygoing guy; I'm sure you two will hit it off."

"I like a good mystery now and then. Keeps me on my toes," Brady replies

"Hey, I was thinking... how about we go for one more horseback ride before you have to leave."

"I'd love to. You said you had a block or something to help me up onto the horse?"

"It's called a mounting block. We use them when riders are older, or handicapped..... or injured."

"Nice save, Cowboy!"

"How 'bout tomorrow morning? Before it gets too hot." "Sounds like a plan. Let's get some dinner so we can continue this cowboy theme later," I say, holding up a DVD.

"'The Good, the Bad and the Ugly!' An excellent choice," he nods in approval.

After dinner we settle in to watch the movie. Brady sits down next to me on the plush couch, draping an arm over my shoulder, and I feel a sense of contentment wash over me. The warmth of Brady's presence beside me and the familiarity of his ranch makes me wish for time to stand still.

Halfway through the film, a knock at the door interrupts our cozy moment. Brady gets up to answer it while I pause the movie.

When he returns, he's holding a tray with two steaming cups and a plate of freshly baked chocolate chip cookies. "How?"

"I texted the kitchen. I thought we could use a snack," he says with a grin, setting the tray on the coffee table. "Cocoa or tea?"

"Tea, please. You are too good to me," I say, reaching for a cookie.

"Only because you deserve it," Brady replies, handing me one of the mugs before sitting beside me again.

We enjoy our treats and continue watching the movie with some kissing breaks scattered in between.

As the credits roll and the movie comes to an end, Brady turns to me. "I'm so glad you came into my life, Finley."

My heart swells at his words, and I squeeze his hands gently. "I'm glad too, Brady.

Brady walks me back to my bungalow, and we linger longer at the doorstep. The cool night air carries the scent of a distant campfire, and the soft chirping of cicadas fills the silence between us. Brady cups my face in his hands, his eyes searching mine with tenderness and longing.

"I don't want this week to end."

"Me neither," I murmur, leaning in closer.

Our lips meet in a gentle kiss, filled with the weight of impending goodbyes. He trails kisses along my jawline, sending shivers down my spine. His hands slide down my back, pulling me closer as if afraid I might disappear.

As we sink into the embrace, everything else fades away—the worries about the future, the distance between us when I return home. All that matters is this shared heartbeat, this unspoken promise of something deeper than words could ever convey.

When we finally pull back, Brady rests his forehead against mine, our eyes locked.

"I'll see you in the morning for our ride," he whispers before pressing one last kiss on my lips.

I watch him walk back to the main house, feeling a sense of longing in my chest.

Chapter Thirty

Brady

Finley should still be using the Gator, so I decide to wait for her on her porch so we can ride together. I hear her rustling around fussin' about something, so I knock to see if everything is okay.

"Come on in."

She opens the door and continues searching for something.

"I can't find my bandana anywhere. I know I left on this bench the other day. I have looked under and around everything. It's not here."

"I'm sure it will turn up. I have several in my office. We can grab you one on the way to the stables."

"Then I guess I'm ready."

"I'm driving!" she declares as we step outside. "Hold on tight, Cowboy." She floors it, and we take off toward the barn.

"I get why you call this Zippy. You're gonna give me whiplash at this rate," I tease as we bounce along the path.

"I don't get to drive much in Boston. It's too hard to find parking, so I usually walk or take public transportation. My little car sits in the underground parking lot more than it's on the road. It's fun to be the one in control."

This woman is something else—calm and professional with a bit of a rebellious streak.

Finley steers the Gator towards the stables, a thrill evident in her eyes as she navigates the twists and turns of the ranch's dirt paths.

I hop off the Gator and lead her to where our horses are saddled and ready to go.

"I'm gonna run in my office and grab you a bandanna. Do you need anything else?"

"I've got my water, so I think I'm good."

"Be right back."

I run into my office and grab a water from my fridge and two bandannas from my credenza drawer.

"The mounting block is in the arena," I say, handing her a floral bandanna. She looks at it and looks at me. "I am comfortable enough with my masculinity that a floral bandanna is no big thing."

I take the leads from the post and walk the horses into the barn.

"Oh wow. This is cool," she says, climbing the steps of the block.

"When you reach the top, sit down so Rosie's back aligns with the platform, then just slide your good foot over."

She quickly gets onto Rosie and gently pats her neck. "I've missed you, girl. I thought our riding days were over."

The horse responds with a whinny.

"This is such a clever idea, Brady."

"I wish I could claim it, but it really is. My gran needed it in her later years, and I'm sure my parents will, too, someday. I don't even want to think about being unable to get into a saddle. "

"Let's make the most of the morning," I say as I mount Bandera.

We meander through the familiar paths of the ranch, and I feel a sense of freedom and joy being on horseback with Finley by my side. The worries of the future fade away, replaced by the simple pleasure of the present moment.

We reach a clearing where the sun hangs low, casting pink and gold across the sky. I turn to Finley, watching her take in the beauty around us with awe in her eyes.

"This is why I love these morning rides."

Finley nods, "Lead the way, cowboy."

After an amazing ride and a delicious lunch, I suggest a swim in the pool so we can cool off and Finley can have a break from the orthopedic boot.

When we arrive I see Geoffrey engaged in a conversation with my sister, Maddy, who is thankfully dressed in a more suitable swimsuit today.

He greets us with a smile, though he seems a bit uneasy.

"Good afternoon, Finley, Brady."

"Good Afternoon, Geoffrey, Maddy. How is the water?" Finley asks as she sets her bag and towel on a lounge chair.

"It's a bit too warm, so I asked Joseph to toss in some ice blocks earlier. That should help."

"Do you have to do that often?" Finley asks.

"This isn't even the hottest part of the summer. Even the ice blocks don't help in August," Maddy replies.

Finley sits on the steps and removes her boot. "Brady, will you please put this up on my chair so it doesn't get wet?"

I take the boot to her lounge chair.

Geoffrey announces he needs to finish some work as he retreats to his bungalow.

"Enjoy your swim," he tells me. Then, to my sister, he says, "I'll email you the contract, and we can discuss it later."

I give her a wary glance. "What contract, what email? Mads, that guy is bad news."

"Relax, Brady," she replies as she slips off her chair and joins Finley in the pool.

"I agreed to help him with a new marketing campaign. He's trying to move his real estate business away from outdated platforms. Many Gen Xers have money and are buying homes, but we never pay attention to Facebook ads. He needs someone who knows what younger people are looking for."

I join them in the pool.

"I know this is your area of expertise; just be careful."

"Brady, I've dealt with men like Geoffrey since I was fifteen. Most of them are all talk, and the ones that aren't are easily put in their place by my money or my bodyguard."

"You have a bodyguard? Since when?"

"For the past four years, dear brother. How else would I be able to make personal appearances without chaos ensuing?"

"I had no idea."

"Of course you didn't. You only ever see me as your goofy-but gorgeous, extroverted baby sister. But I have a successful business and my own life outside of this place. I know how to protect my interests."

"It sounds like you don't need my help."

"I understand you're protective, Brady. But I can handle myself. And if this guy tries anything inappropriate, I'll shut it down immediately." She adds.

"I'm sorry, Mads. I didn't mean to pry."

"It's all good, Brady. Now, let's enjoy the swim."

We spend the next half hour swimming and relaxing by the pool—the tension from earlier a distant memory.

Maddy excuses herself, and Finley and I are left alone by the pool.

I watch as Finley leans back on her lounge chair, her damp hair cascading down her shoulders. She looks content in this tranquil setting.

"You were right, Brady. This is exactly what I needed," Finley says, her smile reaching her eyes.

"You know, back in Boston, everything is always so fast-paced," she muses, gazing at the sprawling landscape around us. "I'm always rushing from one thing to the next, barely stopping to catch my breath. But here..." She trails off as if searching for the right words.

I settle into the chair beside her. "Here, it's different," I finish for her.

"Exactly." She turns to me, her eyes meeting mine. "You have this incredible way of making everything feel so... simple. Peaceful."

I feel a warmth bloom in my chest at her words. "Well, that's ranch life for you. It has its way of slowing things down."

"It's not just the ranch," she says softly. "It's you."

I hold her gaze, feeling a rush of emotions swirling inside me. Before I can respond, she leans over and presses her lips against mine in a tender kiss. The world around us fades away as I melt into the moment, savoring the softness of her lips against mine. Everything feels right, like this is where we're meant to be.

"Finley..." I begin, my voice barely above a whisper. But she places a finger on my lips, silencing me.

"Brady, please don't say anything just yet," she murmurs. "Let's just be here, in this moment."

Chapter Thirty-One

Finley

I stand in front of the mirror, adjusting the strap on my boot. This isn't the boot I imagined I'd have in Texas. Four days have passed since I sprained my ankle, and Brady has been fussing over me constantly. Who would have thought that this grumpy cowboy could be so nurturing?

I hear the crunch of gravel as Brady pulls up in his truck. I snap out of my thoughts and take one last look in the mirror. I've got on one of my favorite sundresses and a single cute sandal. I still have on this ugly boot to keep my ankle stable. Stupid ankle, stupid boot.

I open the door to see Brady stepping out of his truck, looking more handsome than ever in his cowboy hat and boots. His eyes light up when he sees me, and I feel a warm flush creep up my neck.

"Ready for our date, Boston?" Brady's voice is playful as he helps me from the porch.

"As ready as I'll ever be, cowboy." I try to match his light tone, but my voice catches. I can't bear the thought of leaving in just two days.

He holds out his arm, and I link mine through his as he helps me navigate the steps down from the cabin. The boot makes me clumsy, but Brady is steady and strong beside me.

"Where are we going tonight?" I ask him as we make our way to his truck.

"Thought we'd try the Italian place in town," he says, opening the passenger door for me.

"Sounds perfect," I tell him, smiling as he drives us down the dusty road toward town.

He parks in front of a cute Italian restaurant, and I feel a mix of excitement and sadness. This could be our last date before I leave, and I'm sure that I'm not ready to say goodbye to Brady just yet. But for now,

I push that thought aside and focus on enjoying the evening with him.

Brady reaches over and touches my arm. "Where'd you go just now? You've got that little crinkle between your eyes."

"Just thinking how much I love it here." Love it with you, I add silently.

"It's not so bad, is it? Even with me for a tour guide."

"Are you fishing for compliments, Cowboy?" I retort. "I suppose you'll do."

His laugh fills the cab of the truck. The sound wraps around me like a cozy blanket. I'm going to miss this; miss him so damn much.

Brady helps me out of the truck, and we walk towards the restaurant. I admire the charming atmosphere of this small town. It's so different from the bustling streets of Boston, yet it feels like a warm embrace that I never knew I needed. Twinkle lights hang above the main street, and people greet each other with friendly smiles as they pass by.

"Everyone seems to know each other here," I observe, feeling the warmth of the community.

"Yep, it's one of the things I love about this place," Brady replies, offering me a smile that makes my heart race.

"Here we are, the best lasagna in three counties." He hurries around to open my door, ever the gentleman.

The savory scents of garlic, tomatoes, and fresh bread envelop us as we enter. A hostess greets us with a welcoming smile and guides us to a cozy table near a window, offering a picturesque view of the town's main street.

I slide into the red leather booth while Brady settles opposite me. His blue eyes twinkle in the candlelight.

"Your waiter this evening will be Tony," the hostess says before gliding away.

"Great choice," I say, looking around at the rustic decor and flickering candles on each table. "This place is beautiful."

"Thought you might like it," he responds with a grin that ignites the butterflies in my stomach.

Right on cue, a lanky teenager in an oversized bowtie bounces up to our table. "Welcome, folks! I'm Tony, and I'll be taking care of you tonight."

His mouth drops open as he spots Brady. "Uh, Mr. Cavanaugh! I didn't realize it was you!" His cheeks flush bright pink. "Sorry for being so informal, sir."

Brady waves his hand. "At ease, kid. I'm just here on a date." He winks at me.

"Yessir, Mr. Cavanaugh, sir." Tony fumbles. "Umm. Can I, can I start you off with some drinks?"

"A beer for me and..." Brady glances my way.

"I'll have a glass of red wine, please."

As Tony scurries off, Brady leans towards me with a concerned look. "Think I scared that poor kid half to death."

I roll my eyes. "Only you could reduce the staff to a flustered mess without even trying."

Brady leans toward me and whispers so only I can hear him, "Tony worked at the ranch last summer; a sweet kid, but a terrible cowboy. He's all arms and legs, not a single visible muscle on him. The cows scared the heck out of him. But I've got to give him credit; he worked hard and stayed the whole summer."

I smile at Tony as he returns with our drinks, visibly bracing himself before speaking. "Are you folks ready to order?"

"I'll have the lasagna, extra sauce." Brady hands him the menu. "And the lady will have…"

"The eggplant parmesan sounds delicious. I'll have that."

"Excellent choices!" Tony chirps. As he leaves, Brady lifts his beer in a toast.

"To our last date night together." His voice softens. "I'm sure gonna miss you, Boston."

I touch my glass to his, blinking back sudden tears. "I'll miss you too. But this isn't goodbye yet. We still have two days."

Brady nods, his jaw tight. "Two days to make some memories. So let's start here."

He leans forward, placing his hand on top of mine. The touch grounds me as warm and comforting as the glow of the lights outside.

I take a sip of wine, savoring the rich flavor as I glance around the restaurant. Soft Italian music drifts through the intimate space.

"Cozy little place, isn't it?" Brady asks, following my gaze.

"It's lovely. And so charming, just like this town."

Brady hesitates for a moment as if unsure how to proceed. "Would you... would you consider staying with me?"

His question catches me off guard, and my mind races with thoughts of what it would mean to stay on Brady's ranch. I think about my life in Boston, the friends and career I've built there, and how different things would be if I chose to remain in this small town with the grumpy yet endearing cowboy who has captured my heart.

"Brady, that's... that's a big decision. I..." I trail off, searching for the right words to express the whirlwind of emotions coursing through me. "I care about you so much, and it's terrifying to think about being apart."

"These past few weeks with you have been amazing. I finally feel like myself again. And I'm not ready to lose that. To lose you." He runs a hand through his hair. " I know it's a lot to ask, and I don't want to pressure you. But I feel like we are meant to be together, and I'm willing to do whatever it takes to make this work."

"Brady..." I reach across the table, lacing my fingers through his. "You have no idea how much I've loved being here with you. But my job, my life is in Boston."

He nods, shoulders slumping. "Yeah, figured it was a long shot."

"But that doesn't mean this has to end when I leave. If you're open to trying long-distance, I am, too. I care about you, Brady. So much."

His eyes widen, then he breaks into a grin. "Yeah? I'm game if you are. We'll make it work." He lifts my hand, brushing his lips over my knuckles.

"I know this isn't going to be easy, and we don't have to have all the answers right now. But I truly believe that if we are meant to be together, we'll find a way to make it happen."

I nod, my eyes stinging with unshed tears. "I want that too, Brady. I really do."

"Then let's promise each other that we'll do everything we can to keep this relationship alive, no matter the distance," he says, his gaze locked onto mine.

"Deal," I reply, my voice barely a whisper.

We clasp hands across the table, sealing our promise. As we sit there, lost in each other's eyes, I feel hopeful for our future together.

"Whatever challenges come our way," Brady murmurs, "we'll face them together."

"Together," I echo, my heart swelling with love and determination.

Tony appears and places our plates before us, steam rising from the generous portions.

"So..." I twirl pasta onto my fork, buying time to gather my thoughts. "How exactly are we going to do this long-distance thing?"

Brady leans back in the booth, brow furrowed. "Well, visiting each other as much as possible is a start.

I can come to Boston some weekends when things on the ranch slow down."

I nod slowly. "And I can try to take some extra time off work to come here." But will that be enough? A few stolen weekends here and there?

As if reading my doubts, Brady reaches across the table again and squeezes my hand. "I know it won't be easy. But we'll make the time count when we're together. And as much as I hate to say it, technology will help—we can video chat, text, and all that. Long-distance relationships are tough, but they're not impossible."

"You're right," I say, feeling warmth spread through me as I meet his gaze. "We just have to be willing to put in the work, and I believe we can make it through anything."

"Agreed," he says, giving my hand a reassuring squeeze. "Now, let's enjoy this amazing meal and toast to our future together."

I lift my glass, clinking it against his. "To us."

Our meal winds down, and I wish we could linger here all evening.

As we step out into the cool night air, I turn to him, my heart beating fast in my chest. "I don't want the night to end," I admit, taking a step closer to him and breathing in his comforting scent.

Brady stops and turns to face me. The intensity in his eyes makes my knees weak. Slowly, he lowers his mouth to mine in a kiss that steals my breath. His lips are soft and warm, and I melt into his embrace. The world around us disappears as our lips meet in a dance of passion and longing. Brady's touch ignites a fire within me, his hands gentle yet firm as they pull me closer. Every brush of his lips against mine sends electricity coursing through my veins, and I cling to him as if he is my lifeline.

When we finally break apart, a rush of emotions wash over me, leaving me dizzy and breathless.

Brady gently rests his forehead against mine, our skin warm where it touches. "We've got this, Finley," he whispers.

I smile up at him. "We do?"

He nods, a smile spreading across his face, as he takes my hand, and we walk to his truck.

Brady opens the passenger side door for me and carefully gets me into the seat. Once he's settled into his seat, "I think you should know that I'm already looking forward to our first long-distance date."

"Me too!"

Chapter Thirty-Two

Finley

I stand in the middle of my bungalow, my suitcase on the bed, and survey the mess of my belongings. Clothes are strewn about haphazardly, a pair of cowboy boots begging to be packed. I sigh, realizing that my time at the ranch has come to an end. As much as I try to focus on packing, memories of laughter, adventure, and unexpected romance dance through my mind.

"Okay, Finley," giving myself a pep talk, "time to get your act together." I begin folding shirts and jeans into neat piles, trying to fit them all into the suitcase while leaving room for the jeans and two pairs of cowboy boots I bought here. I had hoped to be out of this brace before I left so I could wear a pair home on the plane, but the ankle still isn't ready for that, so I'm trying to make room in the bag for three of the four boots. I never imagined that this city girl would fall in love with the country lifestyle, but here I am, dreading the return to my Boston office.

Over the past few weeks, this ranch has become a home away from home. I've fallen into an easy routine here and found a good man with a heart of gold. Leaving him - and this place - will be more difficult than I imagined. Returning to my empty loft and office at BryantMed fills me with dread.

A sudden commotion outside jolts me from my reflections. I hear frenzied barking. What on earth?

I hurry over and peer out onto the porch. A blur of black and white fur streaks past. It's Bandit. He's got something in his mouth. I catch a glimpse of brown leather just as he disappears around the corner of my bungalow.

"My boot!" That little thief has stolen one of my cowboy boots. And not just any boot - my one good boot that I can actually wear with this blasted ankle sprain.

"Bandit!" I call out, hobbling onto the porch. "That's mine!" I look around, but he's long gone.

As I reach the porch steps, a voice calls out, "Finley! We saw the whole thing!"

I see Sam and Albert approaching, their arms linked and matching grins on their faces. Claire trails just behind, phone raised.

"That was some slick boot-nabbing!" Sam crows. "And we caught it all on video."

"You didn't," I groan, though I can't keep the smile off my face.

"No, Claire did," Albert confirms.

"I'm thinking of making Bandit's thieving ways go viral," she adds. "The people need dog content. Boot-napper is going to be TikTok famous. I'm thinking...BanditBanditsBoots, the Cowboy Hound. Or something like that. It's still a work in progress."

"Bandit sure knows how to keep things interesting around here," Albert adds.

"Alright," Albert announces, stepping up beside me. "Looks like we have a boot to retrieve."

"Operation Boot Recovery is a go," Sam chimes in, grinning from ear to ear.

Their antics are amusing. Having these three around has made my time here so much brighter.

"All right, lead the way then, detectives," I say, linking my arm through Claire's. "Let's go catch us a boot bandit."

"Finley, you should consider yourself lucky," Claire teases. "At least it's just a boot. Barbara lost half her wardrobe to that furry little kleptomaniac."

"True," I concede, chuckling softly. "But I'd still like to leave the ranch with both of my boots, thank you very much."

"Speaking of leaving," Sam says, his tone suddenly somber. "We're going to miss you, Finley. Promise you'll keep in touch."

"Aw, guys," I say, touched by their words. "I'll miss all of you too. This vacation has been one for the books."

With that, we set off across the ranch, following Bandit's pawprints down a winding dirt path. The summer breeze whispers through the tall grass as we walk.

We follow Bandit's trail past the stables and down to a small creek shaded by cottonwood trees. He's leading us on quite the meandering route, but we're happy to play along.

Suddenly, Bandit darts off again, a mischievous glint in his eyes. "Oh no, you don't!" I exclaim, taking off after him with my friends right behind me.

"Finley, the one-legged bandit chaser!" Albert hollers, laughter bubbling up in his voice.

"Does this mean I get a cool nickname too?" Claire asks, panting slightly as we continue our pursuit.

"Sure thing," Sam replies. "How about 'Claire the Camera Conqueror'?"

"Ooh, I like it," she says, lifting her phone to record the chase for her followers.

As we race across the ranch, dodging horses and hay bales, I can't help but smile at our playful banter. This is not how I envisioned spending my last day on the ranch, but I wouldn't trade this moment for anything.

Finally, Bandit reaches a small grove of trees, and we watch in disbelief as he dives into a large bush. "We found it!" Sam announces, breathless from the sprint.

Bandit jumps out of the bush and sits by me with an air of triumph; my missing boot is proudly clutched in his mouth.

Hand it over, buddy. I reach out to take the boot from Bandit, who looks up at me with his tail wagging furiously. "You little rascal," I chuckle, tousling his fur. "Thanks for the workout this morning."

"Nice Detective work, Hon," Albert jokes, patting him on the back as we gather around the bush.

"Alright, let's see what treasures Bandit has been hoarding," Sam says, reaching into the foliage and pulling out a familiar-looking bolo tie. "Hey, this is mine!"

"Looks like you're not the only one Bandit has taken a liking to," Claire teases, grabbing the tie and snapping a picture before handing it back to Sam.

As we dig further into Bandit's stash, we uncover an assortment of random objects: a frisbee, Sasha's water bottle, an old horseshoe, and even a neon-pink feather boa – no doubt belonging to Barbara.

"Wow, Bandit sure knows how to pick his prizes," laughing at the absurdity of it all. "He's like a furry little magpie."

"Can you imagine if all these things went missing for good?" Claire wonders aloud. "The ranch would be in chaos!"

"Maybe that's his master plan," Albert suggests playfully. "Bandit, the dog who brought the ranch to its knees!"

"Or maybe he just wants to make sure we never forget him," Sam adds.

"Either way, I think we can all agree that Bandit is one unforgettable dog."

"Okay, everyone," Albert interrupts our reverie, holding a pair of fluffy pink slippers. "Who's going to claim these?"

"Definitely not mine!" Sam exclaims, and we all burst into laughter once more.

"Wait a minute," I say, my eyes widening as I dig deeper into Bandit's pile of treasures. "This is my bandana... and my sunglasses... and my favorite pen!" My astonishment grows as I pull out item after item that belongs to me.

"Looks like you're Bandit's new favorite victim, Finley," Sam teases, but his words only serve to deepen my connection to this place. The fact that Bandit has taken so many of my belongings is strangely endearing – as if the dog himself has recognized how much the ranch means to me and is trying to keep a piece of me here with him.

"Seriously, Bandit has stolen half of my suitcase!" I exclaim, pulling out a book I'd thought I lost on the cattle drive. Despite my frustration, I feel touched by Bandit's thievery. It's as though he has sensed my attachment to the ranch and its inhabitants and has decided to make sure I don't forget them.

"Maybe he's just super attached to you," Claire suggests.

"Or maybe he's got a crush on you," Albert adds, earning a nudge from Sam.

"Guys, let's not give the dog too much credit."

Just then, Brady strides up to the group with a curious expression. "I saw y'all run by the stables. What's going on here?" he asks, surveying the scattered items before us.

"Bandit's been stealing everyone's stuff, but it looks like he's got a soft spot for Finley," Sam explains, grinning at me.

"Really?" Brady raises an eyebrow as he takes in the array of my belongings in Bandit's stash. A small smile tugs at the corners of his lips. "Well, maybe he doesn't want you to leave either."

His words send a warm shiver down my spine. "Maybe he's onto something," I admit softly, meeting Brady's gaze momentarily before returning to the pile of treasures. The connections I've made here – with the people, the animals, and even this mischievous dog – have become more important to me than I ever imagined.

"Alright, let's get this stuff back to its rightful owners," Albert announces, picking up a gaudy necklace that undoubtedly belongs to Barbara. "I'm sure she's been missing this beauty."

"My LuLu bag! This dog's got good taste," Claire says, flipping her hair dramatically. "I am positively going to make this dog my TikTok co-star. What do you guys think?"

"I think you could make anyone a star, Claire. Or anything in this case." Albert adds as he fills his pocket with as much as he can.

Sam retrieves an assortment of his belongings from the pile. "You're just lucky Bandit didn't steal your heart, too, Finley."

"Too late for that, I'm afraid," I quip as I collect my things.

Brady fills my boot with my things and carries it for me as we all start back towards the main ranch house, chatting and laughing. This lighthearted moment reminds me that life is full of surprises – like a mischievous ranch dog stealing my belongings and a cowboy stealing my heart.

Chapter Thirty-Three

Brady

"I can't believe you have to leave already," I whisper, my voice thick with emotion as I pull her close. Her warm body fits perfectly against mine, but the tears in her eyes make it hard for me to smile.

"I don't want you to leave," I murmured into her hair.

"Me neither, Brady," her voice trembling. "But my job is in Boston, and I can't stay here forever."

We hold each other for a long moment, and neither of us is willing to be the first to pull away. I stroke her hair, breathing in the floral scent of her shampoo one last time. I'm trying to commit every detail of her to my memory. Our time together has gone by too quickly.

Finally, Finley lifts her head from my chest. Her eyes glistened with tears. "I have to go," she whispers.

I gently wipe a tear from her cheek. "I know." I hug her tightly, not wanting to let go. "Promise me you'll call as soon as you land?"

"Of course," she replies, brushing away a tear. "And we'll talk every day if you want."

"Every day would be nice," I say, trying to lighten the mood. But my heart feels like it's breaking into a million pieces as we share a tender kiss goodbye.

"I'm going to miss you so damn much," I said gruffly, emotion clogging my throat.

"Oh, Brady, I'm going to miss you too."

Unable to resist any longer, I capture her lips in a searing kiss. She responds immediately, matching my passion and urgency. We cling together, the world narrowing to just the two of us.

"Take care of yourself, cowboy," she whispers, pulling away just enough to look into my eyes.

"I will, Boston. You do the same." We share a sad smile before she steps back and gets into the shuttle that will take her to the airport.

I stand motionless as the driver starts to pull away. I want to chase after the car – to keep her here with me.

I kept staring after the car until it disappears down the long dirt road leading away from the ranch. My heart sinks further when I can no longer see the vehicle, leaving an empty void in my chest that grows larger by the second.

Bandit sits by my side and lets out a little whine.

"I know, buddy; I'm already missing her too." I rub the soft fur behind his ears. "Let's try to get some work done to distract ourselves," I tell him, trying to convince myself.

I shove my hands in my pockets, and we trudge to my office. Bandit makes himself comfortable on the floor while I watch the clock and try to focus on something productive.

My phone chimes.

> Hey, Cowboy. I just wanted you to know we made it to Dallas; I'm waiting to board my flight to Boston. Miss you already.

> Good to know.

I'm trying to keep my emotions in check.

> Miss you too!

It's been hours since her flight left, and I stare at my phone, waiting for any sign that she's arrived safely in Boston. The screen lights up, and my heart leaps as I see her familiar number.

> We finally landed. There was a bit of a rain delay, but all is good. Wish you were here.

I exhale a sigh of relief, and my body relaxes at the thought of her being safe.

But my heart sinks at the thought of her being so far away, but I try to keep my composure in my reply.

Me too. I hate this. But we'll see each other soon.

I feel a pang of sadness, knowing it'll be weeks, maybe months, until we see each other again.

I spend the next few days in a haze, trying to keep my mind off Finley while going through the motions of ranch work. It's not that I don't love my job – I do – but without her, everything feels a bit... duller.

Weeks pass in a miserable fog. The details of each day fade into the next, but my heart isn't in it. My appetite is non-existent - food tastes like ashes in my mouth. At night, I lay awake for hours staring at the ceiling. When it finally comes, sleep is fitful and filled with dreams of her.

I live for our phone calls. Hearing her voice soothes my soul, even if it makes me miss her even more fiercely.

I'm pulled from my brooding when my phone buzzes with an incoming call. It's from Finley.

"Hey you," she says softly when I answer. "How are you holding up?"

"I'm alright," I lie. Alright is the furthest thing from what I am.

Her sweet voice is like music to my ears. "I miss you so much."

"I miss you more than you can imagine," I tell her honestly. "The ranch hasn't been the same since you left. Bandit misses you, too. He hasn't taken anything from this session of campers. I've checked his little hidey-hole several times, just in case - Just a few sticks and an old tennis ball. I think he's depressed. He sleeps in my office all day now."

"Maybe he's just keeping you company,

We talk for over an hour every evening, catching up on everything in our lives. But mostly, we savor hearing each other's voices. It's soothing and painful at the same time.

Each night when we finally say goodbye, I always feel elated yet hollow. I need to get her back here with me; and soon.

I am in a daze as I wander over to where Logan
is working on renovating one of the ranch's
bungalows. He is up on a ladder, hammering away
at the roof, while Wyatt is hauling a piece of lumber
from the back of his truck.

"Hey brother, you're looking a little lost," Wyatt
calls out as I approach.

I sighed, leaning against the truck. "Is it that
obvious?"

Logan chuckles as he descends the ladder.
"You've had that moony look ever since Finley left.
It's written all over you, man."

"Before Logan here enlisted me as his free labor,
I came over to talk to him about a kidnapping."
Wyatt adds. "We're taking you out tonight, Brady
– getting you off the ranch."

"Where are we going?"

"Doesn't matter. We can shoot some pool or
check out who's playing at 'Over Yonder' - heck, we

could even hang out at Ms. Joanie's knitting circle. Anything to get you out of this funk."

"I'm not sure getting me out of this funk is possible. But a change of scenery might be a good idea."

"I'm sure one of those sweet old ladies would love to knit you a nice sweater," Logan jokes, nudging my shoulder. "In a nice shade of blue to match your mood."

"Hilarious Logan. Is Ally okay with you being out tonight?"

"She and Olivia have a mother-daughter art class tonight. They won't miss me at all." Olivia is Logan's daughter from his first marriage. His wife died of a brain aneurysm, leaving him with a toddler to raise on his own. He married Ally about a year ago, and I have never seen him happier. Ally is the younger sister of our other best friend, David, which was a messy situation for a while. But it all worked out, and they are the perfect little family now.

Thinking of family makes me think of Finley. Am I crazy to want her to be a part of mine? We've only known each other for a few months, but it feels like much more. Maybe it is too soon; perhaps I need more time to figure out what I want. But every time we talk, I can feel the pull, the desire to be with her again.

"Come on, Brady," Wyatt interrupts my thoughts, clapping a hand on my shoulder. "Let's go blow off some steam and forget about women for a few hours."

I nod. "Alright, let's go."

Wyatt and Logan fist bump each other, and we part ways to get cleaned up.

After a quick shower, Wyatt and I head out in his truck to drive to town and meet Logan.

We end up at 'On Cue,' a small pool hall in town. The kind of place where mostly just locals hang out, so everyone here is a familiar face.

We walk in, and the familiar sounds of clacking pool balls and chatter fill the air. Logan is already there, leaning against the bar. Wyatt and I make our way over, greeting familiar faces along the way.

As we approach, Logan grins at us. "Gentlemen, you're just in time. I've got refreshments. He hands

Wyatt and me each a beer and picks up the tray of balls off the bar. Wyatt immediately starts chatting up a group of girls at the bar while Logan and I grab a pool table and pick out some cues.

We play a few games, cheering each other on and trash-talking the whole time. For a little while, I forget about everything else and enjoy the company.

Wyatt strolls off to the bar for another round of beers, and I watch as the ladies take notice. He has such an easy way about him. He never seems to get himself worked up over any one woman. I briefly wonder if his bachelor lifestyle is a better option than the deep emptiness I feel right now with Finley over two thousand miles away.

While Logan figures out his next shot, my thoughts inevitably return to Finley. I can't escape the feeling that I need to do something to show her how much she means to me.

"Brady, you good?" Logan's voice snaps me back to the present.

"Yeah, sorry. Just distracted."

"He's just thinking again. Is it your shot, Logan?" Wyatt says as he hands me another beer.

"Guys, I need your help with something," I blurt out, interrupting Logan's shot.

"What's up?" Wyatt asks, leaning against his pool cue.

"I miss Finley and want her back in Texas with me. I'm not cut out for this long-distance thing, but I don't know where to start."

"Aw, our little cowboy is in love," Logan teases, giving me a playful shove.

I roll my eyes at Logan's teasing but can't contain the small smile that tugs at my lips. "Yeah, yeah. But seriously, I need some ideas. Something to show her that I care. I need to get Finely back."

"You sure she wants to come back to Texas, Brother?"

"No, but it's not like I can move the Ranch to Boston, Wyatt. What am I going to do? I don't want to let her go, man."

"Alright, alright," Wyatt says, "Seriously, bro, if you're feeling this way, you've got to do something about it!"

"Like what?" I ask skeptically, already regretting opening up to them.

"Like some grand romantic gesture," Logan suggests, his eyes lighting up. "You know, something to show her how much you care and want her back here with you."

"Exactly," Wyatt agrees. "Women love that stuff. It's what all those romance books they read have in them."

"How would you know?" Logan and I both quiz him in unison.

"Hey! Don't judge me - I read. Besides, where do you think I get some of my best moves, gentlemen? I don't just pluck them from thin air, ya' know!"

" Alright, Romance Master. What should I do though?" I muse. "I want it to be special, something meaningful just for her."

Wyatt's eyes lit up with mischief. "Ooh, I've got it. You could hire one of those planes to write a message for her in the sky over Boston."

I consider it. It's flashy but doesn't quite capture the depth of my feelings. "Too impersonal," I say.

Logan laughs. "Or even better, learn how to play guitar and serenade her over FaceTime."

"Ooh, how about this," Wyatt says. "You show up at her office with one of those singing telegram guys. He'll serenade her with a love song in front of all her stuffy colleagues."

I chuckle, picturing the look on Finley's face if I did that. "Tempting, but I'd like to avoid humiliating her at work."

"How about a marching band to play outside her office window?" Logan suggests excitedly.

"You guys are crazy. But I appreciate the ideas."

The ideas keep coming, each one more outrageous than the last - flash mobs, a hot air balloon, a jumbotron. As fun as it is to joke around with Wyatt and Logan, none of their suggestions feel right.

"Okay, I've got it! Hear me out," Logan begins, rubbing his hands together in excitement. "You could surprise her in Boston – maybe even plan a whole day of activities that remind her of the ranch and how much she loves it."

I raise an eyebrow, intrigued.

"See, Logan's got the right idea," Wyatt agrees. "And if you need help planning, we're here for you, man."

"Thanks, guys," I say, feeling a sudden sense of relief. "I appreciate it."

"Of course. Now, let's get back to playing pool before you get too mushy on us," Logan says teasingly.

I grin, feeling lighter than I have in weeks, and we return to our game. But now, instead of feeling weighed down by the distance between Finley and me, I feel a sense of purpose. I will make this work and show her how much she means to me.

Chapter Thirty-Four

Finley

I keep glancing at my phone, half-expecting to see Brady's name flashing across the screen. It doesn't, so I set it back on the desk and try to refocus on the documents scattered before me. The words swim together, making no sense. They're merely placeholders for the thoughts of a captivating cowboy.

"Come on, Finley," I mutter under my breath, forcing my eyes to trace the lines of text. "You're a lawyer, not some lovesick teenager." But my concentration wavers, and all I can think about are those piercing blue eyes, the way he would look at me from beneath his cowboy hat, and the way he could see right through every wall I'd ever built around myself.

"Focus," I command myself, rubbing my temples to clear my thoughts. But, like a moth drawn to a flame, my gaze drifts back to the phone, willing it to ring with that southern drawl on the other end.

"Brady Cavanaugh, you've got me wrapped around your finger, and you don't even know it," I whisper, my fingers tapping restlessly against the desk.

I try to dive into the contract file before me. Surrounding myself with the familiar legal jargon usually brings me solace, but today, my mind keeps wandering back to Brady.

"Finley Prescott, you are a professional!" I scold myself, trying to regain my focus. My internal pep talk is interrupted by Donna, my legal assistant, who enters the room carrying a steaming mug of coffee.

"Here you go, Finley," she says cheerily, setting the mug on my desk. "You look like you could use the caffeine."

"Thanks, Donna," I reply, grateful for the distraction. I reach for the mug, hoping the warm liquid will help anchor me back into reality.

"Everything okay?" she asks, her eyes full of concern as she glances at the scattered paperwork on my desk.

"Fine, just... thinking about the merger documents," I lie, forcing a smile. She nods knowingly, giving me a conspiratorial wink.

"Keep fighting the good fight," she teases before leaving the room.

I take a sip of the coffee, but my hand trembles from my restless thoughts, causing me to spill some of the hot liquid onto my paperwork accidentally.

"Great," I groan, grabbing a tissue to sop up the mess. Just as I'm blotting the damp papers, Donna pokes her head back in the door.

"Did I hear a coffee catastrophe in here?" she quips, her eyes sparkling with amusement.

"More like a caffeine calamity," I answer, rolling my eyes at my clumsiness.

"Sounds like someone needs a break. Maybe step away from the desk for a bit?" she suggests, her tone lighthearted yet concerned.

"Maybe you're right," I admit, feeling the weight of my unspoken emotions pressing down on me. I stand up, stretching out my stiff limbs as Donna grins knowingly.

"Go take a walk, clear your thoughts," she says. "A clean, dry contract will be here when you return."

"That's a good idea." I wonder how she always knows exactly what to say to make me feel better. As I exit the office, I glance back at my phone, hoping it'll buzz with Brady's name while I'm gone.

A cool breeze hits my face as I walk around the block. It's almost fall in Boston. Being outside is great for my mood, but it doesn't do much in terms of keeping Brady off my mind. My phone buzzes in my pocket as I'm considering returning to the office.

"Hello?" I answer, hoping it's Brady.

"Hey, Fin! It's Kaitlyn," she chirps brightly, her voice instantly lifting my spirits. "I just got off shift and thought we could catch up over dinner tonight. What do you say?"

"Sounds perfect," I reply, my heart swelling with excitement at spending time with my best friend. "Meet you at our usual spot?"

"Of course," Kaitlyn confirms before we hang up.

As I stroll back to the office, I feel a renewed sense of energy. The anticipation of catching up with Kaitlyn over dinner is enough to pull me through the rest of the day. I manage to focus on my work, pushing thoughts of Brady to the back of my mind for now.

When the workday finally ends, I gather my belongings and hurry to my loft, eager to get ready for dinner with Kaitlyn. Standing in front of my closet, I ponder what to wear. It's been a while since we had a girls' night, so I opt for a casual yet stylish outfit – a pair of jeans and a flowy blouse with a flattering neckline.

After applying my makeup and slipping on some comfortable heels, I take a moment to appreciate my reflection in the mirror. I may be a bit of a mess emotionally, but at least I've managed to pull myself together physically.

"Alright, Finley, time for some fun with your best friend."

I don't spot Kaitlyn right away when I arrive at the restaurant.

"Hey, Finley! Over here!" she calls out, waving her hand excitedly. I weave through the crowded restaurant, taking in the warm lighting and the delicious aromas wafting from the open kitchen.

"Long time no see," I hug her and slide into the booth across from her.

"Please, you've been knee-deep in that merger these days," Kaitlyn retorts. "I'm surprised I even managed to lure you out of your office."

Our laughter fills the air as we banter back and forth, picking up where we left off. It's always so easy with Kaitlyn – like slipping into a well-worn pair of jeans that hug you in all the right places.

"Alright, enough chitchat," Kaitlyn commands, grabbing the menu. "Let's order some food. I'm starving!"

"Me too. I am in the mood for some pasta," I declare, tapping the menu triumphantly.

"Pasta, huh? Well, I'm ordering the scallops," Kaitlyn shoots back with a satisfied grin.

"Sounds delicious," I acknowledge. The waiter arrives, and we place our orders before turning our attention back to each other.

We chat comfortably about our jobs, and then Kaitlyn asks how I'm doing.

"I'm fine. I've been so busy with the merger, and I have a lot on my mind."

"Seriously though," Kaitlyn says, her expression becoming more serious. "How have you been, Finley? We haven't seen each other in ages. And, we haven't talked; I mean, really talked since you returned from Texas."

I fidget in my seat, reluctant to talk about what's honestly bothering me. But Kaitlyn narrows her eyes, giving me a look that says she's not letting this go. With a sigh, I decide to come clean.

"Alright, fine. I can't stop thinking about Brady," I confess, poking at my salad. "I don't know what's happening between us, and it's driving me crazy."

"Ah, Brady," Kaitlyn replies, nodding knowingly. "I had a feeling. So, tell me everything. How is it going with your handsome cowboy? How's the long-distance thing? "

"He seems good. But I don't know how long we can keep this up. I'm questioning everything."

"Yeah, he doesn't strike me as the Facetime kind of guy."

"He's not, and apparently, I'm not either. I'm so confused," I admit. "My feelings for Brady are all over the place, and I'm unsure what to do about them."

"Finley," Kaitlyn says gently, "It's okay to be confused. You've been through a lot, and feeling uncertain about jumping into something new is normal."

"Was this just a vacation fling? Could it ever be something more? I don't know when we will be able to see each other again in person. Would it be crazy to consider leaving my entire life here for a cowboy?"

Kaitlyn listens intently, her brow furrowed with concern as she processes my emotional outpouring. Finally, she offers her thoughts.

"First of all, you're not crazy," she reassures me. "I mean, if I had a dime for every time I've questioned my love life, I'd be wealthy enough to buy my own private island. Finley, I know it's not easy, but try to imagine some possible outcomes if you were to pursue this relationship with Brady," Kaitlyn suggests, her eyes full of empathy. "What do you think could happen?"

I take a deep breath, focusing on the coolness of the wine glass cradled in my hands as I consider her question. "Well, one possibility is that we could find happiness together," I begin, excited at the thought. "Or maybe the distance will drive us apart, and we'll both end up heartbroken."

"True, but what if you don't take the risk? How would you feel then?" Kaitlyn asks, taking a sip of her wine.

"Regretful, I suppose," I admit, the word tasting bitter on my tongue. "

Kaitlyn chuckles, her laughter a soothing balm to my troubled thoughts. "Unfortunately, there's no such thing as a guaranteed happy ending, Fin. But I can tell you this: Love sometimes has a funny way of working things out, even when it seems impossible."

"Maybe you're right," I concede, feeling a tiny spark of hope ignite. "I just wish I had a crystal ball to show me whether or not this whole thing is worth pursuing."

Our conversation ebbs and flows as we delve deeper into my thoughts and feelings, with Kaitlyn offering her unwavering support and understanding.

"Whatever you decide, just remember I'm here for you," she reassures me. "And if you need help figuring things out, I am always just a phone call away. Unless I'm in surgery, but of course, you know what I mean." She adds, reaching across the table to squeeze my hand.

"Thank you, Kaitlyn," I reply, feeling immense gratitude for our friendship. "You're the best."

She lets go and leans back so the waiter can remove our salad plates and place our entrees down. "Of course," she smiles. "Let's devour this amazing food and have some fun tonight!"

Kaitlyn tells me about some of her recent cases at work, the annoying intern she has to watch over, and about a new male nurse in her department. "He's like Brad Pitt and David Beckham had a baby – Tall, blonde, blue-eyed with just a smattering of visible tattoos."

I nod along, feigning interest in her latest hospital crush. As she chatters away, I feel my mind wander.

"Finley, are you even listening to me?" Kaitlyn asks, waving her fork in front of my face.

"Uh, yeah," I lie, quickly snapping back to reality. "You were talking about that new nurse at the hospital, right?"

"Actually, I was asking if you'd like to try some of my risotto." Kaitlyn laughs, not believing my attempt to cover up my distraction. "Okay, spill it. What are you worried about now?"

"What if I leave everything I know behind? What if... what if it doesn't work out with Brady?"

"Then you put your butt on a plane and come home to Boston!"

"Finley, listen to me." Kaitlyn's voice is gentle but firm, her eyes locking onto mine. "You always play it safe. You analyze every situation and chart out the safest course, but sometimes in life, you need to take risks."

I know she's right. I've always been cautious, especially after losing my husband. The fear of getting hurt again has held me back from taking chances and embracing new experiences.

"Remember when you first met Brady?" Kaitlyn continues, a sly smile spreading across her face. "You were so annoyed by him, but then something changed. You started to let your guard down, and you experienced happiness with him."

I smile at the memory. Brady's gruff exterior had initially rubbed me the wrong way, but as I got to know him, I was drawn to his compassionate side and the joy he brought into my life.

"Life isn't about avoiding risks, Fin," Kaitlyn says earnestly. "It's about embracing them, learning from them, and growing. I know you're scared but think about the happiness you could have with Brady. Is that worth the risk?"

My mind races as I weigh my options. On one hand, moving away from my life in Boston would mean stepping into the unknown and potentially facing heartbreak once more. On the other hand, I can't deny the happiness that Brady has brought into my life.

"Kaitlyn," I say softly, my voice wavering as I take a deep breath. "You're right. I need to take risks and follow my heart."

"Exactly," she replies, her eyes shining with pride. "And remember, I'll be here for you no matter what happens. We all deserve a shot at happiness, Fin. Don't let fear hold you back."

"Speaking of not holding back, are we splitting the Sacher Torte or the cheesecake tonight?"

"I need some chocolate, so definitely the torte."

As Kaitlyn and I share the last bites of our sinful chocolate dessert, I am excited for what is to come.

"Alright," Kaitlyn says, setting her spoon down and wiping her mouth with a napkin. "We've tackled the heavy stuff; now let's move on to something lighter. What do you say we hit up that karaoke bar we've been talking about forever?"

A smile tugs at the corner of my lips as I imagine belting out cheesy love songs on stage. "You know what? That sounds perfect."

Chapter Thirty-Five

Finley

It's just another Wednesday morning in Boston, and as usual, I'm sitting at my desk, buried in stacks of legal documents; our office is buzzing with complaints of horrible traffic jams and delays. I feel a little smug about my easy commute and being able to walk to work most days. I am trying to concentrate on the documents spread across my desk, but the chatter is making it difficult.

"Are they doing construction on the Washington Street bridge again? Traffic was so backed up on my way in this morning I had to detour and come in on 93. It's like they want us to be late," a colleague grumbles.

"Ugh, tell me about it. My train was delayed for twenty minutes!" another chimes in.

Amid their griping, Donna breezes into my office with her usual air of confidence. "Finley, you've got to see this!" Her sudden interruption is unexpected; she would usually knock but seems too excited for formalities today. My curiosity piques when I notice her flushed cheeks and bright eyes.

"Okay, Donna, just give me a minute to finish this paragraph." I try not to sound annoyed; after all, She's usually quite respectful of my work time. There must be something important happening if she's this worked up.

I put down my pen and follow her gaze towards the office window, half expecting to see some vehicular catastrophe or an unfortunate collision between a pedestrian and a pothole.

"See what?" I ask, walking toward whatever is consuming her attention.

"Take a look out your window," she instructs, her eyes twinkling with excitement.

I peer out the glass, and at first, I don't understand what she's pointing at. But then, my eyes widen in disbelief, and a smile tugs at the corners of my lips. Instead, What I see leaves me speechless, my jaw dropping in disbelief.

Twenty stories below me is a man riding a horse. But not just any man... my man! I press closer to the glass, not quite believing my eyes. But there's no mistaking that handsome face, those broad shoulders, that easy grin. What on earth is he doing here, on a horse, outside my office?

"Is that... Brady?" I stammer, staring down at the scene unfolding below. There he is, astride a magnificent horse. The sight of him brings a flood of warmth to my chest but also a healthy helping of confusion.

"Yep, that's your cowboy, alright," Donna confirms with a grin of her own, enjoying the shock plastered across my face. "Looks like he is taking the grand romantic gestures to new heights. Or streets, rather."

I laugh at the absurdity of the situation, and my heart swells with a mixture of affection and amusement. Of course, Brady would do something like this – grand, unexpected, and just a little bit reckless.

"Come on, Finley," Donna urges me, her phone ready to capture every moment of this spectacle. "Let's go say hello to your knight in shining Stetson."

We hurry through the office, my colleagues amused and teasing as they catch wind of what is happening outside. Their good-natured jibes do little to dampen my spirits as I practically fly to the elevator, jabbing impatiently at the first-floor button. As I wait, with butterflies fluttering in my stomach, I smooth my hair and straighten my shirt. I wonder what Brady has planned.

"Finley, you're practically glowing," Donna teases, snapping pictures with her phone as we make our way down to the lobby.

"Am I?" I ask, self-consciously touching my face. "I can't help it. This is just so...so unexpected."

"Unexpected is an understatement, honey." She chuckles.

With a ding, the doors slide open. I hurry across the lobby, my heels clicking rhythmically on the marble floors. I burst through the front doors into the crisp Boston air with Donna on my heels.

And there he is, sitting on a horse, grinning at me like I'm the best thing he's seen all day.

I stop at the top of the stairs to take it all in. I want to ingrain this moment into my memories forever. Brady dismounts the beautiful horse with grace and swagger and smiles at me. The sight of him, standing tall and confident by the magnificent animal, sends a shiver down my spine.

"Brady!" I call out, waving at him from the top of the steps. He waves back, an infectious smile plastered across his face that mirrors my happiness. I practically run down the stairs toward him.

"Hey there, Boston!" he says as he hugs and spins me around. "Thought I'd bring a little taste of Texas to you!"

I giggle as he pulls me closer to him. His scent invades my senses, a tantalizing mix of leather, horse, and a hint of cologne. For a moment, I forget where we are and don't care who's watching us. All that exists is him and me, wrapped up in this crazy moment.

I reach up and touch his cheek, feeling the bristle of his beard against my fingertips. "I missed you," I say softly.

"Yeehaw! Ride 'em, cowboy!" someone calls out from the crowd gathered to watch the spectacle. I roll my eyes in amusement, knowing I wouldn't trade this moment for anything despite the potential embarrassment.

I look at the crowd and spot Donna, her phone still documenting everything. She lets out an excited squeal. "Surprise!" she cheers.

"Ready for a ride, Finley?" Brady asks, extending his hand to help me up onto the horse.

"Are you sure this is allowed?" I ask hesitantly, glancing around at the curious onlookers.

"Boston, when it comes to you, sometimes you have to bend the rules just a little," he replies with a wink.

I laugh at his bravado. "Alright then, cowboy. Let's go for a ride." With that, I take his hand as he helps me onto the saddle, feeling like I am in a fairytale. I am so glad I chose to wear trousers to work today instead of a skirt.

Brady climbs onto the horse behind me, and I lean back into his chest. "Let's go on an adventure, Finley," he murmurs into my ear, sending shivers down my spine.

"Ready, Belle?" Brady asks the horse, giving her a gentle nudge.

"An adventure it is," I agree as we make our way down the busy city streets. Pedestrians stop to stare, but I barely notice them. All my attention is focused on Brady - his warmth, his solid strength. I feel safe here with him.

We cross the bridge over the Charles River and into Paul Revere Park. An elaborate picnic awaits us in the picturesque setting of lush greenery and a breathtaking view of the harbor. A soft blanket has been laid out beneath the shade of a tree, and an array of delicious-looking treats is spread out before us. It is very apparent that he has gone above and beyond.

Brady brings the horse to a stop beneath a sprawling oak tree. He hops down and then lifts me off, his hands lingering on my waist. Our eyes meet, and something powerful passes between us.

"Wow," I breathe, taking in the scene before me. "Brady, this is... incredible."

"Well, I figured if I was going to go big with the horse, I might as well go all out with the picnic, too."

"Thank you," I say sincerely, my eyes shining with gratitude and affection. "This means more to me than you'll ever know."

His arms wrap around me, pulling me close as he whispers, "I'd do anything for you, Boston. Anything at all."

"Will there be anything else right now, Mr. Cavanaugh?" A man in a tuxedo, whom I overlooked when we first road up, interrupts our intimate moment. He is holding a silver tray with two glasses and a bottle of champagne.

Brady turns to him. "No, thank you, Robert, we're good for now," he replies, still holding me close.

The man nods, sets the tray on the picnic blanket, and takes the reins from Brady before turning around and walking away. Brady opens the bottle of champagne with a flourish, the cork popping loudly in the quiet park. He pours us each a glass.

"To us," he says, his eyes shining with happiness.

"To us," I echo, tears prickling at the corners of my eyes. This moment is so perfect, so magical, that it almost feels like a dream.

Brady leans in slowly, his eyes locked onto mine as if asking for permission. Our lips meet with a gentle touch. His are soft and tender against mine, sending a shiver down my spine. The world around us fades away, and I respond eagerly, pulling him closer with one arm wrapping around his neck, unwilling to break the connection even for a second. My other hand holds onto my champagne glass, which threatens to spill as I lose myself in the intoxicating swirl of passion and warmth. Brady takes my champagne glass from my hand, setting it aside, and the brief separation sends a wave of desire through me. He returns, and our kiss intensifies, becoming more like a fire burning wild and uncontained. His hand cups my cheek, his thumb gently caressing my skin, and I feel the tenderness in his touch. I melt into him, every nerve ending alive with anticipation and longing.

Then, softly pulling away, Brady rests his forehead against mine, his voice low and rich. "I have something very important to tell you, and I didn't want to say over the phone."

My worry is quickly soothed by a tender kiss on my nose,

"Finley, I love you," he says, his voice barely above a whisper.

"I love you too, Brady," I reply, feeling my heart swell with emotion.

We stand locked in each other's arms, the world around us dissolving as if time itself has halted. I pull him closer, almost in disbelief, "I can't believe you're really here."

"Finley," he murmurs into my ear, his voice warm and tender. "I've missed you so much."

"Me too," I whisper back.

"Before you even ask, I had some help...A lot of help, actually." His grin is sheepish. "I wanted everything to be special and perfect for you."

I give him a playful nudge. "It's perfect. Thank you for this romantic surprise."

We settle onto the blanket and admire the assortment of meats, cheeses, and fruits artfully arranged on a wooden plank. Brady plucks a grape and pops it into his mouth, a victorious glimmer in his eyes as he basks in the success of his elaborate setup.

But where did you get a horse in the middle of Boston?"

He flashes me a smile, a hint of mischief in his eyes. "Let's just say I have some connections," he says as he scoots closer. "And I couldn't resist surprising you like this."

I shake my head, still in disbelief. "You're crazy, you know that?"

He leans in, his lips brushing against my ear. "Crazy about you, Finley."

Brady takes both my hands in his and looks deeply into my eyes. "From the moment I met you, my life has changed in ways I never thought possible. I've tried to fight it, but I can't deny it any longer. I am head over heels for you, Finley, and I want to be with you. I've had some preliminary conversations with my siblings about transferring many of my responsibilities to them so I can spend as much time up here with you as possible. I hope that's okay?" He says it like it's a question - Like I wouldn't want to be with him.

"It's more than okay. But you may not have to do all that. I have a surprise for you, too."

He fixes his gaze on me intently, his eyes filled with expectation.

"I've arranged to take the Texas Bar Exam!"

"Finley, that's fantastic!" he exclaims, sitting up straighter. "When did you decide to do that?"

"I've been thinking about it for a little while now," I admit, smiling at his excitement. "I want to be with you, and I know how hard it will be for you to leave Texas. I wasn't expecting you to make a similar sacrifice to be with me here in Boston. I'm kind of in shock but in such a good way."

Feeling a sense of contentment and happiness settle over me, I lean in to kiss him. I take his face in my hands and press my lips to his, feeling the warmth of his body against mine. I run my fingers through his hair, pulling him in closer. Our kiss deepens, and I feel Brady's hands running down my back, sending shivers down my spine. Our mouths explore each other with a passion that leaves us both breathless.

As we pull away from each other, Brady's eyes are full of a fierce desire that takes my breath away. My heart is pounding in my chest as we remain entwined in each other's arms.

"I'm so glad I found you, Finley," he whispers against my lips, his voice full of emotion."I love you!"

My heart swells with joy at his words. "I love you too," I reply, my voice trembling slightly.

We kiss again, this time more tenderly. I feel like I'm floating on air, my body buzzing with warmth and happiness.

"I just thought of a small problem," Brady adds.

I worry for a brief moment, but he continues, "I won't be able to call you Boston anymore."

"You can still call me that if you like."

"I'll think of something better."

We enjoy the rest of our picnic, talking, laughing, planning, and kissing. Lots of kissing!!!

Chapter Thirty-Six

Brady

I pull up to the small craftsman house on Oak Street that Finley has rented and park my truck out of the way of the movers who are busy unloading. As I get out, I see Finley on the front porch, surrounded by boxes and looking overwhelmed.

"Hey there, beautiful," I call out as I walk up the front steps. "I'm here to help get you settled in. And...I brought coffee!"

Finley smiles, brushing a strand of hair behind her ear. "Thank goodness." She says, hugging me and taking the paper cup from me. "I had to rush over from the B&B this morning to meet the movers and I didn't get to finish mine. There is so much to do today, and I didn't realize how much stuff I had until they started bringing in all these boxes."

I pick up a box labeled 'Kitchen' and carry it inside. I set the box on the counter in the cozy kitchen.

"So what's the game plan?" I ask. "Unpack the kitchen first?"

"Yes, let's start with the kitchen," she confirms. "Coffee maker first. Priorities, right?"

"Can't argue with that,"

She starts opening up cabinets. "Let's unpack these boxes, and I'll try to find a place for everything."

We work side by side, and Finley tells me where she wants things to go. She's got a system for everything. Me, I just shove stuff wherever it fits. But I don't mind following Finley's lead on this. I like seeing her get comfortable in her new home.

Within an hour, we've got the kitchen in mostly working order. Finley has set up the coffee maker and leans back against the counter with a satisfied sigh.

"One room down," she says. "Only the rest of the house to go."

I smile and wrap my arms around her, planting a kiss on her head. "Don't worry. We'll get there."

"Shouldn't you be at the Ranch at least part of the day?"

"I think Carter and Sawyer can handle things for a few days, and if not, they have me on speed dial. I'm all yours till you kick me out."

One of the movers comes into the kitchen to tell us that the furniture is all assembled, and they are about to bring in the last few boxes. Finley and I walk outside to verify that everything is unloaded.

"It's so nice of Ally to rent me this place while I get settled."

"She's happy to help. And Cramer's lucky to have you."

"Okay, so where do you want these?" I ask, balancing two boxes in my arms.

"Those will go to my office in town, probably tomorrow. You can put them near the back door for now."

We move on to unpacking the living room. Finley directs me where to place the furniture while she opens up boxes and starts shelving books.

"Have I mentioned how much I love this house?" she says, running her hand over the built-in bookshelves. "It's like something out of a magazine."

"Ally's got great taste," I agree. "She and Logan did a nice job fixing this place up."

Finley sets a framed photo of her late husband on the mantle. I know how much his memory still means to her. She catches me looking and gives a bittersweet smile.

"I wish he could see me starting over here," she says softly. "Does this bother you?"

I wrap an arm around her shoulders. "Not in the slightest. I'm sure he'd be real happy for you, Finley."

We share a quiet moment, standing there together. Then Finley takes a deep breath and turns to me with a more upbeat expression.

"Alright, enough of memory lane. We've got work to do!"

I chuckle. "Yes, ma'am."

We spend the rest of the day unpacking and organizing. With each box that's emptied, the house starts to take shape.

"Wow," she says, surveying our handiwork. "It's truly starting to feel like home."

"Thank you for helping me unpack, Brady," she says softly, taking my hand.

"Anything for you, Finley," I reply, squeezing her fingers gently. "Welcome home."

I am so glad she's in Cramer and near to me, but I hope that this cute little rental house is just her temporary home.

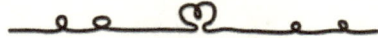

"Ready to tackle your new law office today?" I ask Finley as I arrive the following morning. She is sipping her morning coffee on her new front porch.

"My law office. That sounds so crazy, doesn't it?"

"Not at all," I say, taking her hand as she rises to take her mug back to the house.

"Okay, Cowboy. Let's do this."

I grab the two small boxes by her back door, and we walk toward her new office in town.

"I am so glad to still be able to walk to work," she says.

The morning sun beams down on us as we step onto Main Street, heading towards her new office across from the courthouse in the town square. Cramer is already buzzing with activity, and the scents of coffee and fresh baked goods float from the nearby coffee shop. Finley inhales deeply, a smile playing on her lips. "I could get used to this," she murmurs.

As we approach the modest brick building that houses the law office, I can see the anticipation in Finley's eyes. This is a fresh start for her – a chance to build something of her own.

"Here we are," I announce as I unlock the side door into her private office and step inside. A familiar smell of old books and polished wood greets us, along with what used to be George's enormous wooden desk, which now belongs to Finley.

"Wow," she breathes, taking in the room. "This is all mine, isn't it?"

"Sure is, darlin'," I reply, my chest swelling with pride. "And George couldn't be happier. He's finally retired and moved to Port Aransas to be with his daughter and her family. He's thrilled you're here and taking over things."

"Speaking of which," Finley says, gesturing to the boxes piled beside the desk, "we've got some unpacking to do."

"Let's get to it," I agree, grabbing a box marked 'law books' and carefully slicing through the tape.

As we work, unpacking books, files, and a few of Finley's personal touches, I marvel at the woman beside me.

"Hey, Brady," she says suddenly, pointing to a large potted plant with a brightly colored WELCOME tag sticking out of it. "Looks like it's from your sister. Where do you think this should go?"

"Probably closer to the window?" I suggest, watching as she tries to move the greenery to its new home, the sunlight streaming through the leaves casting dappled patterns on her face.

"Here, let me help you with that," I say, moving the large plant toward the window.

"Perfect," she murmurs, stepping back to admire our handiwork. "Thank you."

"Anytime," I reply, my heart swelling with love. "Anything for you."

As we continue to unpack, the office slowly transforms into a space that is distinctly Finley's. Her diploma hangs proudly on the wall, while photographs join the books lining the shelves.

"Finished," Finley announces, standing in the center of the room with her hands on her hips. "What do you think?"

"Looks perfect," I tell her honestly, wrapping an arm around her waist and pulling her close. "Just like you."

"Flatterer," she accuses, but I can see the happiness shining in her eyes.

"Only speaking the truth," I insist, kissing her temple. "And I'm proud of you, Finley Prescott."

"Thank you, Brady," she whispers, arms winding around my neck. "For everything."

"Come on," I say to Finley, gently tugging at her hand. "There's someone you need to meet."

"Evelyn?" she asks, raising an eyebrow inquisitively.

"Yep, your new right-hand woman," I reply with a grin. "Evelyn Springer."

"We've talked quite a bit on the phone; I like her."

"Trust me, she's the best of the best," I assure her as we step out of her office into a small waiting room and approach another office.

As we enter the room, we find Evelyn diligently organizing files at her desk. "Evelyn, I'd like you to meet Finley Prescott."

"Finley! It's so nice to finally meet you in person," Evelyn exclaims, her warm smile reflecting the genuine enthusiasm in her voice. She crosses the room to shake Finley's hand firmly. "Welcome to Cramer and our little legal family."

"Thank you, Evelyn," Finley replies, studying the woman who will be her partner in this new venture. "I'm excited for us to work together."

"Me too." She adds, "I have tied up most of George's loose ends, but I'll have a few things for you to look over after you get settled. Nothing urgent."

"Wonderful. Thank you. I should be here bright and early Monday morning," Finley tells her.

The two chat comfortably about the practice and clients while I linger nearby. It's clear that they will work well together, with Evelyn's experience and Finley's calm confidence.

They talk for a few more minutes before Finley and I return to her office. As we walk, I can see the excitement in Finley's eyes.

"She seems great," she says. "I like her a lot! And I think we'll make a great team."

I smile, happy to see Finley so at ease already. "I do, too."

"She's very knowledgeable in ranching and oil drilling legal matters," Finley continues.

"Yes, Evelyn was instrumental in keeping George's law practice running smoothly for years; everyone in town knows her. You'll learn a lot from her."

Back in her office, I watch Finley sit at her desk, and she takes a deep breath. "This is a REALLY big desk!"

"George was a big guy," I laugh, taking in her small frame behind the ridiculously big desk. "We can get you something more suitable if you like."

"No, it's fine. I'll just get a pillow or a booster seat to sit on." She jokes, settling into the chair.

"I still can't believe this is happening," she says as if trying to convince herself.

"You're going to be great," I assure her.

"I hope so," she says, turning her attention to her computer. "I need to start drafting some emails to clients to let them know I've taken over George's practice."

"Oh, I can assure you. The Cramer chatterboxes have already announced that for you. Welcome to Small Town Texas, where everyone knows everyone's business," I tease with a grin.

"Well, I guess that makes my job a little easier. I have to prove myself now."

"And you will," I tell her. "The folks in town are real glad you're here."

She beams at the encouragement and looks around with satisfaction.

"It's coming together," she says. "I think I'm going to love it here."

I pull her into an embrace. "I know you will. And I already do."

As the day winds down at the ranch, I glance at the clock and realize it's time to call it a day. I get cleaned up and drive to town. Finley has gotten settled and has been working for a few weeks now.

I step into the waiting room, and the chime announces my arrival. I find Finley and Evelyn in the conference room. "Finley," I say, catching her attention between stacks of files. "Are you almost done for the day? How about we go to Grizzly's for dinner?"

Her eyes light up with excitement, and she nods eagerly. "That sounds perfect, Brady. The day has just flown by. Evelyn and I can finish this up tomorrow."

"Sounds good," adds Evelyn, stifling a yawn. "I'll see you tomorrow, Finley."

"Goodnight, Evelyn," Finley replies as she gathers her things and prepares to leave the office.

We walk side by side through the quiet streets of Cramer, the fading sunlight casting a warm glow on the quaint buildings lining the sidewalks. The atmosphere is peaceful, and I feel grateful for this moment and the woman walking beside me.

"Can you believe I've only been here a few weeks?" Finley asks, breaking the comfortable silence.

"Time flies when you're having fun," I reply, reaching for her hand. "And I can't imagine being anywhere else."

"Neither can I," she says softly, gently squeezing my hand.

We arrive at Grizzly's, and the amazing smell of Tom's cooking wafts through the air as we enter the cozy restaurant. We are seated at a table near the back, settling into the comfortable booth and scanning the menu.

"Everything sounds so good," Finley muses, her eyes dancing across the various options. "What are you having?"

I smile as I watch Finley flip through the menu.

"I think I'll go for the chicken fried steak," I say, closing mine and placing it on the table. "What about you?"

Finley hums in thought, her finger tapping against her lips. "I think I'll try the meatloaf. It sounds delicious."

Once we've ordered, Finley reaches across the table and places her hand on mine. "Thank you for everything, Brady. This move has been a huge change, but you make me feel so at home already."

I rub my thumb over her knuckles. "Of course, darlin'. I want you to feel like you belong here because you do. Cramer may not be Boston, but it can be home if you let it."

Finley smiles. "As long as I'm with you, any place will feel like home."

Chapter Thirty-Seven

Finley

November 6

Dear Andrew,

As I sit here in my new home, I feel a mix of emotions swirling within me. This journey to Texas has changed me in ways I never expected. There are moments when I feel your presence as if you're guiding me through this new and exciting chapter of my life.

Brady has shown me kindness and a way to smile again. I never thought I could find joy after losing you, but here I am. Yet, despite this newfound happiness, I feel the weight of your absence. I miss our late-night talks, your laughter, and the way you always knew how to comfort me. You were my anchor, and letting go has been the hardest thing I've ever had to do.

This isn't a goodbye forever. You will always be a part of me, woven into the fabric of my memories and my heart. I promise to carry your love with me as I embrace the future.

Thank you for the love we shared and for helping me find my way back to happiness. I hope I'm making you proud.

Forever yours,

Finley

Epilogue

Brady

The sun is sinking low in the sky, casting a warm golden glow over the ranch as I walk outside, my heart pounding with anticipation. I texted Finley this morning asking her to meet me at the skeet shooting range at 6:30 tonight, and now all that's left to do is wait.

I smile as I think back to the first time we came here together. It was right here, surrounded by the sights and sounds of my family's beautiful ranch, that I first realized I was falling for the brilliant, confident lawyer from Boston. And now, after everything we've been through, I'm ready to take the next step in our journey.

"Hey, cowboy," Finley calls out, approaching the range with a curious smile.

"Hey there," I reply, trying to keep my voice steady. "You got my message."

"Of course! What's going on?" Finley asks, her eyes sparkling with curiosity. "It's kind of late to be shooting anything, right?"

"Finley," I begin as I walk closer to her. I take a deep, steadying breath as I pat my pocket to ensure the small velvet box is still there. I don't think that I have ever been so nervous.

I drop to one knee before her and pull the box from my pocket. "From the moment you walked into my life, you've turned it upside down in the best way possible. You've shown me what it means to truly love someone, and I can't imagine spending the rest of my life without you by my side."

Her eyes widen, and she covers her mouth with her hand, evidently not expecting this turn of events.

"Finley Prescott, will you marry me?"

As the words leave my lips, the world seems to stand still. The setting sun casts a warm, rosy hue over

Finley's face, making her look more radiant than ever before.

"Brady Cavanaugh," she whispers, tears brimming in her eyes, "you have no idea how happy I am to hear those words. Yes, yes, a thousand times yes!"

I slide the engagement ring onto her finger, and as the diamond catches the fading sunlight, it feels like the perfect symbol of our love – strong, beautiful, and enduring.

Finley throws her arms around me, tears of joy wetting my shirt. I hold her tightly, my heart swelling with love.

"I can't wait to spend the rest of my life with you, Finley," I whisper into her ear. "I promise to love and cherish you always."

"I can't wait either," she says, kissing me.

Want to see how Finley and Brady finally deal with Amber once and for all?

Download BONUS SCENES on BookFunnel

https://dl.bookfunnel.com/rv9zso9zfe

A Note from Desiree

Hey, my Lovelies!

Thank you so much for taking the time to read my book! Your support means the world to me. I started writing as a way to destress after leaving a particularly toxic corporate job that drained my creativity and joy. In the midst of that chaos, I found solace in binge-reading romance novels, getting lost in the stories and characters that made me believe in love and second chances.

One day, I woke up with a surge of inspiration and a few story ideas swirling in my mind. I decided to take the plunge and put pen to paper, and the rest truly is history!

I'm thrilled to let you know that I have several more books in the works, each filled with heartwarming moments, laughter, and, of course, a dash of romance. I can't wait to share these stories with you, especially those featuring the charming folks of Cramer, Texas, and the irresistible Cavanaugh Brothers.

Just a quick note—Cramer is a fictional town born from my imagination, so let's keep the haters at bay! I wanted to create a place where love and adventure intertwine, and I hope you enjoyed visiting it as much as I loved writing about it.

Stay tuned for more tales that celebrate love, resilience, and the beauty of new beginnings. Your feedback and support inspire me every day, and I'm so grateful to have you on this journey with me.

With all my love,

Desiree

Acknowledgments

I want to take a moment to express my heartfelt gratitude to everyone who has been part of this journey.

First and foremost, a HUGE thank you to my husband. Your unwavering support and encouragement mean everything to me, especially on those days when my creativity feels like it's running on empty. You believe in me when I doubt myself. I am so grateful for your patience and love.

To my wonderful girls, thank you for being my first draft critics. Your insights and honest feedback were invaluable and helped shape this story into something I'm genuinely proud of. I couldn't have done it without your keen eyes and thoughtful suggestions.

I also want to extend my deepest appreciation to my editor, Lindsey. You transformed this manuscript from a rough draft into a polished piece of art. Your expertise, attention to detail, and unwavering dedication made all the difference. Without your guidance, this book would have been, well, let's just say it wouldn't have been nearly as good. Thank you for believing in my vision and for your tireless work to bring it to life.

A special shoutout to Claire, whose distinctive personality inspired the character in this book. Your uniqueness allowed me to embellish and add fun elements to the story, making it all the more enjoyable. Thank you for being a constant source of inspiration and for letting me share your wit and charm with the world!

Lastly, to my amazing beta readers—y'all are absolutely killing it! Your enthusiasm, insights, and willingness to dive into my world have made this process so much more enjoyable. Thank you for your constructive criticism and for helping me refine this story.

To everyone who has supported me along the way—thank you for being part of this incredible journey. Your encouragement fuels my passion, and I can't wait to share more stories with you in the future!

With all my love,

Desiree

Also by Desiree Hammond

My Grumpy Cowboy Boss

Grumpy Single Dad

If you loved My Second Chance Cowboy, you can
help other readers find this book by leaving a review
on Amazon and Goodreads.

https://www.amazon.com/stores/author/B0C1S13
364

https://www.goodreads.com/author/show/304101
39.Desiree_Hammond

If you'd like to read my first novella, it's free to
download on bookfunnel

https://dl.bookfunnel.com/40oluu7otm

About the Author

Desiree Hammond is currently living her own second-chance romance in a charming small town near Dallas, Texas, where she shares her life with her supportive husband, wonderful daughters, and an assortment of lovable dogs. Her family is the heart of her stories, and their adventures inspire her writing every day.

Desiree has a deep passion for romance, especially sweet romance—the kind of stories you wouldn't be mortified about if your kids picked them up. She believes in happily-ever-afters that make you swoon, where readers can fall in love with the characters just as much as they fall in love with the stories. For her, there's nothing quite like the thrill of a well-crafted plot that leads to a satisfying conclusion, leaving readers with hope and joy.

When she's not busy writing, you can find Desiree indulging in her favorite books, cooking, or spending time with her family. She loves connecting with her readers and sharing her journey through the world of contemporary romance.

If you want to keep in touch and be part of her literary adventures, feel free to join her Facebook group at https://www.facebook.com/DesireeHammondAuthor/

or follow her on Instagram at @desireehammondauthor.

She loves hearing from her readers and sharing insights into her writing process, upcoming projects, and the little moments that inspire her stories. Thank you for being a part of her journey!

www.ingramcontent.com/pod-product-compliance
Lightning Source LLC
Chambersburg PA
CBHW020540120726
47903CB00001B/51